Onyx Shadows

D.B. Forest

CONTENTS

To anyone who wants a book dedicated to them. Here you go. This is for you. Hopefully it's cool enough for bragging rights.

CONTENT NOTE:

This series contains graphic violence, torture (including psychological torture), child abuse, PTSD and trauma responses, body horror, suicidal ideation, and themes of mental deterioration. Content intensity increases significantly in Books 4-5. Please take care of yourself and read at your own pace.

CHAPTER 1

ELLORY

"Stop that boy! Stop him!" echoes down the narrow, stone corridor with the accompanied crushing 'clunk, clunk' of the knights' armor. I turn, seeing a young man leaping over crates, dodging townsfolk and merchant shacks, a proud grin splitting his face as he turns to laugh at the less agile, less flexible guards.

"You're a skunk's tail!" he shouts back at them, still barreling down the street, and with a jolt in my chest, I realize he hasn't noticed that he's going to collide with my stand.

"Watch out!" I scream at him, but it's too late.

Time moves achingly slow as he turns his head, and his eyes widen. His raucous smile melts from his face, pulling his mouth into an 'o.' He tries to stop, arms flailing, feet skittering, but it's too late.

I dive out of the way, rolling into the street, as he plows into the shelves with a crunch. They don't stand a chance; wood whines and splits, crashing to the ground with a cacophony of cracking and shattering ceramic bowls and pots. The young man reaches out, trying to grab anything solid. But instead, he catches the wool blanket that *used* to be my shade, yanking the shelves on the other side down on top of him with a crash. The image of pink and green herbs spilling through the air from an upturned basket presses on my mind like a memory I'll have forever.

He moans as the dust settles, and the scent of strong, earthy herbs wafts.

Rubbing my forehead, I assess the damage. My mind hiccups as I stare at the pieces of wood and broken things. What am I going to do about this? I can't sell this stuff now. And it will take forever to clean up and put everything back together.

The oaf pokes his head out from under the wool blanket, staring around wildly, his mirth subdued.

"We've got him!" one gravelly voice shouts, as the young man wriggles himself out from under the shelves, squishing herbs, nuts, and fruits under his hands as he pushes himself to his feet.

He darts through the crowd with a faint, "Sorry," whipping behind him.

I glare daggers into his backside. Thrashing metal armor rings in my ears, clashing off the walls as the guards part around me, still chasing their quarry.

I sigh, pursing my lips, narrowing my eyes, breathing deeply, and pinching the bridge of my nose to keep the rage at bay.

This is the last thing I need right now. My family can't afford this. We're poorer than the dirt we stand on. Barely able to scrape by with the earnings we get from the shop.

So, this is less than ideal.

The bare-bones shop is in pieces. Normally, it stands upright, rickety shelves holding aloft a bare blanket to keep the sun off my head, strong scents and spices invading my nose until I can no longer smell anything. It's usually meager at best. Now it's less than that, I bemoan internally as I stoop to pull the shelves off the goods. The splintered supports creak as I push them against the wall.

I get a few curious looks in passing as I clean. Not because people want to *buy* from me, but because people love drama. It breaks up the mundane.

Snatching the largest basket, I scoop handfuls of debris into it, tossing shattered ceramic, crushed fruits, and smashed herbs inside. I don't know how long it will take to replace it all. Mother has a few bowls I can borrow for now. I can trade for a couple of baskets. The stand, though, I'm not sure how it'll piece back together.

I don't have the time or energy for this.

We can't afford an apprenticeship for Cassian, my younger brother, and Mellen, my younger sister, is too small for hard labor (nor would I want her to have to put herself to some trade). Mother's energy is expended by taking care of them both, but she does a little mending on the side. Small favors for neighbors, for which we sometimes get a scrap of bread in return. In short, we don't have options.

I grab the dusty blanket and stuff it in the basket too, before making my way down the street to the lower town, into the quarter known as Muck Water to the locals. The name started as a joke about the terrible sewage system, but kinda stuck (Muck Water is actually the "nice" name for it). There's also Mouse Next near the northeast end of the lower village, which was a slur against an ancient people who mostly settled in that section and whose descendants still live there. And Bad Wine Row near the taverns that line the street, where traffic comes through the city gate. It's notorious for obvious reasons and leads up to the main street where the merchants gather to sell their wares. And the guilds are strict on where and when the taverns are allowed to solicit traffic to their own establishments. And to be clear, they don't run up this far. There are a few on the upper side of town, but not as persistent as the ones on Bad Wine Row. And with better wares, so I hear.

And as my stand sits at the crossroads between the main road and the one that leads into the lower town, you'd think the traffic would help with sales, but everyone knows the best wares are in the richer parts of town, so some people just hurry by.

Sometimes I wish I could live off the land, simpler, freer, harder perhaps, but less dependent on the shaky goodwill of others. I long for a trade more reliable, money more sustainable, and freer flowing. I just don't know how to make it out of this hole. I feel stuck. No matter what I do, I can't wrench myself from this dismal living. Can't save my family from going hungry.

I dump the contents of the basket into the scrap heap where skinny mongrels and beggars (and sometimes poor peasants like my family) try to make a meal. Two flea-bitten dogs snarl over the mushy fruit I've just tossed in, lips curling back, heads down, ears flat. I'd feel sorry for them and might try to help them, but I might just as soon lose a chunk of myself if I get near enough, not to mention the sickness or bugs they probably carry. So, I just hold my nose against the atrocious smell of rotting things and waste, and head back down the street, eager to put distance between me and the stench.

With nothing left to do, I head home. The stone houses give way to hut-lined streets where the one-story houses touch each other. Sad, sun and rain-worn homes with streaks in the wood, some tilting precariously, sit propped up with beams of wood. Old thatching, dirt floors, rickety doors that creak and flap in stiff breezes. My small home tucks between a cramped barn and another small home with an older, raucous mead-bibber and his old maid of a daughter.

Sunlight stabs the dusty living space when I open the door, and Mother's head jerks up. She sits in the worn chair near the empty hearth, with mending in her lap.

"You're early," she says, taking in my sullen appearance as she stretches her neck. "What happened?"

"Some idiot crashed into the stand. It's broken, and everything's crushed."

She has mousy hair with strands of gray, high cheekbones, a slightly rounded nose, and a thin face. There's a freckle above her left eyebrow and another along her jawline. Her hair is usually pulled back into a knot with a ratty rag to cover her head. I've always thought of her as pretty, but through the years, her age and stress have pulled her features, making sad lines in her brow and around her mouth.

She sighs, and her face tightens as she fights the concern away for my sake. It's too late. Her fears are my fears.

"I'll gather more," I say, rubbing my temples. "But the stand will need to be rebuilt."

She smiles tightly as if to belay my worries but can't quite bring herself to believe we *shouldn't* worry.

"I can ask Gerdor to look at it," she offers softly, looking down at her work, purposefully avoiding my gaze. She knows I hate to ask anything of anyone, and especially of him.

The hut feels strangely empty suddenly. No sound, but for the creaking chair when mother shifts. No children messing about, helping mother with cleaning, mending, or playing. That's not normal.

"Where are Mellen and Cassian?"

"Mellen is down the way with Aidela learning to make pots and weave baskets. It's not an apprenticeship, though," she adds the last part quickly. "Aidela offered to teach Mellen a few things as long as we do mending for her. Her eyes are getting worse, and she has to strain to see these days. She said she could use the help."

I nod, breathing away my stubborn pride. "And Cassian?"

"Apprenticed to Gerdor," she answers, cheeks coloring, even as she keeps her gaze on mine because she knows what's coming.

"We can't afford that," I burst out. "Mother, his sleeping arrangements. His food and tools."

"Gerdor told me not to worry about the money. Cassian can come home every night. Gerdor said he has some old tools for Cassian. I can send him with some food," she answers, her face turning down as she draws the needle through stiff cloth. She means *her* food if it comes to that. I doubt it will, though. Gerdor will most likely feed Cassian. I know because I've seen Cassian munching on this or that as he sits atop the fence, kicking his feet and watching Gerdor at work. Sometimes small presents of food make their way home in his pockets. He always shares with Mother and Mellen, but that's not the point.

"We can't keep asking Gerdor for things. You can't keep relying on him like this," I admonish.

"And what would you have me do?" she questions, voice rising. "We have no alternatives."

"It makes us beggars," I counter, tears pricking my eyes at the implication. "All we have left is the roof over our heads, the little porridge or bread the mending brings in, and what we can scrounge from the forest."

"I am doing the best I can," her pitch rises, but she catches herself, regret etching her features a moment. "Gerdor can help us. I know you don't like him, but it's not his fault that your father left us in such dire circumstances. He wants to help. And we are fools to refuse. We *need* help."

Silence coats our outbursts. We do nothing to counter it, letting it hang while we lose ourselves in our thoughts. She continues stitching.

I know that Gerdor has feelings for my mother. I know she has a degree of affection for him that she tries to hide from her children. Well, me mostly, because she's afraid I won't approve. She's also afraid to love anyone. The social conventions surrounding her standing in society as regards relationships don't ease her fears.

My father disappeared when I was young. Rumors abound, and everyone in the lower town is always eager to share the story with anyone who asks. Seems everyone knows what 'really' happened. Everyone but his family.

Some people say he ran away with a younger woman. Or that he's a fugitive of justice. Or a magic-weaver assessing the castle's weaknesses. Or he was murdered.

Since his death can't be proven and the circumstances that would prevent his return cannot be corroborated, it appears to society as if we were rejected by him. We're 'damaged goods.' People don't like dealing with damaged goods. Unfair as it is, rumors are enough to hinder any progress we might make in the world. My mother is, in essence, a widow with mouths to feed, but worse than a widow, she's a woman seen as unworthy of a man (and it should be noted that this is a curse borne largely by the poorer classes rather than the rich...People with means don't have to deal with some of our limitations because they have money. Wrongs can be made right with money).

So, it is unlikely that she'll ever marry again, even if a man did want to take on children that weren't his. Which few men do. Making a living is hard enough. And for those children not to be his own...not to bear his name and continue his lineage...It's not exactly ideal for him. Thus, not a very tempting option.

Gerdor puts himself in a precarious situation helping us like this. Rumors will spread. His kindness might be interpreted in another way.

I should be grateful that some of our closer neighbors offer us these charities like Aidela. She's old enough to know that society's rules are dumb. And cranky enough to flout them if she can. Gotta love old people.

But even still, my mother doesn't deserve this life. She's tried hard to keep a brave face for us, but I've seen her at night with the firelight tracing tears down her face. She deserves more, and I shouldn't begrudge the help she's received from Gerdor. Nor should I fault her for accepting it. Life is hard enough.

I breathe slowly, taking the leather purse from my waist and handing it to her.

"If this won't cover the work on the stand, ask him if we can pay him over time, or maybe I can work it off somehow."

She takes the leather purse. Her thin, rough hands quiver. This is all the money we have.

I should have scavenged for food in the scrap heap before coming home.

It's fine. I'll bring home extra food for us when I scavenge from the forest. Mushrooms, onions, and fruit. Whatever I can get. Mother's Forest Soup will have to do for tonight. A probably tomorrow too.

"I'm going to pick more herbs," I say, slinging my hammock-like leather pouch over my shoulder and hooking the basket on my arm. Mother nods, trailing the thick leather string on the pouch through her fingers. Her cheeks seem more hollow than usual. Has she eaten in the last few days? I can't remember.

I step through the tiny door into the sunlight, the brightness brings my headache to a small throbbing pain in my temple, and I guard my eyes against the sun till they adjust. Kicking at stray stones in the road, I make for the southern gate.

It's not that I don't like Gerdor. For his quiet gruffness, he seems a kind soul if a little simple and slow with his words, but a true artist with his work. I only resent his kindness because I miss my father. Gerdor is a reminder of what I've lost. Like a hole that needs to be filled. I can't let it be filled because that means the one who left the hole isn't coming back. But if I keep it open for him...he'll be welcome when he does.

If, whispers through my soul but I refuse to hear it.

My father ran the shop when I was younger. I'd sit and watch him selling herbs, discussing the qualities of each, and terms of sale. Watching him was how I learned how to haggle, what certain wares were worth in terms of money, and fair trades (I prefer to deal only in money, but sometimes I take food or wares if my family needs them). After a hard day's work, he'd take me into the forest to gather herbs and fruits. I remember the feel of his rough hand holding mine as we walked, so I wouldn't run off and get lost. He'd point out the best spots to gather, which wares were ripe enough to take, and quantities based on the regulars who always expected him to have certain items. He always had the best to be found. We did well when he was here. With time, we might have even thrived. Moved up to the richer parts of town with our shop.

But anyway, one day when I was young, I'd stayed home to learn to make bread with my mother, at her insistence, but I soon broke free. Eating sticky dough from my fingers, I wandered off to find my papa at the stand, but when I arrived, he was gone. The wares were left out and unattended as if he'd been there moments before and had just disappeared. Thinking perhaps that he was just playing a joke, I just smiled and sat on his stool, waiting for him to pop back up. I watched every passerby, eagerly kicking my legs and giggling occasionally at how funny it was going to be when he returned. But as the crowds died down, he didn't show.

Dusk settled its blue-gray mist over the town, and all the other merchants closed up to head home. In a deserted square with the night coming on, I was sure my father would come soon, but he never did. I may very well have stayed the whole night waiting if my mother hadn't come searching. She found me calling out for my father, telling him he could come out now.

My mother spent the next few days asking the other merchants if they'd seen him. Not one of them had any information about his whereabouts. Abandoned with mouths to feed and no trade skills, my mother returned home defeated. I saw the panic etched into her brow, and silent tears of my own began. All that night, they didn't stop coming, and the next morning, without discussing it with my mother, I rose to take my papa's place at the stand.

It was my job. Or at least I knew enough of the trade to make it work, though I did have to learn to be sharper with customers who thought they could slip an unfair trade by a child. It was rough going, especially with customers who would push and bully to get their way. It taught me to be wary, to call for the guards when thieves attempted to steal things or things got too heated, to value the things I still had, and to take care of my mother whenever I could.

The memories fade as reality descends. Images in my mind dissipate into the corners and dark crevices of the stone walls around me as I walk, and my heart hardens against the incessant question before it surfaces. Always the same question whenever I think of him: Where did he go? I know there's no use wondering anymore. Wondering doesn't bring him back.

"I'm innocent. I've done nothing wrong. Please," a small voice cries, echoing off the walls as I turn down the street toward the main gate. Clumps of people have gathered to watch. I stop on the fringes out of curiosity.

"You know the penalty for using magic," one of the guards dragging her says. Her bony hands are in shackles that look way too big on her small frame.

"It wasn't a lot of magic. Please, the children were starving." Her eyes are wild with fright, her thin, white hair sticking out, and her back and shoulders are rounded.

"Isn't that Ol' Woman Ferdy? From Ilfrain?" someone asks.

"The one with the goats?"

"No, the one with the lame cow."

"If she has magic, why didn't she fix the cow?" someone jokes, and a few laugh. But I don't.

"Magic is magic," one of the guards says, pinning the laughing people with a warning gaze. The crowd falls silent and stiff.

"It was just enough to feed the children. That's all. They would have died," she says, pulling back in the weakest and most pathetic way, it almost hurts to watch. Her thin arms are like sticks bent at odd angles from the men's fists, and her knees are bent as she plants her feet. But it does no good. She's dragged along anyway. And I can't watch anymore, so I turn and go about my business. I try not to think about things like the old woman. Thoughts turn into whispers. Whispers are dangerous. As dangerous as rumors.

The guards barely glance my way as I approach the gate. I barely glance at them.

Outside the city walls and across the drawbridge, I veer from the worn road to the deeper parts of the woods where hardly anyone else goes. Wild raspberries, grapes, apples, crab apples, and pears grow aplenty in the forest, though not all at once. I suspect this place may once have been a farm before the wild took it back over.

Blackberries, mushrooms, watercress, any edible leaves I can find, and wild onions make their way into my basket, and then I begin searching for medicinal herbs. I wish winter wouldn't come and kill all the green and rot the fruit with its icy touch. I could feed my family from the forest if the plants didn't die, but already the spring fruits rot, and the flowers get replaced by ones hardier and more acclimated to the warmer weather. Later in the year, there will be apples and gourds.

I gather as many of the strawberries as I can. The King's Stable Master has a taste for them, and he was a friend of my father. He takes enough pity to visit my stand on occasion. When the strawberries die, he buys wild carrots and apples for the horses. His patronage keeps us afloat. Another form of pity that I begrudgingly take.

Then there's the King's Physician and the King's Cook, who come occasionally when they can't find the exact herbs they need from the other merchants. I always keep their favorites on hand. One is an old man who doesn't like to walk far, though, so he tries to stay in the main square, which is closer to the castle. I only see him in emergencies. The cook sends his apprentice to shop, and the apprentice has eyes for the servant girl at Verdon's stand, so the boy spends his time wooing her and shopping at the stands closer to her.

Still, I try to have the best of everything each of them could want. And my family eats the leftovers, so they don't go to waste.

My mind turns to my two younger siblings.

Cassian and Mellen don't really know our father. They were very young when he disappeared. But Cassian looks like him, same shape of the face, nose, and brow. Mellen has Papa's gray eyes and a slight figure like a wisp. She's always been quite small for her age. For a while, Mother wasn't sure she'd make it. Mellen had to have special milk, and she was sick often, keeping Mother up at night. But the tiny bundle pulled through somehow. Mother swears we could have been twins with the shape of our faces and noses, though I have more freckles than Mellen.

We all have dark hair. Mellen has to make do with my hand-me-downs, and Cassian wears Papa's old clothes, which are too big, but Mother insists he'll grow into them. Mother and I have two dresses between us, which we've worn nearly threadbare. Her mending won't hold them together forever. We'll need new ones soon.

I'm seventeen. Cassian is thirteen, and Mellen is eleven. Mother's right to apprentice Cassian. It's beyond time. It's years later than most boys. And Mellen needs to learn skills she can't learn from our mother. I know that. My issue lies with the money.

It's always the money.

Hours drag, passing me by, and darkness falls as I wander slowly, sometimes on hands and knees, to find the plants I need. Finally, I decide that there's enough to fill the stand and feed us for tonight and tomorrow. Mostly, I just can't fit anything more in the basket, the pack, or my pockets, so I stuff one more apple in my mouth, cringing at how the sourness bites back. I shoulder my pack and head for the city gate.

As I near the road, I hear muffled screams and yells from the forest, probably travelers on the road. A sharp, cutting howl rips through the air. I freeze breathlessly to listen, heart thrumping in my throat. It doesn't sound like baying wolves or the high-pitched cry of a hunting bird. It sounds larger. Much larger. I hasten my step toward the city gates, eager to put distance between the blood-curdling squeal and myself, but it slices through the thin veil of night like a blade. Shaking, I desperately hope it doesn't hear or smell me as I break into a run, hoping I'm far enough ahead to get to the gates before it catches wind of me.

I break through the tree line and see the torches on the city walls like fireflies against the night. So far away still. So much space between safety and me.

The ear-splitting scream is closer now, raking through the descending night like a wolf declaring territory.

"What was that?" one of the guards asks.

"Close the gates!" orders the Captain, and a flurry of men along the walls position themselves for defenses just in case.

"Wait!" I call out. A deadly choice if the animal hears me. It might even see me running and give chase, but if the guards don't hold the gate for me, I'll be trapped outside the walls with the creature.

"Hold! There's a girl," one of the men calls. I pump my legs harder, wind whipping my skirt, basket jostling in my arms, pack shifting across my back. I hope the contents survive. I can't afford another day out of work.

The screech pierces my ears. Louder. Closer. Malignant and hungry.

"Drop the basket, Girl!" one of the guards shouts. It weighs me. Even though I know it's slowing me down, I can't leave it. I *can't*.

Breathing harder, face heating with fear and exertion, I run harder, but the earth begins to sway under my feet as a sudden burst of pain in my head flashes white across my vision. I try to shake it away. The frenzied guards blur into spots of color. The breath catches in my throat as I fight through the panic.

"Someone fetch her," a voice floats through my ears. My legs grow heavy, and my heart thuds in my ears. I try to pull fuller, deeper breaths, but my lungs convulse, and I stagger, dropping the basket, and watching the contents scatter in a beautiful cacophony of color that soothes the vision and calms the mind.

I don't feel afraid, though I know I should. I just feel tired as the world grows farther and farther away, grayer, and my dulling senses watch it all happen with tired curiosity. I fall, but the jarring pain loosens my grip on reality rather than drawing me tighter. Instead, I float in a sea of gray, wondering at the beautiful dark blue sky with silver stars peeking out.

"She'll recover?" a hushed voice asks, worming its way into my foggy brain. The surprise in the tone hangs in the air like a hammer waiting to strike.

"Yes. It's remarkable. As if the beast passed right over her. She was covered in blood when they found her, but once the maids cleaned her up, she was completely unharmed. Not even scrapes or bruises from the fall."

"Yes, remarkable. Must have just been the blood of the others," the first voice reasons. It's significantly smoother than the second and has the sophistication of the upper classes.

The voices pull me from the darkness. A soft glow of light penetrates my eyelids, and I smell the tangy, potent scent of mashed herbs. My fingers twitch, sliding against smooth, soft, sleek material that feels too rich to be anything my family owns. Which leads me to believe I must not be home.

I suppose that makes sense, though. I passed out. I remember that. The guards must have come to drag me back through the gates. Which was brave and kind of them since they could have just left me. I owe them my life. Of course, they wouldn't have known where I live, so they *wouldn't* have taken me home. Mother must be worried. I should go. And I have a lot of work to do before the shop opens.

I turn my head, preparing to get up. My limbs feel heavy, though, like they aren't strong enough to move just yet. They don't lift like I tell them to, instead lying like logs across the admittedly soft bed and sheets. I'll rest for a few more moments. It seems I have no choice anyway.

"She's waking," the second voice points out as I open my eyes. Sharp sunlight blinds me. My brow crumples in an attempt to ward off the offending brightness. Sometimes it gives me a headache, and I really can't afford one right now.

"Get the curtains," one of the voices commands. "Are you feeling alright?"

I suspect that the question was directed at me because it was said in a much softer tone. I blink back the light as the curtains block out the sun. Then I nod at the man's question as I rub my eyes. Bright spots shoot across my vision for a moment. And finally, my eyes start to adjust.

One of the men, the upper-class sounding one, wears an ornate doublet, black with gold brocade. His gray hair tumbles in loose curls, brushed and shiny. He looks too fancy to be in the same room with me. Befuddled by him, I turn to the other man.

He has wispier hair grown long under his bald cap, but it sticks in different directions like a cow licked it. He hunches in his less grand overcoat and plain white shirt. His wiry brows lift and crunch as he feels my forehead, cheeks, and wrist. He seems to calculate his findings inwardly, humming as he does so. I recognize him as the old physician from the castle. At least he's familiar, and he must know me from my stand.

The room is large, and that's all I really notice before my dry throat clicks. I cough to loosen my voice a little so I can speak.

"Water for the Lady Heiress," the fancy man says. An amused smile cracks the bottom of my mouth at being termed 'Lady Heiress.' He must have a sense of humor. I couldn't be farther from such a person. Lady Heiresses are noble beings set to inherit an estate, hence "heiress," although sometimes that term is dropped for simplicity, as the term "Lady" can refer to any level of nobility for a woman, as "Lord" can for men. Sometimes it's easier than sharing a specific rank. Especially when they get to be long.

A servant pushes through the door with a bucket of water, sloshing as he enters.

"Easy," the rich man scolds, moving swiftly and checking his black boots in distaste.

"Sorry, Your Highness," the boy's voice cracks, as he bows awkwardly, narrowly avoiding a second slosh. He hurries to the bedside, dips a cup into the pail, and holds it out to me, dripping water down the sides.

"Olid, your boy needs training," the rich man states, his mouth in a thin line, and color rises in his face.

"Of course. Please forgive him. He's new," the physician answers, taking and mixing herbs in a bowl. "Edwin, now the whole pail is dirty because your hands have been in it. Fetch another."

The boy's mouth pulls down, but he nods, head down, as he hurries from the room.

"Apologies, Lady Heiress Orielle," the rich man says, placing his hands on his hips. "Good help is hard to find. I'm sure your father has this problem as well, but he'll be happy to hear that you're safe at least."

I look around, expecting to see the Lady Heiress Orielle, but no one else is there, and the man's pinning gaze never wavers from my face.

"My father?" I question.

"Yes, your father. He must know what it's like to have problems finding good servants," he answers as if that clarifies the subject. The physician nods sagely in agreement.

I'm still lost. Does he know my father? But that doesn't make sense. I mean...the physician, yes. But not the nobleman. And the thought of my poor merchant father having servants is laughable. The closest he ever came to having a servant was having me help at the stand. And I loved it, so that wasn't servitude.

My brain is foggy, but I recall the fancy man called me by another name. Perhaps he's merely mistaken my identity? I must look like the Lady Heiress they believe me to be.

I shouldn't be here, and this is starting to make me uncomfortable.

"I'm Ellory," I reply, but the words stick in my throat, sounding mumbled. Both men flash confused glances at each other and then at me. The Physician even stops stirring his concoction for a moment. He places the backside of his long, bony fingers against my brow again, then removes his hand, confusion and concern pressing his brow and settling over his mouth. He stoops to stare at my face, looking for something.

"She must have hit her head," he says finally, brows raising as he straightens to peer at the fancy man. "No telling what really happened out there, but it would explain why she was unconscious and took a while to come around. She's burning up too. It will take some time for her to recover."

"Best let her rest then," the rich man says, hands on his hips.

"I think so, Sire. I'll send word on her progress, though."

"Do that. I'll inform the prince of her condition. He was beside himself. I had to order him away." The fancy man's eyes swing to me. "I wish you a speedy recovery, Lady Heiress."

I smile weakly in reply, waiting for him to turn and leave before scrunching my nose. How can they think I'm a Lady Heiress? My clothes, my smell, my hair, and the dirt embedded in my nails must be obvious to them.

"Who was that man?" I ask the physician. He shoots me a quizzical look.

"That is King Beregon. Surely, you know him?"

I shake my head. "The King? Why would the king be here? Why would he be concerned with me?"

"A bad fall indeed," the old man says to himself, shaking his head in pity. He goes back to mixing his concoction. "But I intend to fix you up as best I can. You'll be as good as new soon. Never worry about that, My Lady."

Enough is enough. I've got to get home and let Mother know I'm alright. She'll be worried. Then I have work to do, collecting new herbs and setting up the bare makings of a shop so I can sell something at least.

I put all my focus into rising, but the physician shakes his head at me.

"Not yet. You need to rest. Here," he says, handing me the cup that he's been mixing. "Drink this."

I recognize the foul odors as a sleeping draught. Strong and designed to let the body rest and heal. I shoot him a confused look.

"I can't drink that. I have to get home," I say, "My mother needs me."

A profound sadness crinkles his old eyes, and his wiry gray brows frown.

"My Lady, your mother is dead. And *this* is your home now."

My skin tingles with hot pricks of fear and dread. Mother is dead?! How? Why? Did the creature get her? What happened? What do I do? No. She can't be dead. I need her. And what about my siblings? Cassian and Mellen need her, too. Oh, Great Kings! How am I going to take care of them on my own? Do they know? Where are they? I need to find them.

But it's too late...While I panic, the physician pours the contents of the cup down my throat. I feel it taking effect.

Time seems to stop as the image of the room stretches before my eyes. Tiredness like a weight on my eyelids, my eyes start to close against the numbness.

Wait...No...have to find them. They'll need looking after. And with that thought, a wave of exhaustion lands on my brain like a field of black, knocking me into a stupor once more.

Chapter 2

Maehdiorah

"There may have been someone there who needed our help," Elonrod says, flashing that 'I'm innocent' grin of his. "We won't know if we don't check now and then."

"You're not supposed to expose yourself in town," says a gray-haired woman with sunken eyes. "You might have been caught."

"I had it under control," Elonrod insists, like he's comforting the woman. "They'd never catch me. Besides, they're not gifted like we are. There's no way they could hold me even if they weren't slow and lumbering."

"They have ways," someone says.

I wait for someone to point out that *if* he were caught, his breaking loose and subsequent disappearance, certainly utilizing magic, would spark speculations of magic-users among the city folk, which would insight panic. The knights would be called from all corners of the kingdom to ferret out the offenders. It would be chaos.

"If someone had seen you-"

"But no one did," Elonrod says, his eyebrows pulling up earnestly. "I didn't do magic inside the city. Just some harmless pranks, and the guards got upset. That's all."

"Getting their attention is unwise," says a crinkly old man named Gomthen. His back must be bothering him today, because he's grimacing a lot. His thin, old arms lean heavily on his cane. "They will begin to know you by sight."

"I understand, but you know..." Elonrod keeps talking, but his mouth turns up as if he's not in trouble at all. As if this council hasn't been called for *him*, so the elders can dole out their warnings and potential discipline for his reckless behavior. He won't get in trouble. He knows it. *They* know it. This is just keeping up appearances.

The truth is, they *need* him. And they'll excuse his jaunt into Thorondar just like they've excused every other time because he's their darling. Their rising star. The next to take up his seat on the council, not as a member but as their leader.

They've not had one for some time. The council of elders makes decisions for our small community (only a few members of which are here now, like Erian, Reathl, Theliod, and me). We all pitch in to some degree, which is why I'm here now despite not being a sitting member of the council. I am one of the peer regulators chosen for today. Meaning, I'm to give my opinion if called upon or if I feel it necessary to chime in. I rarely do. Instead, I make sure my face doesn't echo my sentiments that this is a complete waste of my time.

In our community of five hundred and six magic-users, the leaders are chosen by their abilities with the gifts, intelligence, and character.

And Elonrod is the most talented being they've ever seen, which marked him from a very young age. He's been groomed by them. And despite his penchant for causing minor trouble in the cities and villages (like bored young men are prone to do), he's exactly what they want in a leader, and many are eager for him to take his place.

That's why he'll be lightly reprimanded, if at all, and sent on his way while they smile at his exploits as he tells tales around the fires tonight.

I'm not jealous, just annoyed. And only slightly. I don't care what he does as long as he doesn't ruin anything. I wish he were more careful.

If he's caught, there will be consequences. And more so if the guards in Thorondar ever find out what he is. Not just for him, but for all of us. And a future leader should take that into account at least, no matter how confident he is in his abilities. Putting his people at risk is no virtue.

The council shifts, ready to hand down his reprimand. It is as I thought. He's told to be careful, and the council disbands with their warning demeanors slipping away into familial love for the boy.

He merely grins and nods at their words as the children who'd been waiting by the tent door for it to be over rush inside, eager for the trinkets he's brought them. They swarm Elonrod, chattering at once, reaching for the things he pulls from his pockets. Asking him what it was like in the city, what he did to the guards, and how he got away.

He leads them outside, and they trail along. Some mention the brave pranks they'll pull when they're old enough. I see the elders exchange looks, but no one says a word.

I hope Elonrod sets the children right about the dangers of his exploits...though likely, he won't.

No longer needed, I take my leave.

Life is always happening "right now." That's what most people think and feel anyway. What's in front of their faces, what they see, hear, feel, think, and why those things are the most relevant and important. It's a very short-term view.

But life is the extension of it all, the overview. The many lifetimes and generations that come and go. The flow of civilization. The expansion of knowledge. The development of new technology that builds on what came before. The process of millions of lives pushing towards a goal, and over time, either failing or succeeding. It's the lives that existed from the beginning down to this moment and continue beyond.

The problem with people is that they have short lives, which makes them shortsighted. They think no one's ever felt the way they feel. No one's seen what they've seen, been through what they've been through. They're stuck in a field of corn, only able to see as far as the furrow. But they believe the furrow is what matters. But what truly matters is the whole field. There are countless furrows. They may catch glimpses of another's furrow-I'd call that empathy-but they are stuck traversing their own rut.

A simple metaphor, and far from perfect or exact. But it does illustrate the depth of humanity's perceptions as opposed to those who see much, much more. And watching these humans can get...exhausting. On one hand, I pity them. On the other hand, I wish I could make them see the bigger picture. But if they did, it might break them.

And they want it all 'right now.' 'Right now' is not always the best time to have the things one wants. But impatience has a way of distracting the mind from logical thinking. A way of twisting people's ambitions and making ends justify the means. And people will do horrible things to get what they want sometimes.

'Right now' isn't calculated. It isn't levelheaded or strategic. It's the petulant cries of an undisciplined toddler. But these people who want to be free of the oppressive laws against magic and the people who wield it...to them, this tyranny is far bigger than their furrow. It encompasses it. It's all they see. They feel the pain of it 'right now,' and pain is an intense motivator. They're desperate to find a way out.

Magic-users. Magicians. Witches. Sorcerers. Enchanters. Many strains. Many combinations of gifts. Many potential professions. All enveloped under the single domain of magic-users. That's the technical term used in royal decrees, so Kings can get away with killing anyone who has any ounce of magic at all or the potential to wield it. And sadly, even those who don't. People have been executed simply for rumors, whether or not they've used magic. Without proof, the kings reason that it's better to rid themselves of even the suggestion than to let it alone.

The relationship people have always had with magic is complicated. It's seen as a disease by those who can't wield it. Call it jealousy. Fear. Or logic...since it can be wise to fear what others can use against you. But it's treated with caution, wariness, disdain, hate, anger, and even mobbish frenzy.

But there was a time before the Dark Risings when magicians sang the crops to life during hard years. There were times when magicians could encourage rain, dispel rot, and disease that infested crops and livestock. Kings themselves used to use magic or use those who wielded it. Sometimes for conquering or defending. In times of war, magic-users of all occupations and talents were called upon for their abilities. They weren't just allowed to walk freely through all the lands; they were celebrated. Beloved. Paid well for their talents and contributions. Encouraged to thrive. It was an honor to be a magic-user. A gift.

It wasn't always like *this*.

We weren't always hunted, shut away in dungeons, forced to endure suffering and an existence of degradation. But a few bad apples have spoiled the bunch, which is why here and now, magic-users are forced to hide their talents, and often, flee for their lives.

They're not just second-class citizens like the peasants. They're not even the dirt under society's boots. They're the creepy crawly things that decompose bodies in the earth. At least that's what the ungifted believe about them. And the reward for turning in magic-users can be great. Bounty hunters have made life incredibly difficult, so the magic-users are always on the run or ready to pull up stakes and move.

Which is how we ended up here on the banks of a small river. Our scouts caught wind of bounty hunters in the woods. Those men didn't seem to know about us yet, and we were able to evacuate the camp quietly in the night before they knew what they'd nearly stumbled onto.

Now, these outcast magic-users tentatively set up their tents and makeshift corrals for their animals. The small children play near the river or hide and pounce in the tall reeds. Some help their parents; some begin their lessons with the teachers. Every so often, one can see a streak of gray on the wind: magic-users patrolling the area to make sure we're still safe. Especially since this place is new to us.

I know my evaluation of humans seems harsh. And I don't blame them for wanting so much in their short periods of existence. It makes sense to do so. Otherwise, life is only suffering, and when a short period is all one has, of course, they want it to matter. And most of them want peace and joy.

Luckily for these particular humans, the time to get what they desire draws near. Soon, they won't have to pitch their tents in hidden valleys. They'll roam the cities once more with our non-magical counterparts. They'll protect kings, heal the sick and wounded, and provide help that non-gifted people can't do on their own.

That's why I came to them years ago...because I know it can be done. We can put off the oppression of the kings. Be a celebrated people again. Build our schools like in the days of old and encourage magic again. Build a better life not just for our kind, but for others as well.

Soon, but not yet.

They want to fight 'right now,' but I urge caution. I tell them we don't have the numbers or the strength just yet. But they don't want to listen, because they want to be free 'right now.' It doesn't work that way. It can't. I've been fighting this war for centuries, little by little, so I know.

It will be difficult. It will be deadly, and many of these people here before me will not make it to the end. But those that do will be free. And their children will be free. And that flow of civilization, Life, will move on that way.

Even now, I lay the groundwork, stone by stone, until everything I have planned is in place. It is a lot to do by oneself, but I have time and resources. And I know it will be done correctly. Once I am ready, the time will be 'right now.'

Chapter 3

Ellory

Wet tears haunt my cheeks before I become conscious of anything else. The crackle of the fire glows soft orange against my eyes, the slight sting of smoke singing as my eyelids slide open. The small fire gurgles over the wood, dancing happily in the fireplace. Immediately, the deafening cloak of night and the steady, relaxing drone of home press upon my mind. My fear and the pain of loss melt away under the comforting scent. Everything is where it should be, including me on my small straw pallet in the home I grew up in.

I must have been dreaming. A very realistic dream, but I'm home now, and relief tingles across my skin as I look for my family.

Sure as the light of day, my mother sleeps nearby, sitting on a stool, leaning over the table with her head on her hands. The rise and fall of her back and the sound of her long, drawn-out breaths let me know she's fine.

Relieved, I swipe at my wet cheeks, laughing a little, feeling silly for crying at a dream. The stress must be taking a heavier toll than I thought. But it's alright. We'll be okay as long as we're together. And maybe that's all I need to focus on right now. Life could be worse than it is. I just needed to put things in perspective. I'll try to be more positive and less afraid.

I stretch, and my arms pop. I don't remember how I got home. I must have been out cold. How embarrassing. The guards must have thought I panicked and passed out because of fear. I shake my head in disgust at myself. That's *not* the reason I passed out. I'm not a waif. I was terrified, but...my head...

Oh well. It's not like I care about their opinion of me. At least I'm home safe, but the herbs? I look around, hopeful, but knowing I won't find them here. The image of my hard work spilling out of the basket as it fell out of my hands flashes across my mind, and I sigh, disgruntled and angry at myself. There's no way anyone went to pick up the things after I dropped them. And they shouldn't have. Not with the beast out there. I wonder what became of the animal, whatever it was? And what of the people I heard screaming?

But I can't really think of that now, or I'll lose my nerve, because I have work to do.

I toss back the thin blanket and throw my legs over the bedside. The rustle wakes Mother, who jerks upright on her stool.

"You're awake," she breathes, the stool toppling as she dives at me and crushes me into a hug. Her chest heaves in silent sobs. I pat her back, realizing how scared she must have been.

"It's okay. I'm alright," I soothe. She pulls away, wiping tears with one hand, the other pressed against her chest to calm herself.

"We weren't sure if you would be okay or not. We couldn't wake you," she says. "I didn't know what to do. I sent for the healer, but she was attending others and couldn't come."

I rise and pull her into a hug, letting her cry against my shoulder, hiding my own tears because I hate having scared her like that. She doesn't deserve to fear losing a child. Not again. She's already been through that. And not just with Mellen as a small, weak baby, but with me as well.

I was stillborn. Mother and Papa were heartbroken, but I managed to draw breath. Sometimes she still calls me her miracle baby. But being that to her puts just as much pressure on me. I'm already the eldest, but to be her miracle baby too...Makes me feel like if I'm only alive due to a miracle, what am I alive for? If not to take care of my family, I don't know. And I feel like I'm letting them down. Her *miracle* is letting her down.

But I have to stop thinking things like that.

We stand together for a moment, sniffing and crying quietly so we don't wake the children. Finally, when she breaks to wipe her face, I ask how I got here.

"Gerdor went looking for you when we heard that terrible screeching sound. He and the guards brought you home."

I breathe through the embarrassment, hoping it doesn't show on my face.

"And the basket?"

"They were more concerned with getting you safely inside the gate," she answers as if I shouldn't worry about that over my life.

I knew the basket would have been left behind, but hearing it said gives no comfort.

I curse silently. My stupid luck to faint and ruin everything.

"It's just stuff. *You* are more important than stuff," she says, brushing my hair back, as her brow lifts sternly. That look she gives to remind me who the mother is here. And I can't argue. Especially after the night we both had.

"I'll go salvage what I can," I reply quietly.

"No, you won't," she counters. "You lie back down and rest. Tomorrow can take care of itself."

"I can't afford to rest." It's odd, isn't it? The concept that even rest costs money. Every second costs something.

"Yes, you can. And you will, because we'll survive another day or two without the shop." Her face is still stern, but her breath catches in her throat. "Please."

Oh...

I'm worrying her *too* much. I sit, or rather, fall back onto the bed.

"I have to go," I say, meeting her gaze as she stands, wrapping her thin shawl tighter around her shoulders. The fire is dying down. "Even if the guards never kill the creature, we still need to eat."

She shakes her head vehemently. "We'll find another way. Gerdor has already offered-"

"We can't accept."

"We don't have the luxury of picking and choosing," she shoots back. She takes a deep breath, closing her eyes. Her hands clench in frustration. She's searching for a way to make me understand, but I'm trying to find a way to make *her* understand.

"There's no use getting yourself killed going after the basket," she says evenly. "That creature killed an entire camp of knights. All of them dead except those who went missing. And you go out by yourself into the deeper parts of the woods all the time. That's not safe. What if something happened when you were out there? No one would find you, and I'd be worried sick. I can't bear the thought of you not coming home, so you can't go out anymore."

Anymore? Like...ever?

It rings in my ears like the warning bells on the gates. Hair raises on my head, tingling as my eyes pop open.

"Mother, I don't know how to make this work otherwise." I burst, tears crowding my eyes. Desperation takes over, and I hide my face in my hands because I can't hold back the fear any longer. Despite the revelation that we'll be okay if we have each other, we *can't* make it if I don't have an income.

We can't do this. Gerdor's charity is proof of that. Proof of my inadequacy and my faults. And it hurts, burning a hole in my chest and reminding me of the failure I am, the hopelessness of our situation. We might as well beg on the streets for all the world to see, to pity, to spit on, and kick and mock.

Poor peasants. That's all we are. Virtually useless. An eyesore to the upper classes to be sneered at and looked down on.

The warmth of Mother's hand on my shoulder pulls me back from the brink of complete despair. I still have to keep it together. For her. For Cassian and Mellen.

I've got to think of a way out of this.

I hold on to her hand until the sniffling subsides, and I breathe normally again.

"Let's get some rest," she suggests. I nod, pulling back the thread-bare blanket on the straw pallet. She slips onto the other with Cassian and Mellen, cuddling her two growing babies. Suddenly, they don't seem as young as they used to be, and I think of them both trying to earn a living for us, too. And someday...their future families.

Seems just yesterday I was coming home after a day at the stand, watching the two eat their dinner at the small table. Cassian always gnawed at his potatoes like a wild beast. Mellen always picks the skin off hers before eating it. She always looked so young and prim in those moments. But she's not a baby anymore. She's had to grow up.

I've shouldered this responsibility for so long and tried my best. But I'm terrified. And I fear I'll buckle under the weight of my failure.

When I'm sure my mother is asleep, I sneak out of bed and through the door. I don't mean to worry her. And I'll get in trouble for this later, but it will be worth it if we can eat without having to ask for help. I need this.

The haze of graying morning snuffs the lower village, but it's enough to see my way. I hasten toward the city gate, determined to retrieve something, *anything* I can sell today.

The guards stand formidably, if not a bit tired, atop the gate. One snoozes in the gate tower.

"Can I pass?" I call out to them. The sleeping one shoots upright.

"Are you mad?" They ask, peering at me. "There's a dangerous creature out there, and we're under strict orders not to open the gates at night for anything but crown business."

"Oh, this is crown business," I call back in my 'haggling' voice, nodding assuredly. "The King's Physician needs special kinds of herbs. Only I know where to find them. He sent me." I just hope they believe me.

"I wasn't notified," the gate tower guard joins, looking me up and down. "You don't look like a servant of the King's Physician."

"I'm a merchant from the lower village. The physician is a customer of mine," I answer, which is technically true. "These are special circumstances, and he can't find what he needs in the city."

"Must be for the Lady Heiress," one atop the gate reasons.

"Yes. She needs special care," I answer quickly.

"Fine. Then you may pass but be quick about it. The gate closes behind you and doesn't open till you get back, understood?"

I nod, and the gate tower man gets to work raising the gate just enough to let me through.

"Hurry back," one warns as the gate closes behind me. The sound echoes through my chest with the thud of my heart. Barred against the walls and the safety of the inner town, my courage ebbs, but I force one foot in front of the other, walking a little stiffly because I feel loose like jelly.

Out in the open, I feel exposed, and the woods interject themselves darkly and ominously into my view, because the forest could be hiding anything. Belligerent with night, they stare back at me as I watch for the faintest traces of movement in their midst, waiting for the creature to clear the trees and charge me. I shake off the chills, breathing shallowly and rubbing the pricks of fear off my arms.

The basket lies where I dropped it. What a fool I am, I think as I practically fall over myself to gather what I can.

Some of the softer fruits are bruised, but the heartier of my bounty has survived like the onions.

The light still dull, I can barely make out a few of the herbs that scatter through the tall grass. I scoop handfuls, wondering at how they crackle in my hands. They've withered more than they should have for just one night. Almost as if they've been out here for a whole day. I can't have been out that long...

Heat rises in my face. I must have been, which also explains Mother's fear. She had to watch her child lie unconscious for over a day. I sigh, dropping my head into my hand for a moment and rubbing at my face. It's worse than I thought, and mother didn't tell me I'd missed a whole day in the shop already.

She didn't want me to worry.

This whole not worrying thing is really starting to mess with our well-being, though. *Not* telling me things is worse than telling me. At least I can *do* something with the truth, with reality. I can't if I don't know what I'm dealing with.

Frustrated, but resolved, I continue snatching at all the herbs I can find, still casting furtive glances at the woods and expecting a shrill cry to announce my impending doom.

I lift the basket and head back without so much as a leaf stirring...that I know of.

The strange stillness in the morning confuses me as I walk back to the gate. The guards let me in without hesitation but say nothing more.

I walk through the waking streets to my regular place on the market street to set up for the day. Mother will be upset with me when she wakes, but she can't argue now that it's done.

The stand lies in the sorry state it was in before I left. It's actually quite lucky no one stole the wood, but I guess they could have gotten better elsewhere. I set to work, getting the space worthy of at least *some* business today. Even if it's just a little.

Mid-morning lies heavy in the streets like an old dog lazing. I've propped up the half-shelf that survived and display the best of what I was able to gather. It's not much, but it's worth trying to sell today. I try to pretend it's not as dismal as it seems, but I feel like a child again, sitting cross-legged on the ground, waiting for some soul to buy the bracelets I had made out of weeds. Papa had indulged me, letting me set up my dandelion, woven grass wares because he approved of my eager spirit. Now I don't even have rudimentary weed wares, but it's still just sad. I'm having a hard time putting that feeling off as I stare at the measly spread. It's a fraction of what I'd normally have for sale.

And I feel off. More tired than usual. My mind feels only half awake today, dazed and feverish. I hate feeling this way.

I glance at my makeshift clock. The shade of my corner pole (which I've reset based on the marks on the ground) has reached the midpoint mark. The subtle marks I've made along the wall indicate times of the day so I can determine when I'll get the most business.

Generally, the day starts with the first wave of customers as the sun has barely risen. It's cooler, and the men are heading out to the fields or going about their work. Then, sometimes, the 'courtlier' folk arrive. Mostly to gander at the pretty things up the way. Another rush will come when wives and mothers come out to get dinner supplies for their families, who'll be home around dark. Until then, the occasional meanderer will wind their way through the marketplace. They'll look, but they probably won't buy. When the sky yawns, and the sun dips below the tall forbidding mountains in the west, the farmers and tradesman make their way home, maybe stopping by for something extra, but that is the last opportunity of the day. After which, I usually pack up my stores and head home.

It's the same every day unless there's an event going on. Then we get even more merchants vying for positions in the better spots. Some come from the villages and set up big tents, muscling some of us out of the way and causing nasty fights over space.

But most of the time, the market is manageable.

I rub my eyes, half in frustration, half because the sun glares off the stone wall opposite me in the street. It's blinding this time of day, so to keep my focus off it, I watch roving customers whose eyes roam over the wares of merchants up the street. The general muttering amongst the wandering groups of twos and threes, barking dogs, and yelling children isn't loud, but the sounds add up, creating a buzz of voices that bounces off the stone walls and echoes down the corridor. Between the sun, smell, and the noise, my daily headache begins.

I press my hands into my temples and rub hard, but the ache doesn't subside. Unfortunately, the headaches are getting more frequent, more painful, and my body grows more tired with each passing day, despite the amount of sleep I get.

I *have* to be here. That's just the way of the world. We work for a living, and if we fail to work...I think about this too much, though. My mind loops over it because I just can't find the answer.

Around me, similar shops sprout along the street and up through town. Varying from my embarrassing excuse of a shop to larger, full buildings with larger, more colorful blankets, which garner the most attention from the passersby with the promise of more merchandise or at least a less gritty experience. Even the first levels of houses become shops, offering more permanent locations. Thorondar's market is the largest in the kingdom, running from dawn to dusk, collecting the largest portion of buyers of any in the kingdom because it sits in the capital city of Drene. And it's popularized by the rare visits of royal family members. As a result, merchants enjoy a variety of buyers, sometimes stemming from outer regions just to say they've been here, some taking souvenirs back.

It's too bad I can't afford a spot further up the street where the mobs are attracted by the fancy banners and the criers offering 'better' merchandise and competitive pricing. Gimmicks are prevalent. Annoying, but they work. Ish. By my estimation, it'll take me seventy years to save up enough to pay taxes on a spot like that. But the sales would be considerably better and would compensate for that. Eventually. Then I'd be doing fine.

I can feel my mood turning sour like watching a homemade boat toy sink in a pond. Bad humor sticks on my cheeks and darkens my brow as I slump over, propping up my face with my arm. Some of the would-be customers cast me fleeting glances as they pass me by. I simply follow them with my gaze until they're out of sight.

A head of dark brown hair pokes into view from behind the wall just up the street. I notice because of how slow and calculated the movement is, like stalking prey, and that's odd for the city. I squint against the sun to get a better look, and the figure notices me watching them. Sheepishly, the degenerate from the other day, the one who destroyed my stand, stares at me with a goofy grin on his face and an uncomfortable blush across his cheeks and nose. He shuffles closer, hands in his pockets, as he stares at my pitiful shop. He's on the taller side of average, gangly even, with strands of dark brown hair hanging haphazardly over his brow, and patchy dark hair on his face like he's trying to grow out a beard but hasn't quite matured enough yet. And he's got a confident, cocky stance and set to his shoulders despite how his foot scuffs the dirt. It's like he already assumes he'll be forgiven, and that rubs me the wrong way.

"What do you want?" I snap.

"I came to apologize for the other day," he answers with his annoying grin in place. I stay seated, tucking my hands under my legs.

"They didn't catch you? Too bad. They should have thrown you in the stocks. Then I'd at least have a *fun* way to dispose of the fruit you ruined."

He bats a nod at me like and shrugs like 'that's fair.'

"I deserve that. And to answer your question, no. They didn't catch me. They couldn't catch a cold."

I don't know how to answer that, so I remain silent, hoping he'll feel awkward and leave.

He shuffles. "Anyway, I wanted to say I'm sorry for destroying your shop, and-" He stops dead suddenly, brows screwing together in an urgent, but confused way as he stares at me. Almost as if he's assessing a threat, and his hands find their way out of his pockets now. He leans closer, as if trying to read something scrawled on my face. Too close. I lean as far back as I can.

"What are you doing?" I ask.

"What are you?" he whispers so as not to be overheard. His eyes dart around quickly and then land back on my face.

"A merchant," I answer, wrinkling my nose and staring back in confusion.

"No, not that. You know..." he says, nodding his head like I should understand what he means.

"What?"

"You know. Like...like what can you do?"

"Pick and sell stuff?" I offer, gesturing to my meager goods. "I sell herbs and fruit. I'm pretty good-"

"No," he answers shortly, shaking his head in annoyance. He casts furtive glances around at the people nearby again to see if they're listening. Then he leans closer. "Like magic. There's magic in you. What magic can you do?"

I stare dumbfounded and afraid. Is he *nuts*?

"I don't do anything like that. That's illegal," I snarl back in a hushed tone, glancing at the merchants nearby to see if they've heard. I'm affronted that he would even bring something like that up. Even the suggestion of magic can get someone in huge trouble around here. Stocks. Torture. Execution.

"Oh..." he trails off, pulling back a little and regaining himself and his surroundings as he ascertains my confusion. His face clears of emotion as he realizes he's said too much.

"I have to go," he says, turning on his heel and striding through the crowd.

"Yeah, get lost," I breathe, watching him purposefully cutting directly down the street without wavering. I try to put it out of my mind, but nobody's ever looked at me like that before. I've seen faces contorted with anger, disgust, mischievous mirth, contempt, loathing, and despair. I've even seen joy in some and pity in others, but never the look he just gave: an intense, soul-boring gaze meant to unravel every fiber of my being and lay it bare for inspection. It was incredibly vulnerable, and I don't like it.

What did he mean by asking what I am? It's a little rude. No, it's a *lot* rude.

I knew he was rude because of the incident. A decent person would have helped clean up their mess. Still, the odd look worms its way to the forefront of my consciousness because it doesn't make sense. And because it was unsettling.

And what was he thinking, bringing up magic in public? Idiot.

Put it away. It's nothing. It won't matter in five minutes. In fact, it hardly matters now.

Can't argue with that.

"...still haven't killed the beast," a woman's voice cuts through the usual noise as she walks with a friend down the walled corridor. Both peasants but better off than my family. Probably servants in the King's household.

"I hope they kill it soon."

"Me too. To think it's just outside the city walls..." They share a shiver, continuing past my stand without a glance. "Traveling isn't safe anymore."

"No one has even seen it. Well, apart from the Lady Heiress Orielle, but she hasn't recovered. I hear the physician doesn't know if she will."

My head swivels in disbelief, and I strain to hear more of their conversation as they walk away.

"I heard the animal ripped the entire armed guard to shreds. Blood everywhere," one of them indicates with a gesture. And then they disappear around the corner, taking their conversation with them. I curse silently. I wish I could have heard more.

I shudder with the memory of the beast's screech, and the hair raises on the back of my neck as goose bumps skitter across my arms. Seems a random coincidence that the ladies speak of Orielle. It brings up my dream with the physician and the king. How strange...

The screams I heard in the forest...That must have been her party then? And the guards who helped me could have talked of her while I slept? That could have conjured the dream I had.

That poor girl. She must have been terrified, and to be the only survivor...What was her party out there for? On the road here, maybe? Not that it matters, I guess. Wrong place, wrong time. And part of me understands the fear she must have felt. To a small degree...I didn't see the things she saw. Obviously.

My headache worsens like a child throwing a tantrum. It refuses to be ignored. The light burns my eyes, and sounds ricochet through my brain incessantly in an overwhelming cacophony. Even the scent of the herbs stings my throat. All I can think of is wrapping myself in the blanket and hiding in the shade of the wall behind me, but that doesn't look very professional, so I sit, glaring at the light, rubbing my face, batting the sweat off my arms, and wishing time would pass faster so I can go home and press a wet cloth or even a salve to my burning head.

I can't go home, but I can rest my eyes for a moment. Yes, a little rest sounds nice. I feel myself slumping before everything goes black.

CHAPTER 4

MAEHDIORAH

There are three kingdoms on the mainland. And a few smaller scatters of people who'd rather be left alone and have fought viciously to be such. That doesn't stop the kings from occasionally trying to rein those ferocious peoples in. Or there are vassal states that pay homage to particular kingdoms. Or those kingdoms of the seas.

Drene currently occupies the northern and eastern territory of the mainland. I say "currently" because borders shift over time. In days past, they've been known as Mountlan, but that was when the mountains were much taller than they are now. Drene's king is Beregon, and he's fiercely against magic. As are the other kings.

Merendhere comprises a decent part of the land that was once Farlan, which touches the sea on the west and butts up against mountains on the east and south.

Cordain squishes between the northern parts of the kingdoms of Merendhere and Drene. It is much smaller than the other two. But it is the richer, with various mines of gold, silver, precious stones, iron, and salt (which would have been taken long ago by one of the other two if not for the army of mercenaries Cordain was able to buy from the ferocious people they welcomed into their land). Its territory stretches over a varied landscape, running north to the mountains past which humans do not often go because of the cold, uninhabitable climate, and down to the territory once known as Rimfar, which was destroyed long ago by Thagyn the Dark Magician, but has since healed.

I have watched these lands shift and change: be reborn, renamed, territories clawed out with swords, borders bought with blood. They are ever changing. As is history. Being rewritten as it can be.

And we, as specks of dust on the wind, have the audacity to think our lives mean something...

But I digress.

Kings live well. Their subjects...as well as they can. Money is distributed from the top down. It filters up and up and up through the classes. And then being filtered back down as the kings see fit. To their vassals for their loyalty. Knights are bought this way, favors too. Land estates are passed down, sometimes falling into the King's hands through wards, unpaid debts of the nobles, or lost by unfaithful Lords or Ladies. And he distributes some of his lands at his discretion.

And all of this is extremely boring...But humans like this game for some reason. They've played it for centuries and never seem to stray from it. Always, someone seizes power and, in essence, recreates this system in his own regime.

There are some kingdoms over the seas, and sometimes ships return laden with exotic goods. But often, these territories are seen as inferior. Once a king of Merendhere launched a navy to take these territories, but the navy was lost in a storm. He was furious. The territories had not been worth his navy, and the incident left a bad taste in all the kings' mouths. There has not been a navy sent since. Only privately owned merchant ships take the burden of potential loss on themselves. And on occasion, have to pay that price.

It is written in the historical records that ships went out much more often. Seafaring and piracy abounded. Great cities sprang up along the coasts and thrived, bringing riches to those who sought them. Not so much anymore.

History saddens me. Thinking of things that are no more. The stories amuse and entertain me. And knowledge is always something to be sought after. But history denotes a wisp of what was and will never be again.

Thoughts like this sober the mind. Here and now will happen once and soon be the past.

I step away from the campsite. Though I can keep my mask on with people, I prefer space and aloneness. Years of being part of their community have been awful. To keep my sanity, I walk in the woods often, craving that solitude.

I'm not a being of many words. I don't like speaking often to the members of the community. Partly because I know they're not long for this world, and partly because I find their small-mindedness confined and hard to deal with on a regular basis. It drains me.

One never feels more alone than when one can't be understood. To be honest, *I* don't mind being misunderstood or alone (As long as their misunderstanding of me causes me no grief). Alone is one of my favorite things. I never feel lonely. There are no other minds to disturb me with incessant, meaningless chatter. And the emotions they have...Such beings have a hard time seeing past their emotional nature to what should be done. It's tedious and inefficient. My energy is best spent elsewhere.

At what point do feelings become thoughts? Or emotions logic?

And on some level, I understand that emotional beings react emotionally, and it is logical to allow them to choose things that satiate their emotional sensibility since they are and will remain as such. But their emotional sensibilities might be better suited if they took hold of their emotions and suffered a little more in the present for greater reward in the future.

Most just wish the pain would subside and do anything to make it so. Fools. They could have everything they want and more if they simply worked a little harder. But...perhaps they don't really want what they say they want. Perhaps their emotionality blinds them in ways they don't understand (yes, this happens. I've seen their ignorance in the face of their own feelings firsthand. Point that out, though, and they get even more emotional and self-unaware. It's almost as humorous as it is obnoxious, only serving to prove my point).

For example, sometimes they say they want to practice their gifts to hone their craft, but they spend more time fishing or gabbing with their friends and family than doing anything resembling practice. Point this out to them, and they make excuses for why they *must* fish or talk instead of practicing their gifts.

"I'm tired from a day of working."

"I can learn tomorrow."

"This other thing really needs to be done. I'll just finish it first."

I don't fault them for their choices in leisure time. I just prefer honesty in action. I wish their words aligned with their choices. It would make it much easier to understand and sympathize with them, and nothing irks me more than dishonesty. Especially to oneself. Logically, it only puts a strain on themselves by creating a dishonest relationship with their own minds and spirits. Besides, if one cannot be honest with themselves, how can they be honest with another? But another point...no progression in one's life can be made without the honest, clear introspection that lays bare their weaknesses. Hardly anyone wants to truly face their own demons.

But they say they do...

Frustrating humans.

But...humans are *human*. Confusing, complicated creatures that insist on their rightness even if the evidence clearly states otherwise, and they will fight to the death simply because they can't admit to being wrong.

Which is stupid. Thoughtless.

But I digress.

Humanity disgusts me most of the time, and there were long stretches of time when I left them alone. But there is an injustice in this world that is baser than the humans I currently keep with. And there are old wounds to heal. Too old for anyone living to remember accurately, but for the stories that have been passed down, being distorted as the centuries roll on.

I have some of the original stories. They're etched on my heart. But I don't correct tall tales when they are told. Stories, when told, become more than reality. They become fantasies that humans cling to in order to fulfill a basic need. Therefore, there's no good to come of my telling the stories as they truly happened. Besides, if I *did* correct them, people would question my authority on the subject and how I could possibly know such things. I would either look like a fool or have to drop my mask, so I let it be. And because one story in particular is too precious to me to be told as it happened.

...

Yes. I prefer to be alone rather than constantly battered by illogical humans, but I have to stay. I have to complete my task. Once it's finished, I'll be free to return to my cottage in safety and solitude. I'll tend to my garden once more and cultivate the wildlife that linger there.

There will be no more need for my expertise and planning. My work will be done. At least for a time. I can choose to remain immortal or pass on to the next life.

But here and now, I have a problem.

Elonrod is the key to my plan, but he could ruin everything.

His recklessness and arrogance make him an easy target for the king's men, yet he insists on pushing his limits.

He thinks because he's the greatest magician in ages, he can't be caught or taken down. It's unwise to think that way. Even the Dark Magician Thagyn couldn't rule forever. He failed eventually.

I need the boy to be careful.

"Telisan?" a voice breaks into my thoughts. A small voice of a child from the community. I turn to engage with the child, because that's the name I'm known by here. I'm unhappy at being found, not having vented properly, but the tone of her voice suggests that the 'grown-ups' told her to fetch me.

"There's a magic-user Elonrod doesn't know about in the city. They said to get you."

"I'll be along shortly," I say, but the child waits, so I move toward her with slow strides over the patchy grass. She holds out her hand for me to take as we walk back to the camp. I take it to comfort her, giving her a quick squeeze. It is 'Telisan's' way to be kind to the children, at least. And to be fair, the children aren't as annoying as the adults.

"What did he say about the magic-user?" I ask.

"That she's a merchant. He has no idea what she is, though. She doesn't know she has magic. So, he left."

"What do they want me for?"

"To make plans to bring her here. He says you're smart."

"Ah, of course," I say as if that's all that needs to be said. Sometimes we rescue those we find who have magic. And it's unusual that the boy's gift *can't* tell him about the girl's talents.

I must admit I'm curious myself. The boy's gift has never failed him in the past. But if it has now, I need to know why. Might have been because of a magical suppressant the king has deployed in the city, which I will need to know how to counteract. Or it might be the boy is slipping. And if he is, he might need to be pushed to work harder. Or perhaps the girl herself is something different.

Either way, I have work to do.

CHAPTER 5

ELLORY

"No change?" the voice asks, hovering somewhere above me. It sounds familiar, but I can't place it.

"She has some color back now," another says. "It's strange. She was fine before. Seemed like she would recover. I can't explain this last turn. It's as if she were near dying."

"Perhaps a bout of weakness? A wound you did not know about?"

"I'd never be so careless," the man asserts. I can tell now it's the physician, and he sounds almost affronted. The other voice must be the King. And as I think it recognition sets in.

"Then what was it?"

"I can't explain it any other way. She was well, and then she wasn't."

"But you say she seems to be recovering again?"

"She was paler an hour ago. Her blood flows a little stronger now. You can feel it. Here." Something rough holds my wrist tightly, and I feel my own pulse against a calloused finger.

"No. I trust you." The man's hand leaves my wrist, and cool air pricks my skin.

"Let me know if there's any change," the king commands, and the door squeaks as his boots on the stones fade.

I don't like the way they talk about me like I'm not here. I'm not comfortable with the attention, nor have I ever been. And where is Mother?

No. She wouldn't be here. This is the dream again. Which would explain why everything is dark and hazy, or why I can't wake myself up despite being fully aware of the sensations around me. It's almost like I've been entombed in my own body.

That thought springs at me like a cat coiled on its haunches, wrapping its claws around my brain. Panic surges through my body like lightning, livening my limbs. I sit upright, sucking in a deep breath as if I'd been drowning.

"Relax, My Lady," the physician says, "Nothing to fear."

"Dream. Just a dream," I say, calming myself. I'm not actually dying. I wasn't actually stuck. It's just a dream. That's all.

"Yes, you're finally awake," he counters as he continues mixing a foul-smelling paste. I purse my lips because I don't want to waste a dream arguing about something pointless. Besides, the dream will change soon enough, and all of this will be but a strange memory. Why am I dreaming this again, though? It's like I picked up where I left off last time. Probably just because I was thinking about it before I fell asleep.

Generally, my dreams shift away the more I try to focus, so I do in the hopes that this will pass.

There are two windows along the wall bearing the warm, white-yellow glow of the sun. They light the tiny space better than the torches, which stand along the walls and in the corners. Many shelves line the walls, and some are even suspended from the ceiling above a worktable. Along these shelves are spices, herbs, bottles of various shapes, sizes, and contents, as well as leather-bound books. Bowls and grinders, measures and balances take up much of what I can see on the shelves directly ahead. Turning, I see the rest of the herbs and things that would be useful for medicine. There is also an armoire, which I assume contains the dangerous varieties.

The room is shaped sort of like an 'L' with the medicines in the toe. The bed is in the corner, and the entryway is in the stem. In the stem is more of a receiving area for guests and a couple more beds for the sick. Quick flutters of the birds outside cast flighty shadows on the walls.

The only souls in the room are the Physician, his servant, and me. The only sounds are my breathing, the clinking from whatever the Physician grinds and mixes.

"Alright, Lady Heiress, your medicine is ready," the old man says, rising with cracks in his bones and pouring the liquid into a cup. He hobbles stiffly to the bedside, wielding the medicine. I cast a suspicious glance at it.

"What's in it?" I ask. It smells foul.

"Something to help you feel better. Not to put you to sleep this time, though. Likely, this last bout of sickness was because of something in the last batch. We won't make that mistake again."

"Alright," I agree only because whatever it is won't hurt real-life me, and I can always wake up. Kinda wish I could wake up before having to drink the stuff...

His rough, calloused fingers plug my nose as he pours the contents down my throat. I gag at the taste and the clumps of herbs clinging to my tongue, but I manage to get it all down. As the physician releases my nose and pulls away, I feel the medicine sliding into my stomach and settling. Oddly cold, the sensation spreads through my abdomen and chest.

I shiver.

"You seem much stronger today, Lady Heiress. Less confused. More yourself. How are you feeling?" the man says, placing his hand against my forehead and then my cheeks to feel for fever.

"Fine, I guess," I say. "Other than the headaches."

"Headaches? Do you get them often?"

"Almost daily," I answer. He nods, taking mental notes as he feels under my chin for swelling.

"And do you notice any triggers? Similarities between when you get them or what causes them?"

"I think it might be stress. It's too bright, there's lots of noise, the smell is overpowering, and then my head starts to hurt."

"I see. And how did your last physician treat them?" He moves to my wrist to check my pulse.

"Oh, I treated them myself. I just put something cool on my head," I admit. "Like a rag dunked in the water bucket." Not that it really matters, but I don't want to shatter the man's illusion that I had a 'last physician.' Somehow, playing the Lady Heiress, he thinks I am, is kind of relaxing. I get beyond my own troubles for a moment. I can take this with me into waking life and think about what it's like to be treated as a noblewoman...that'll be a fun fantasy to pass the time at the shop.

"Treated them yourself," he repeats low to himself, turning my wrist back over to a more comfortable position. "Well, I had not been told of your condition, but I'll work on a remedy for you."

"You don't have to," I say politely as if it'll matter.

"Not to disrespect your Ladyship, but I do. As the King's guest, you are entitled to his hospitality. Not only that, but he's ordered me to take care of you better than I'd take care of my own daughter. Not to worry. I'll send the boy for herbs, and we'll fix up your headaches in no time."

I thank him and tilt my ear toward him as he orders the boy to fetch certain things.

"You're sure, you remember?" the physician demands a little sternly as if he has to check the boy often.

The boy nods.

"Name them then."

"Calendime, frurarty, lechistime, peashbaria, and loodenber," the boy recites. I know those herbs. I stock them specifically for the Physician because he's the only one who wants them. It's too bad this is a dream. I'd make a good money on a transaction like this.

"Very well. See that you go all the way down the market to the girl with the fresh stuff. You know the one?"

I scoff at myself. I must be so stressed that my dreams are trying to save me from financial ruin.

The boy nods again, annoyance in his nasally sigh.

"Get going then," the Physician waves him away.

I'm not there, though. The thought leaks through my consciousness.

I'd better wake up.

Strangely, waking up feels like falling asleep. One moment I'm there and the next...

"Hey! Are you ok? Are you dead?" a voice filters through some part of the black consciousness that envelops me. But I can't get out because my mind seems stuck inside a dream. I feel my body. I hear outside noises. I know I need to wake up, but I...can't?

"Hey, girl," the voice says louder. Something smacks my shoulder. I topple, and the falling sensation rips me from sleep. I grab for anything to hold onto, but I'm too late as I hit the ground hard, jarring my shoulder. I suck in a deep breath against the pain.

Everything is bright like the peak of the afternoon. My shop is undisturbed. Thankfully, no one stole anything while I was asleep. I rise, stretching as I rub my shoulder. Sweat coats my brow and lines my hair. I feel its stickiness under my shirt, too. I feel gross and dizzy with sleep, but I meet the physician's boy's gaze.

"Great King of the Ancients," he says, "I thought you might have been dead. I see dead people all the time at the castle, so I know what that looks like. Usually, they're all pale and puffy. Sometimes they-"

"Yeah, I get it. What can I get you?" I redirect, not looking for any more chit-chat than necessary. At least he came all the way down today for herbs. The physician must need them for something special.

The boy closes his eyes and thinks, his eyes scrunching as he rubs his face.

"Calendime...frurarty...um," he pauses, face screwing up as he tries to think.

My blood tingles in my veins. A shiver runs through me as my dream resurfaces like a memory. That can't be right. It must be a coincidence. But my skin prickles with cold, and I ask the boy, "Do you want lechistime, peashbaria, and loodenber too?"

He blinks in surprise.

"Yeah. How did you know?"

"Those ingredients complement each other in specific medicinal concoctions," I answer quickly, hoping he doesn't dig deeper as I search for the specified herbs.

He falls silent, watching me until I come up with what he asked for. He hands me the bag of coins, takes his wares, and saunters back up the street.

I tuck the money away and settle back in my chair, wondering over the coincidences that no longer seem to be coincidences.

Dreams are just dreams, but they did *feel* real. I saw and heard things that have come to pass. Maybe that's what the mischief-maker meant when he said I have magic.

I think they call it a seer? The people who see the future? What about people who see the present? Like through another's eyes? Is that a common magical ability? I know very little about magic. I just keep my head down and ears closed when it comes to those types of things. Don't even gossip.

I shudder violently at the sudden chill that sweeps through my body. Goosebumps rise on my arms despite the heat. I rub them, darting my gaze around at anyone nearby who might be watching me. No one seems to pay me any mind.

I can't have magic. That puts my entire family at risk. But what can I do? Hide it? I guess I have been so far. As long as I don't talk in my sleep. But I'll have to be very careful. And I've never purposefully used magic. I certainly have no intention of using it for ill.

But I'm afraid of myself. Afraid of where magic comes from and what it will do to me. I hadn't really thought about it before, because magic has been banned for many years. It has never been relevant to me other than transactions with questionable figures from time to time, but most magic-users don't make it this close to the castle. Even if they wanted to try, the castle has defenses for such things. Hounds that can smell if someone has magic. Crystals...

If those hounds find me, I'm dead.

But say I *could* use the magic for good? For my family? Could I even control the magic to do so? Would anyone know how? Or am I just a conduit for its will? For instance, will it just take over and work in whatever way it sees fit, and I'm merely a slave?

It's not like these things are taught to the public. Why would the kings want us to know that? We just go on old stories.

Can I tell Mother? What would she do? She'd be worried. It would be one more thing for her to fear. Just another reason for us to sink even lower than we are. Would she send me away? Where in this world is even safe for magic-users?

That trouble-maker would know.

He *must* have magic. Why else would he be able to tell I do too? And the whole concept seems foreign and makes my head dizzy.

He won't come back, though, or shouldn't if he knows what's good for him. Most likely, he'll be afraid I ratted him out to the authorities. He can't risk coming back to the city.

And...in all seriousness, I may be wrong. I may not have magic. But two dreams that reveal things I didn't know? That seems a bit more than just explaining away. And the coincidences? Not likely.

The weight of this terrible secret settles on my shoulders.

Nothing much happens at the stand until the end of the day. Head swimming, nauseated, I try to gather the wares, but give up mostly because the world refuses to stop spinning, and it's messing with my ability to stand. I lean against the wall to rest, disgusted by how weak I feel, especially since I've slept...a lot.

I decide to leave things as they are. I can throw a blanket over. But how will I gather fresh herbs tonight? The thought of making it to the forest seems bleak, and with the creature still out there...

I just don't think I can make it.

My fingers brush the bag of coins. We won't starve. Not yet. Maybe this will buy a few days. I'll have to conserve it, though. Just get it into mother's hands. She'll handle it.

Chapter 6

Maehdiorah

I steal away in the night. One of the benefits of being a lone soul is that no one questions when I go for long walks. I hear Elonrod dazzling the children with his talents at the fires, their awed noises and giggles rising into the night. When the work is done for the night, most of the community sit and talk, but there are some who guard. I pass one with a little nod of my head as he tells me to be careful.

I walk for some time into the woods, listening to the sounds of the forest, reaching out with slight wafts of magic to feel if another is nearby. Through the wind, through the earth, and plants. The scouts have settled for the night, and nothing human stirs around me for quite a way, which feels like pure freedom. The thrill of aloneness never fails to brighten my mood at least a little. I soak it in.

Freedom has the sweetest taste of anything in the world. Others disagree, and that's fine. I'm not them and they're not me. Some seek fortunes, others seek attention or adulation. My peace is freedom.

Aloneness has been my dearest, most constant friend, keeping me safe and warm. It kept me alive and gave me purpose.

But I cannot stand and soak it in for too long. Another needs me.

So, catching hold of the wind, I speed through space to a clearing in a similarly wooded place. Reaching out with magic, I probe the area for signs of life, any life. But I only feel various day creatures asleep and night creatures roaming.

I stick my hand into my pocket, touching the smooth, dark stone, rubbing my thumb over its surface fondly. The sensation sends vibrations through the ethereal plane that call out to my creature, and I wait patiently for him to get my message. I don't have to wait long. Shadow travel is quick.

I feel him coming in the shift of the winds and the darkening of shadows. Then a trail of shadows elongates and draws into the meadow. A pool of darkness gathers like murky fog, taking shape as it grows into a large wolf-like form, and Lelioth tests his surroundings to be sure it's safe before he steps towards me.

I reach out, melding my feeling to his, looking for any pain, physical or otherwise. But it seems his darkness keeps him hidden and safe. There are no new scrapes or cuts to mend tonight. I'm pleased with that. It hurts when he hurts, and though he's strong, he's not entirely impervious to weapons. He cannot be killed with mortal weapons alone, but they still bite.

His eyes glow as he locks onto mine, but his head dips so I can pet him. I rub the space between his eyes and up onto his forehead and atop his ears. He leans into the scritches, eyes closing. He seems well-rested, as though he'll be strong tonight. The darkness attests to his readiness for the hunt.

Lelioth is my pet, a forbidden creature I brought forth long ago. And he is dear to me. I fear the day I will lose him. The thought comes often and saddens me greatly, but such is life. It moves on. And the mortal passes with it. Sometimes the immortal, too.

But there's no reason to dwell on that here and now. I've come to ensure he's safe and well-fed.

I whisper to him as I spend a little extra time rubbing behind his ears. He loves that, and the darkness stretches with him as his shadowy figure plops onto the dead leaves, asking me to rub his belly.

"It's going to be a good night for a hunt. Plenty of good things to eat," I say as I pet him. His paws flick. His ear twitches as he picks up on something too far for my hearing, and he squirms onto all fours, alert and watching.

"Is it time? You can go," I say, and he swings his head to match my gaze before the darkness around him shifts back into shadows. He melts away like a cool summer breeze under a warm sun. And I sense I'm alone again.

I wait a moment, enjoying the stillness. Nothing stirs, and most of the animals have left us for fear Lelioth would eat them. Most things fade away when shadows become dangerous. It's only wise.

And I must fade away too into the night. I don't want to go back to camp. I wish I could visit my cottage, rest, and enjoy the silence, but I have duties. I have a promise to keep. I have people who rely on me.

I will return to camp shortly, listen to the sounds of camp, be annoyed by the strangeness of humans, play my part, and await my freedom. But for now, it's nice to sit in the empty woods and pretend that I'm home.

CHAPTER 7

ELLORY

Anxiety vibrates from the old Physician's fingers as his hand lands on my brow. Familiar scents of herbs fill my nostrils as well as the sounds of the old physician's breathing.

Why do I keep returning to this dream?

I open my eyes, not surprised to see the physician's chambers, but getting annoyed, and wishing I could dream of something else.

Night casts a dark spectral feel across the walls, combated and kept at bay by the torches strewn about. They cast a golden-orange light.

The old man heaves a nasally sigh.

"You keep giving us scares like you're dying," he admonishes.

"Sorry..." is all I can think to respond with as the man backs away to see to his herbs, but his words itch at my thoughts. Dying? Am I dying?

A half-formed thought zings through my consciousness. One that I'd barely notice, except that it catches on my emotions like a sleeve on a doorway. It begins to form as it takes hold of my soul. A thought that I can't believe and can't shake because it's too strange and terrible and makes no sense.

This doesn't feel like a dream. My senses are too sharp, nothing wavers, my sight isn't tinged with gray...Nothing has changed. It's all too clear. Too perfect. Too real.

I run my fingers over the fabric of the sheets. I feel the fibers woven together, the rough wool of the upper blanket, which has tufts clinging to it. I pull my arms together over my stomach, pressing a fingernail into my hand. I stare at the half-moon shape left on the soft palm that certainly doesn't feel calloused like mine.

No...this doesn't feel like a dream.

I conjure thoughts without the haze of sleep blocking me. Thoughts I control. Thoughts that make sense and are backed by memories. Real ones: the last conversation I had with Mother, Cassian, and Mellen asleep on their beds, things I've heard and seen here...I remember them well.

It's definitely not a dream.

What does this mean?

Is this how seers dream? Like reality? Will I be haunted by this forever?

Or is this some spell I'm under? Did that boy from the market do this to me? Because if he has magic...

Whatever it is, it's terrifying. I have no recollection of coming here or of being brought. The Physician doesn't know me as the girl from the stand. He knows me as Lady Heiress Orielle and the King...If this isn't a dream or a spell, I've been in the presence of the king. As a magic-user...

Oh, Great Kings!

I'm going to get caught. I'm going to be found out. And then I'm going to be executed.

I shoot up, immediately regretting that decision as pain radiates from my stomach, slashing at me. The sheer force of white-hot burn knocks me back onto the pillow, a sheen of sweat breaking on my forehead as I grit my teeth. My hands tremble, cold as I place them against my abdomen, searching for the source.

"What happened? What's going on?" I cry out, seeing the physician hobbling quickly to my side.

"What did you do?" he returns, throwing my protective hands to the side and lifting the wool blanket off me to check my stomach.

"Here? Is this where it hurts?" he asks, "Feels fine. Must be internal. What kind of pain is it?"

"Like a stabbing pain. What happened to me?" I ask again, tears slipping from the corners of my eyes. I can't help it. It hurts so bad.

"There was a lot of blood when you came to the castle, but no external wounds." The pain subsides gradually, and I settle back into the blanket, panicking and clawing for understanding.

"How did I get here?"

"Don't you remember? The beast. The patrols found you and brought you here," the Physician says.

"I'm in the castle?"

"Yes, King Beregon's castle. You're safe here."

"Is this real?" I ask hoarsely, needing to hear the words come out of my mouth, to hear someone answer.

"Of course, it is," he shoots back, gray, wiry brows crunching on his forehead.

"I don't know. I don't know," the words come out of my mouth because they loop in my head. I hide my face in my hands for a moment.

What am I going to do? Am I going crazy? What do I do? How do I find out?

I need to stop. I need to relax and think. Panicking is not going to help me right now. I need a solution.

Here's what I know: I keep having these 'dreams,' but I also keep coming out of them, and everything is normal again. The beast *is* real. My family is real. The fruit stand is real.

Anchoring myself calms me a little. I keep going.

My father left when I was little. (Okay, that took a dark turn.)

My family needs money to survive (Not much better.)

My name is Ellory. (That I can get behind.) My name is Ellory.

"There. That's better. Relax. The blood doesn't flow so much," he approves, wiping my forehead with a cold, wet cloth.

I force myself to breathe deeply and let it out slowly.

It's okay that I don't know what this means. I'll figure it out, I tell myself. But since I don't know what's going on, I'm going to need to act it out on the off chance that this is real. The Physician must not suspect me of using magic, but I'm definitely not the Heiress Orielle. I will have to pretend, though...

It's good that he thinks I've hit my head. I can get away with not knowing things. I can ask about this woman as if I have no memory, and that will help.

In the meantime, I need to put the pieces together. Worst case scenario, I can always walk home.

No, I can't...I don't look like *me*.

I'm...in another person's body.

...

This is some sick sort of magic. It's really the only explanation. Someone did this to me. I don't even know what this body looks like. Who she is.

Great Kings...

That must be what the blackouts are. Switching back and forth. Maybe I can get back to my own body?

But how does that work? Can I control that?

Maybe I just need to wake up from whatever this is. Pain doesn't do it. Falling?

But I don't have to worry for long. Panic drained my energy, and I start to feel heavy with exhaustion. Darkness beckons from behind my eyelids.

Ah! Sweet relief! The way home. This time, I just need to stay there. However, that works...

I feel the world float away as I sink willingly into the darkness.

I wake to a pounding in my brain and exhaustion that overwhelms my bones. I can't lift my arms to make them work. It's a little frightening, like being tethered enough not to float away, but not being able to pull myself to safety. I'm aware of sounds on the other side of my consciousness. But I can't interact with them. My eyes won't open. I don't have the energy. Just like before. It's terrifying.

The fog around me lets in pieces of the outside world. Crickets and the sound of footsteps. A voice calling my name. The voice of a boy turning to a man, and I want to call back. The sound grows nearer with his footsteps. And suddenly I'm reminded of when I was little, looking for my father at the merchant stand.

Am I *still* at the merchant stand?

"Ellory?" Cassian calls out, his tone relieved and afraid all at once. The scuff of his calloused feet is loud against the stones. "Mother is worried. You need to come home."

His voice grows louder as he nears, and I can feel him smack my knee.

"Wake up, Ellory. Mother is waiting." He smacks my knee harder. The fog begins to lift, slowly. I groan, feeling like boulders weigh me down.

His hand lands on my forehead, feeling for fever. Then his hand falls away and lands on my shoulder.

"Ellory," he calls louder, giving me a shake. Slowly, my body musters enough energy to open my eyes at least. I find Cassian through the blur of my eyes and the blue of night.

"You don't look well," he says.

"I don't *feel* well," I croak. But the haze is overwhelming, and trying to stand only worsens the dizziness. I fall back against the wall.

"What do I do?" Cassian whispers. His harshness is only a product of his fear, but it makes me feel like a bad sister. I'm terrifying him.

"It's okay," I answer immediately. "I just need a moment to wake up."

"I'm gonna get mother," he says, darting away before I can tell him not to worry her. He disappears down the winding corridor.

I've got to follow him. I try to rise again, but the fury of a pounding headache knocks me down like a thump to the head, and all I can do is swallow back the fear and the pain, holding my head in my hands.

Great Kings! What am I going to do? This can't go on.

I sit stewing in fear, resentment for my situation, and desperately trying to keep awake until my mother arrives.

This is the last thing we need. Hopeless and helpless, I feel the weight of everything that's wrong. Tears slip down my cheeks because I don't have the energy for anger.

I hear them coming up the corridor once more. I think of home and my family and how nice it will be to rest there for a bit. This isn't the end. I'll recover and get back to work soon.

I'll take care of my family.

And the darkness descends once more, but instead of pulling me out to the dark ocean where consciousness exists, I float up. My vision is veiled with a thin whitish layer. I think I'm standing, but I can't feel the weight of my body anymore. It's like falling and flying all at once, being hollow so the wind rushes through me, cold and stinging.

There is no tiredness, no aches. And the world is strangely muffled. The sound of my mother and Cassian arriving stretches and bounces together as if I'm hearing them from the other side of a waterfall. I see people approaching. My mother gasps and rushes to my side, bending down. I look down to see why and start in horror and confusion.

I see myself lying on the cobblestones, still leaning heavily against the wall. My face ashen, lips bruised, eyes wide, lifeless, staring. Haunted by the image, I turn away, gazing at Cassian, whose eyes bulge with fear and surprise. He trembles, wrapping his arms around himself and then clinging to Mother as she tells him to get Gerdor. He walks a few paces to oblige her, but his eyes are riveted on me in horror and fascination.

Mother returns to my lifeless side, covering her mouth with her hand, tears streaming down her face. She sniffs and sobs, petting my tangled hair with a quaking hand, touching my cheek, grasping my hand. She clasps my head in her hands, soft sobs turning to wails, and pulls my body nearer, cradling and rocking back and forth.

Time has very little meaning here. Some moments seem to stretch, while others are fleeting. Gerdor suddenly appears, face grim, jaw set, lips pursed as he kneels next to mother, his hands on her shoulders as if he's soaking up her pain.

"Ophalia," he says to comfort her.

Shock melts away, and I kneel beside her too, craning my neck to look into her face, but she can't feel my presence. She's not aware of my existence right next to her.

I'm...*dead*.

In that place where one might be awake, but probably isn't, I can see the Physician's quarters around me. It's night. I'm alone, and I feel like I'm floating above the bed, but there's a voice that beckons me into a darker place. Something dangerous. Something more than sleep. Terrified, I try to open my mouth to ward off the darkness, but instead I let out a loud snore that wakes me with a jerk. Breathing heavily, I stare wildly at the familiar surroundings with the sharp scent of herbs, and the sounds of wood shelves creaking and settling.

My head feels like a fog has lifted. Like everything is clearer than it's been in a long time. I feel like myself, whole, energized, and without the headaches. In fact, except for the pain, I feel much better. I feel *alive*.

What am I doing here? And what happened to Mother and the children? I should find out. The linen sheet falls away under my brushing hand. I rise, still surprised and relieved at how good I feel, and I think I can run the stand all day without a problem. I wonder what the Physician did to help me feel better. No wonder the King employs him.

I don't know my way around the castle, but I can ask someone for the way out. From there, it's easy to get to the lower town.

What do I say to my family, though? How do I tell them who I am? I can't tell them it's me. How horrible might it be for them to have a stranger show up at their door when my dead body lays in their home? That would be cruel and even if they believed me, it would put us all in danger.

I could tell them I'm a Lady Heiress, just checking on them. But why would I check on them and no one else in the lower town? That would look suspicious. Women of nobility don't go to the lower town anyway. Separation of classes makes that a difficult issue to navigate.

I flip my hair over my shoulder, trying to figure out any possible way I could get home, but then it dawns on me once more that I don't know what I even look like. My eyes fall on a looking glass across the physician's room, and I move towards it a little hesitantly. What if I don't like the face staring back? It won't be *my* face. But I have to know.

So, I look.

Staring into the slightly clouded surface, I see a whole different person who stares back. When I raise my hand to touch my face, she does too. When I touch the icy mirror, she does too. She's as surprised as I am.

That's definitely not my face. That's the face of a noble, soft and pale. She's terrified, her light brows pressing together, her small chin dropped slightly in surprise. Her small, delicate nose points up. Small, plump mouth with pale lips parted slightly. And her gray eyes sweep over my face, focusing on all the details.

The hair is blonde. A light blonde, thick and long, like it's been well-maintained. Like the nobles do. I gather it in my fist for inspection. Long, flowing, pretty like it's been brushed. It's jarring. My hair *was* brown and rougher, oilier, frizzier, and kept in a braid.

She's wearing a silk nightdress with a light blue tint. I've never worn something so elegant and delicate in my life. Against the night air, it cools, leaving very little to warm myself with, and I shiver, hugging my arms to me. My *white* arms and hands. No tan lines from being in the sun at the stand for days on end.

I knew I'd look different, but it's so surreal it gives me vertigo. I no longer have the pieces of me that were my history: little scars from the wild cat I tried to tame when I was little, or the burn mark from the cookpot on my arm. My freckles, my calloused hands, my features that look like my mother and Mellen. It's all gone. Only she remains. This new person who's actually dead and not here at all. A ghost in the mirror.

A ghost that means something to the people here. She had a life. Memories. People she loved who love her still. I'm going to have to meet and interact with those people. See her life, live it for her (if I don't want to get caught). How do I live a life I know nothing about? Especially with nobility?

This is all very overwhelming. And confusing and confining.

I feel trapped.

CHAPTER 8

MAEHDIORAH

The castle gates aren't hard to get into. It's simply a matter of the hounds and whether they are present or not. Also, it does matter if anyone nearby is wearing special crystals that glow when magic is nearby.

The crystals are conduits for magic. And quite useful for various acts of magic. I've found several myself and use them often. It's ironic that the kings use magic to *detect* magic, but no one seems to talk about that.

The hounds have a more scientific way of weeding out magic-users, which is scent. The scent of magic in the blood.

Magic is akin to a life force. It lives within the spirits of the people who have the ability to wield it. It binds to the blood and body of the person or 'vessel' and, with the combined efforts, it becomes a viable 'gift' or talent that one can use and potentially grow.

The depth of magic a being is capable of wielding depends on who their ancestors were. Combinations of magic-wielding potential can grow or diminish within a bloodline over time. Which is also why we have very few truly talented individuals these days, like Elonrod. Talent for natural magic is waning in the world. According to my findings, there's no other magic-user currently living that rivals the power of Thagyn, save perhaps Elonrod. But whether Elonrod is a direct descendant, I can't say. Nor is it important. What's important is that here and now, Elonrod has asked for my help in extricating a girl from the city before she's found out. So, I accommodate even though I'd rather not go to the city.

Our guise: two simple peasant folk from the outer villages. I've talked him through a backstory, should anyone ask. But it's not likely anyone will. We will probably be ignored.

The real difficulty will be extracting the girl without raising questions. Worst case scenario, we grab her and disappear. Best case, she understands when we tell her we're here to help her. She follows us, acting completely naturally, and doesn't say a word to her family about where she's going and why.

Of course, they never choose the best-case scenario. I'm not a monster...well...not to the degree that I don't understand familial ties. But I also understand death and torture, and that goodbyes and explanations can be done once we're safe. That's one of the human things that people have a hard time with, though, even if you explain it to them.

Most likely, she'll be confused when we explain she has magic, go through shock, fear, and disbelief, not want to come with us, but ultimately realize that it's what's best for her and her family, and come with us, but want to talk to them before she goes. We'll have to convince her not to, and she'll come while secretly planning her way back to the city to see them again.

That's how it goes most of the time when we have to 'rescue' someone. It can get messy and complicated depending on how strictly they stick to their convictions that they must say goodbye.

We have speeches for that. And force if it comes to it. It's important that we protect our camp, the people, and the location after all.

Elonrod points out the stand where the girl sets up her shop. She sells herbs and fruits, from my understanding, but as we approach, Elonrod starts looking up and down the street. Instead of the girl at the merchant stand, there's a boy setting wares haphazardly. No one should put kingscrun anywhere near the dillywor, but this boy has no idea what he's doing. He's got a mop of curly dark hair hanging over his eyes. He's in the awkward part of the growing step where he's definitely not a child, but nowhere near being a man.

Elonrod walks right up to the merchant boy.

"Hello. The girl who usually works here. Where is she?" he asks. The boy stops dead, face turning sad and pale as he clenches his jaw. He looks down and starts handling his wares a little slower and more delicately.

"She's dead," his voice cracks.

Elonrod stiffens.

"Dead? How?"

"She was sick a lot. It finally took her."

"She was your sister?" I ask because I see the glint of wet on his cheeks, and he swipes his nose quickly. He nods. "Our condolences."

"Sorry to hear that," Elonrod says, his voice deflated. He's blaming himself. I can tell by the cut of his brow and the clench of his jaw. If he'd been here sooner...If he'd talked her into leaving with him when he ran into her...If. If. If.

But she's dead, and he can take comfort in the fact that she wasn't found out. It was merely a sickness. We might have been able to cure her, but it's no use in feeling sorry now. She's joined the spirit realm.

"Is there anything you need?" the boy asks, gesturing over his goods.

"No, we just wanted to see your sister," Elonrod says, but I step up to the shelves and start switching things around.

"These can't go together," I say, separating the dillywor and kingscrun. "They'll spoil faster, and if they touch while spoiling, they'll let off a noxious gas. Never store them inside your home together, either. Accidents happen. Always keep one outside.

"Also, you'll want to lay these out by size," I say, holding the frurarty up so he can see. "People buy them based on how much they need. It's easier to calculate if they're lined up properly. Place the more popular herbs upfront and at eye level. You'll get more customers that way. Send the less popular ones to the back and the sides. See these? These are rare. Make sure people are aware that you specialize in rare herbs. They'll start coming to you for the stuff they can't get elsewhere. I assume that's how your sister stayed in business?"

I move around his little shop as I go, rearranging and putting a decorative spin on a few of the eye-catching herbs, creating fans with some feathery ones, laying a few flowery ones by color. Then, having optimized his shop, I step away.

"Memorize this layout if you can. I'm assuming your sister was the one who gathered the herbs as well?" I don't need him to answer. It's obvious by how little he knows, but I wait for his confirmation anyway.

He nods, though he's wearing an overwhelmed expression. I'm not sure how much of this he'll retain, but it hardly matters.

"Then you'll want to look near marshes for these ones," I say, pointing to the grubdula in the center. One of his most rare. Very popular despite how little knowledge ordinary people have of the root and how they underutilize it. It's much more versatile than people know. "The others can be found in various places in the woods here but be careful."

"Thank you," he says after waiting a beat. "I was afraid I'd fail at all of this. It's so different than carpentry."

"Remember what I told you. Practice. You'll figure it out," I say, though I know even as I say it, he might not actually figure it out. It's just a nice thing people say to encourage others.

"Sorry again about your sister. Good day," Elonrod says, and turns to go. I follow, giving the boy a quick parting smile to give him heart.

"That was nice of you," Elonrod says when I catch up to him. We walk side-by-side except for when we dodge oncoming traffic.

"He needed help," I say. It serves my purposes for him to think I'm being nice to the boy. Really, I can't stand to see something I know so well being done so poorly. It grates on me, knowing it could easily be fixed. My hard work will most definitely fall apart, but for a moment, it was done right.

"He was the one who found her," Elonrod says. I'm not surprised he looked into the boy's head. It's one of his gifts. "He's still sick about it and feels guilty that he didn't go looking for her sooner."

"Perhaps nothing could have been done," I answer to soften his own guilt.

"Perhaps," he echoes.

We pass through the lower town. Once outside the gate, we'll traverse the road a ways, acting like we're heading to one of the smaller villages, and when no one's looking, in the blink of an eye, we'll be back at camp.

But he hesitates and walks more slowly.

"The strange thing is...I could swear she's still here."

I stop, staring at him for a moment. "What do you mean she's still here? Her ghost tarries?"

"No...I can't explain it. I don't know what it is."

"Thought? Feeling? Sense?"

He shakes his head. "I can't tell." He looks around the lower village, and I can tell he's reaching out with his gifts.

"Don't be too obvious," I warn. He doesn't hear me. He's listening to all of *them*.

"I don't know," he says finally, but he won't give up. He doesn't like puzzles he can't solve. He's too arrogant for that.

"We can come back," I say, because I don't want to stay in the city. We have no idea how to find the girl. And his gift may be failing him. I don't like dealing with things I'm unprepared for, so I'd just prefer to leave.

"I suppose," he answers. A confused look presses his features for a moment, but then he turns and heads out of the city.

I catch up but keep a step behind. This is a problem to solve. It's unlikely she'd have died and recovered. Such forms of magic are classified as 'Dark' magic and hardly touched, even by those who have magic for what it does to the user.

That being said, there are only a few reasons Elonrod still senses the girl.

Either she's a ghost that Death hasn't come for, in which case his gift has taken on a new scope, which would be incredibly fascinating to explore.

Or perhaps he's wrong about what he senses. Misreading someone else as her or he's not interpreting what he's sensing correctly. This could mean his gift his failing (like I've mentioned), or it could mean the king has a new sort of defense against magic that may scramble our abilities. This is a terrifying option considering I'd have a new element of warfare to discover and counteract before I can move forward with my plans.

Or...she's not what she seems. And given that he doesn't know *what* she is, that might be the more likely option.

Obviously, this predicament requires more study. I doubt the boy will give up on finding the girl if he's so sure she's still out there. I'll need to tag along...just to make sure things still run smoothly if nothing else.

CHAPTER 9

ELLORY

S unlight pours into the room, waking me. I rub my eyes, making colors explode across the back of my eyelids. The first thing I notice is the absence of spicy smells. That's odd. And my eyes pop open.

As I thought...I'm no longer in the physician's workspace. And I'm not quite sure how I got here...

I feel like I've sunk into a cloud. I'm lying on a large, luxurious bed, and a slight breeze from a window plays with the draped canopy overhead. Fancy woodwork lines the posts with gold chasing silver inlay. I see a large chest by the bed, gilded with iron and carvings of war. Then there's an armoire of the same dark wood standing against the wall, partially open with colorful silk spilling out. Long divans and soft carpets stretch across the floor, vibrant greens and blues, edged with gold silk threads. The windows are actual glass, seamed by gold panes and garnished by colors portraying scenes from the countryside, a farmer hoeing near his cottage so realistically portrayed I can hear the metal slamming into the earth, spattering stones. Another displays a stag being chased by excited hunters and barking hounds. It's stunning.

A vase of fresh wildflowers graces a small table by the bed.

My heart sinks. I just thought if I could open my eyes and be home, it would be like I dreamed the last few days. Like they'd never happened at all.

But I'm not that lucky.

I stretch my limbs, feeling the soft sheets against my feet and the bedding underneath me. I suppose there are worse places to wake up to. I should be grateful for that at least.

I have no idea how this happened or why. But I need answers. I just don't know how to get them without people getting suspicious. I can't exactly just start asking questions about magic. That's how people get hauled away to the dungeons and executed.

Although there was the mischief-maker, and he might have answers. No one asks those kinds of questions without reason. Especially not the way he asked. And it must have made sense in his mind to ask those kinds of questions. So, how would he have come to that conclusion? Likely, he's got magic himself. Where did he disappear to? That must mean there's somewhere safe where he hides. If I'm to find answers, it'll be with those types of people.

I'll probably never come across him again, though. He might not come back. Even if he does, there are thousands of people here to look through, and I don't look like me anymore.

So...that leaves me with little to go on.

It's fine. It'll be fine. I just have to get a feel for who I'm supposed to be and then go from there.

What I know of the royal family is that the King and Queen had seven children. Three of them died tragically. The whole city churned out to see their bodies somberly brought through the city on funeral carts. The eldest son and heir died from sickness. The third eldest perished in an accident involving a horse. Something to do with it landing on his chest, and he couldn't breathe. From the story, no one could help him. They had to watch him die, struggling to breathe, face turning blue. And the second daughter also died of sickness. She'd been born small, from what I understand, and didn't grow properly. My mother wept when she saw the tiny coffin.

The remaining children seem healthy…not that I hear much. Prince Kalandrel, Prince Kethrain, Princess Sepish, and Prince Tibbeth. I know very little beyond that. Prince Kalandrel, as the second-born son, has been elevated to heir.

That's what little I know. I have massive knowledge gaps that need to be filled. And I'd better get started.

I scoot to the side of the large bed and swing my legs to the floor. The stones are cold beneath my feet until I move to the sleek, black rug made of some large animal. I can't go snooping through the castle in a chemise, so I go through the dresses in the armoire. They're beautiful, of course, but it feels wrong to enjoy them, so I grab the plainest one and slip it over my head. It feels too nice, too delicate. It would definitely be ruined by my usual daily activities. I can't imagine standing at my shop, helping customers looking like this.

And my mother creeps into my mind.

Guilt settles over my mind like a weight. The image of her bent over my dead frame presses on my memory like a hot coal against my palm. I did that to her. Somehow. She's in so much pain and grief that I can't take away. Cassian too. He was terrified. And Mellen?

I have to get back to them somehow. I don't know when. But I need to see them. Make sure they're safe and taken care of.

What can I get away with under the pretense of my 'fall,' I wonder? Can I say I'd like to see the lower village? How does a Lady get away with wanting to see *Muck Water* of all places? Can I say I'd like to set up a charity without it being viewed as strange? Queens have a history of alms...Can I 'sponsor' my family? Or a few families to avoid looking like I'm favoring people.

That is...if I have my own money as a Lady. I'll need to get that sorted. Worst case, I can sell a few dresses. Who knows what else this Lady Heiress might have owned? That could fetch a coin or two.

I pull my hair back and braid it because even I know it would never do for a woman of nobility to be seen with her hair undone.

Her hair is so soft.

My hair.

I'll have to get used to taking ownership of this body, and not just because I'll sound weird if I say the wrong thing out loud. For better or worse, it *is* mine now. I make it move. I control it. It's not like I can go back to my old body. I don't have a choice.

But...does that mean that whatever forces that made this happen killed the girl? Was she going to die anyway, or did I kill her?

Too dark.

Can't go there just yet. Gotta figure life out first.

Once her-*my* long hair is braided, I stare at myself in the looking glass just a moment, trying to convince myself I look fine enough to wander the halls. I'm kind of afraid to dive into Heiress Orielle's life. I'm not sure what I'll find.

The door handle jiggles and the hinges squawk as the heavy door opens. My heart flutters in panic.

"Up already. Good sign," the physician says. The light from the windows illuminates the age spots and smaller cracks in his face as he holds the door open for a maid girl with a brown cloth over her shockingly red hair. She's carrying a basket of linens and doesn't look up.

"Come sit, Heiress Orielle. Let me look at you," he says, gesturing to a small sitting area near the door. The maid moves past me without a word and sets about making the bed. I feel bad as I watch her, wishing I'd already done it. I just hadn't thought to.

I sit where the physician tells me to. He lifts my chin to inspect my eyes and face. He feels my pulse and asks me questions about how I'm feeling.

"Much better," I say.

"Glad to hear it." He nods as if he'd been expecting it. "Any new memories from before you came to us?"

"No."

"That's too bad. Overall, I'd say you've recovered well. Let me know if you start feeling poorly again. This is Ardialle. She's your maid." He turns to go. "I'll let their majesties know you're recovered and able to receive visitors. They'll be happy to receive the news."

"Thank you," I say, "...For everything."

"Of course," he says with a quick smile. Then he closes the door behind him. I hear the maid fussing about with the sheets. She hums a little as she does. I have no idea how to talk to her. But...she'll be able to make me look presentable at least before I venture into the castle or...receive visitors...

"Lady Heiress Orielle? Are you ready for me to fix your hair...I mean, not 'fix' but do up? My apologies. I shouldn't have used that word. It's perfectly lovely as it is. It's just not the fashion, is all. Not that you have to adhere to fashionable standards. It's just common for Ladies..."

The poor girl looks flustered. Her freckled cheeks and nose have turned crimson, her hands are tucked behind her back, and her neck is bent so far so she doesn't look me in the eye.

It makes me uncomfortable. Because in the hierarchy of society, she'd be above me in normal circumstances. Yes, I was a merchant instead of a servant, but I was a poor merchant, and she works in the castle.

"Yes, that would be lovely," I say, because I'm not sure how to respond to the nervous energy she puts off. She moves to the mirror and vanity, waiting for me to sit on the cushioned chair.

Cushions on chairs are nice, I decide, as Ardialle takes out my braid. The cushions are way better than sitting on plain, hardwood like the ones I had at home and the stand.

Ardialle parts the strands of hair. Softly, like she's revering the long silky threads. She must be new to Lady's maid work. That's fine with me. I'm new to this world, too. So, it might be an advantage to have a maid who doesn't quite know her job. Might be easier to get away with things.

And...if there was ever a noble for her to mess up with and not have to expect repercussions, it's me.

"How long have you worked at the castle?" I ask, watching her figure in the mirror because she's bid me not to turn my head.

"Two years as an undermaid. Now I've been assigned to you, since I understand your maid was killed in the attack. I'm very sorry for your loss. It must have been terrifying."

"The attack?"

"With the beast. In the forest."

"Oh yes. Sorry, my memory isn't intact," I say, gesturing to my head and hoping that will be enough.

"Please, your Ladyship. No need for apologies. We've heard of your fall, of course. Must be hard. It must cause you a great deal of pain not to remember your loved ones back home."

"It does," I say, seeing my opening. "It gets frustrating. I've only been able to piece together little things. Do you think you could tell me more?"

"Of course! What would you like to know?"

"Anything you can tell me would be helpful."

"Well...you came to use from Bassenthral. It acts as its own kingdom in the north but is a vassal of Drene. Your father doesn't hold the title of king, but he is the ruler there. The wedding party was attacked in the forest. Such a shame. So close to the city and yet too far away to be saved." She shakes her head, and her hands flutter a bit. "I've heard some of what they found..."

"Indeed...what do you mean wedding party?"

"I suppose you wouldn't know, would you. How delightful for me to get to deliver such good news...You're betrothed to the prince."

I sit for a moment in terrified stupor.

Well, that certainly changes things.

I can't just flit about without being acknowledged by others. I'll be visible to nearly everyone I meet. Learning how to be a Lady will be much more difficult under scrutiny, and I just don't know if I can...

On the one hand, this could be an interesting experience rife with possibilities.

On the other hand, if I don't do a good job...what do they do with Ladies who fail? Banish them from court? What if I end up having to go to Bassenthral? So far away from my family. What then?

I take Ardialle's hand in a hurried, very out-of-character gesture, but I don't care. I'm panicking, and I need something solid to hold onto.

"Okay, here's the thing...I'm going to need you to teach me everything you know about being a Lady, because I don't remember."

Her russet brown eyes meet mine with concern, but she nods.

"I will do my best."

CHAPTER 10

MAEHDIORAH

E lonrod hasn't given up his pursuit of the girl. He feels strangely about her, and it's been clouding his mood as of late. He speaks with the council, insisting that I be there so I can advocate for his story of what happened in Thornodar. It's not needed, though. They believe him well enough, and I stand mutely by, trying not to feel as if this is a massive waste of my time. Highly inefficient. But I did say I needed to stay close to him, so...

"But if she's dead, we don't need to go back," Gomthen says, screwing up his wiry eyebrows at Elonrod.

"I can't explain it," Elonrod admits. "But I don't think she is."

"Then the boy lied?" asks Amtira, the old woman.

"No, I saw into his mind. She was dead."

"Her spirit dwells then?" Gomthen suggests. "There's not much we can do about a spirit."

Elonrod skips a beat. "She's not dead."

"And why are you so determined that she needs to be found?" Amtira asks.

"Because she doesn't deserve to live in fear, even if she's not aware of her magic."

Given my choice, we'd leave the girl be. And if she is deceased, she's certainly in no position to bother anyone. No one asks for my opinion, though, so I keep it to myself.

The council members look to each other, and Amtira leans back in her chair before turning back to Elonrod.

"You may continue your search but be careful."

"Of course," Elonrod says. Then he turns to me. "Shall we get started?"

"I was unaware that you'd need my help," I answer as we slip outside of the council tent.

"I could use amplification," he answers.

"There are others who can help," I answer. He stops in his tracks, and out of politeness, I stop too.

"Please," he asks, and there's something more serious in his tone and earnest in his brow. I don't think I've ever seen him this way. He's usually so...goofy. But it's only there for a second.

I nod slowly. "I'll help you," I say, and he nods before striding off.

The unfortunate thing about this girl being Elonrod's focus is that now it's my focus as well.

So, we sit together in a little clearing away from the camp. Far enough that we can't hear them, nor they us. Out here is peaceful, or it would be if I were on my own, but unfortunately, I'm stuck sitting on a rock across from Elonrod while he sits on a log.

Shifting to get more comfortable, I watch him for a moment as he reaches out, and I can feel the energy of his magic charging the area. Eyes closed in concentration, he searches for the girl's energy. And I stretch and roll my shoulders back before settling in to help him.

Gifts like his and mine are rare, but they're not all powerful. Sometimes we work together when particular problems need attending. Some powers are great, but they can be helped along with another's energy. This is what we call amplification, bending our energy to twine with another's while they mold the direction of the energy with their own talents. It's very like becoming a conduit, seeking out the natural magical energy of the world and then channeling it towards the other magic-user.

That's all some magic-users are good for, not being able to direct magic themselves, but able to feel and call to it. Which I do now, sending a steady stream of energy from the plants, trees, and earth towards him.

Elonrod soaks it in. I haven't seen him apply himself this much since he was a child. To someone for whom things come naturally, not having something come easily is frustrating. But I feel how dedicated his search is from the strength of the energy he soaks in and projects out.

"There's a darkness around her energy," he says, cutting the silence. "It's not *her* energy. It's just...there."

"How does it feel?" I ask, suddenly wary.

"Strange...I don't want to say it's Dark Magic, but I've never felt magic like it before..."

My skin tingles. "If she's dealt in Dark Magic, she'd certainly have markers."

"She has none."

"That you can see or that you can *see*?"

"Both. All I saw was the dark force. It's like a chain. Maybe it dampened her powers? It could be why she doesn't know she has any."

"It's possible," I say. An inkling tugs at my mind. The inkling that she's not what she seems. The chain...The darkness around her. If not a Dark Magician herself, there's a possibility that she's dealt with someone who is. And if someone's gone to lengths to dampen her abilities, there must be a reason.

I need to see the girl. I need to know what and who she is. I need to know what threat we're dealing with, so I can dispose of it.

"Describe her to me. Her physical features."

"She's got brown hair, kinda long. Keeps it in a braid. She's got angry eyes. But I can't blame her. She looked tired and stressed."

"Anything else? Leave out no details."

"How will this help?"

"I can look for her too." He sighs and straightens his back.

"Thought you were only amplifying. Don't you have an aversion to using your gifts?" he teases. I hate it when he jokes about that. It's the lie I've told. It's part of my 'character,' Telisan, but it's not true. I love using my gifts. I just don't like others knowing what they are. People with talents like mine don't get to stay hidden.

"I use them when necessary."

"And when is that? Can't any time be deemed 'necessary?'"

"Depending on one's perception, I suppose."

"And yours is...?"

"That it's necessary when yours can't do the job."

He laughs as if I were being sarcastic. I wasn't. But I play along.

"Alright, you look for her then. She's a peasant. Her name is Ellory. Wears a dusty, brown dress. Knows about herbs. Lives in the lower village with her mother and two younger siblings. Can't tell what her gifts are exactly...it's strange. But she'd be talented if she could develop them."

Her knowledge of herbs means she might smell like them. That's something to go on at least.

"How much of her thoughts did you read?"

"Why is that important?"

"People go where their thoughts lead." He rolls his eyes at me. It's *his* territory, and he doesn't like me stepping in it. It was mine long before it was his. But he doesn't need to know.

"She's struggling with money. Stresses obsessively about it. Loves her family. Is terrified of the guards finding out about magic."

"Do you think she turned you in?"

"No. She was scared, but that wasn't on her mind."

"Anything else?"

"Missing father."

"Possibly taken by the guards? If she has magic, he might have."

"She didn't know."

I let it be. Settling back into the flow. To be clear...No. I don't worry that he'll read *my* thoughts and know my plans, though thought reading is one of his many talents. He tries occasionally. Just to see if he can get past the block. I know because I feel it being probed on occasion. He can't break through, but in his mind, it just creates more of a challenge. More of a question that can't be answered. I understand it's risky to arouse suspicion by hiding my mind so carefully, but it's necessary. If he were to break through, he'd know everything, and depending on his reaction, he might have to be replaced. And such a thing would take far too much time and effort.

"You gonna look for her then?" he asks, because he's felt that I haven't accessed my gift yet. He can't feel *how* I use it, just that I draw it.

"Just...give me a moment. It's been a while."

"That's what happens when you don't practice."

"Oh, is it?" He responds with something I don't pay attention to because I'm focusing on reaching out.

There are several ways to look for this girl if one has the capability to access specific gifts.

One is through sound. If I knew what her voice sounded like, I could listen for her through the wind. This is more easily accomplished in places close by. For example, I can hear the camp more clearly than I can hear Thorondar. It takes a lot of patience, sifting, and care.

Another is through sunlight. I can see wherever the sunlight reaches. It's bathed in faded yellow, a little murky, and the images can come fast and overwhelming like a river.

Both are also ways we can use to travel if we need to. But again...not every magic-user can. In fact, it's a sign of great ability if one can travel through sunlight, and the magic-users tier themselves based on abilities such as these.

None of them know of moon travel, a most difficult feat. More so than traveling through sunlight, and a rarer gift as there is a very specific strain from which it comes that is in danger of dying out entirely (And it must be noted that it may be accessed through the gift of connecting with the sun, but only if one is attuned to such a degree that they can work off reflections of sunlight and not merely sun itself. This is why it is nearly impossible to master if one does not have the strain in their blood. And even then...the bare light is difficult to harness. Less like a river and more like a splash. Hard to get a hold of, let alone manipulate).

These are gifts passed down from the ancients who possessed magic. These ancients weren't human. The humans who have these gifts have no idea how lucky they really are. They could have just as easily been born without magic if a few things had been different long ago. An entire race of magic-users might not exist at all if not for the intermingling.

But back to my search for the girl. I use sunlight. The sun has risen across the kingdom, but I begin my search in Thorondar. It's the last place she was.

The images dribble like a waterfall, soaked in bright, yellow light that hurts to focus on. In fact, when young ones with this ability learn to use it, they're told not to focus directly on the sunlight pouring into their minds. Instead, we focus adjacent to it and let the images sweep by. In a way, it actually makes it easier for me to find what I'm looking for because it takes care of the distracting images. I only look for what matches, disregarding the rest.

It takes a lot of practice and patience to focus on a specific place. And if one doesn't, they can be overtaken by the sheer immensity of what they unlock. It's a depressing sight when one has the capability to unlock that gift but isn't strong enough to wield it. When that happens. The being shuts down. It's like they're in an eternal sleep, even if their eyes are open. Catatonic. We call it burnout.

They don't wake up. They die that way, unable to eat or drink. It doesn't take long.

There's a reason only a few can use the sun. Some even refuse to try their hand at the gift if they don't feel strong enough. There's no shame in it.

As for the search...I focus on what it looks like. How the city is shaped, and gradually, the images shift the more energy I pour into focusing. I look for images that look like the girl. And perhaps of the boy we met in the market. He's easy to find once I make those images the priority. Reaching out, I can sense his familial ties. I also see images of a girl who looks like the boy, but she's harder to see through the window where sunlight pours in. She's young, but nothing in her suggests the use of magic, so I pull away. But now I can get a sense of the family's essence.

Now, if I pair that with the images, it should narrow down the scope of the images that come through. It will help to sift them faster and push out the irrelevant images.

No...I must slow down. I can feel myself going too far, too fast. And I know if I reach out more, I'll surpass Elonrod's capability. I can't do *that,* or Elonrod will know. He might sense and understand that my magic is stronger than his own. He won't be able to ignore that. It'll raise questions.

No one must know. Not yet. And there's no need to tell him how to find the girl either with the family's essence. I'll let him stumble upon that himself...*if* he figures it out.

But it'll be better if I find her first. Then I'll know what should be done with her.

Even still, I pull back through the images in gold, which isn't hard. It's like merely loosening my grip so the current takes me just a little way back. I go back to the images of the city that come naturally and cease trying to drive them. I watch little bits and pieces of people's lives as they happen. Unruly children, barking dogs, people about their business.

I want to make clear that I'm aware that what we do is an incredible invasion of privacy. And thus, I deem it a gift only to be used when I need. These abilities should be used with a strong base of good morality. (Which is why I've seen fit to dampen the gifts of others from time to time or burn them out. Difficult to do, especially under the noses of the others, but there are those who should not have these powers.)

I don't like it. Me...The being who loves to know *everything*. Every angle before making a plan. Every thought in someone's head. Every feeling they have because I need to know everything in order for my plans to be laid sufficiently. I need to know which way the wind blows and why. And when I need people, I need to know exactly what to expect from them.

But even *I* feel it's wrong to spy on people like this.

I know Elonrod feels the same way. I've heard him discuss his reservations before. He'd rather travel to the city and seek out the 'lost' ones than spy from afar. It's also a tactical advantage because, as I mentioned before, gifts are easier to use the closer we are. Less draining. More pointed.

But we also fear discovery by the guards.

I use this gift here and now because this is indeed an urgent situation for one reason. Elonrod has seen Dark Magic. And it's touched the girl somehow. Dark Magic is dangerous. Dark magicians Rise...and fall, generally destroying everything in their wake as they seek to build their own empires. Dark Magicians aren't made. They're created. By the magic itself, twisting the individual into a terrible force of nature.

Most magic-users haven't/won't touch it (not that many have the chance). For good reason. They fear it, shun it. And choose to forget it even exists. All well enough for them.

The girl may not have dabbled in Dark Magic herself, but she's been in contact with someone who has.

And the only living magic-user I know of who's played with Dark Magic is me.

CHAPTER 11

ELLORY

A nervous ball of energy has taken up residence in the pit of my stomach. Ardialle explained all she could, but she's passed my education off to a more experienced Lady's Maid.

This one's name is Thessel. She's not as old as my mother, but definitely older than me. A bit plumper in the cheeks and chin, dark eyes peeking out from under her strong brow, her fingers nimble and hands thin from work. Her face fits her voice. It's not gruff, it's just kind of low and comes from her chest, a smidge craggy at times. And I'm trying to focus on what she says, but I feel like I've been stuffed full of information, and my brain feels like it might burst. It's certainly pounding. I can't take it anymore.

"...you'll need to remember to keep your chin tilted," she's saying with her hand under my chin to show me how high it needs to be held.

"Might I take a break?" I break in. "I'm feeling overwhelmed by all of this. I'd like to let it soak in for a moment."

"No trouble at all, your Ladyship. Sometimes the best way to get something done is to let it soak," she winks. Then she shuffles to the window and takes up her sewing. The yellow light spills over her headpiece and around her shoulders as she works quietly. She casts the occasional glance into the courtyard below.

I keep my chin up in the air. It feels pretentious. Unnatural.

Once Thessel saw the state of me, she set about ordering Ardialle to fix this and that about my attire. She really took to it, handling everything around here and the two of us like we're her children.

She *was* one of the Queen's maids until about two hours ago, when the Queen transferred her duties. She's been a mother-bear ever since. I guess some people are just that way.

Or we look rather pathetic on our own. And in need of direction.

But I like Thessel's straightforward way of talking too much. It's come in handy so far. She's covered a lot of topics in a short period. As long as I remember everything and practice until it's natural, I might have a shot at being a Lady Heiress.

"Tell me about the prince then," I say, starting to get the hang of requesting with a 'command' rather than asking. Still feels funny, but it's necessary, so I do it.

"Oh, you'll absolutely adore him. You won't remember, but you've met him. He's quite handsome and charming."

"Handsome in the natural way or handsome in the way all princes would like their betrothal prospects to see them as?"

Her eyebrow shoots up, but she shakes out her project with an amused look. "Don't believe me then?"

"Just checking."

"He's handsome in the *conventional* way. I've seen him grow from a boy to a man, so of course, I'm biased, but I'm not telling lies when I say he's nice to look at. Ardialle, wouldn't you say?"

Ardialle nods with a quick blush. She doesn't say much as she airs out the dresses and accessories that were recovered from the caravan that was attacked by the beast (apparently Orielle brought her entire wardrobe. She definitely planned on staying, so she must have been in favor of the wedding and marriage). Ardialle hasn't said more than a handful of words since Thessel's arrival. Seems she's content to let the older woman take over.

"See? I'm not the only one who thinks so..." Thessel keeps talking about his looks and prospects, but I cease listening.

I'm not comfortable with the idea of marriage to someone I don't know. I hadn't thought of marriage for myself.

That had been a source of some conflict between my mother and me before I got sick. She encouraged me to 'look around' at some of the young men. I didn't want to. I knew too much about them to be entranced by any of them. There were only a few I crushed on for their looks, if nothing else, but I was never good at encouraging young men to communicate with me. And some I chased off on purpose because I couldn't see myself with them.

I really thought I'd have time to take care of my mother and the children first. I'd reasoned I could get serious about marriage later, but my family would need to come first.

Mother thought I could have found some nice young man with his own income set up. That would mean I'd have to leave the shop and bear his children, leaving my mother without an income. I hadn't wanted to do that.

Seems I've just left her like that anyway.

They can still get by on the coins I got from the physician (thank the ancient kings he was generous). It will last a week or two if they're careful. I will need to make it down there at some point. I'm working on a plan.

And at the same time, I'm trying to keep my anxiety at bay.

"...Princess Merish was entranced. You remember, Ardialle? The way she danced with the prince the night of the Winter Moon?" Ardialle nods. "But no matter, because you're here now. And Kalandrel never was interested in Princess Merish anyway." That last part was directed at me like a motherly pat on the head.

A knock sounds at the door, and I freeze, looking at Thessel for some indication of what I should do. She laughs at my discomfort.

"Shall I see to that for you, My Lady?" she asks. When I nod, she calls, "Who is it?"

"The prince has requested I ask after the Lady Heiress and determine if she's well enough for a visit," a muffled voice calls through the door.

"She is well enough," Thessel answers with a grin on her face. "Tell the prince she's at his disposal."

"Well then, will you let the Lady Heiress know to meet the prince an hour before dinner?"

"I will inform her."

My heart has been pounding the whole time. Now I feel like it's in my throat. The inevitable has arrived.

"Ohhh, don't look so terrified. There's really no need to worry," Thessel says, "Just remember what you've learned so far, and be willing to learn about the things you don't know. You'll see with Kalandrel, there's nothing to worry about."

Grateful as I am for her comfort, I'm panicking.

"I don't think I know enough. What more can we get through before I meet him?"

Ardialle slides the flowy blue dress over my head and cinches it around my waist, tugging roughly against the laces. The sleeves are a see-through material, and a slit runs through them from the wrist to the shoulder. It drips and tumbles like water, just as soft. A golden thread plays like sunlight over the surface, weaving, dancing, and I press a hand against the material at my waist to feel the cold slickness of reality. I've never felt so beautiful. But it's stolen beauty. Real, but not mine.

Ardialle unfurls the dress where it hangs up on my chemise and then tugs on my hair, pinning it up into a bun with Thessel's help. Then they step back and let me see Lady Heiress Orielle in the long mirror. I can hardly believe the woman I'm staring at is bound to my will, but I touch my hair lightly, and the young woman in the mirror does too. When I blink, I see her eyes open at the same time as mine, and as I step closer to examine her, she peers into my face as well. I feel strange, like an impostor, a thief of body and life.

Thessel did her best to teach me. That's all I can ask and say for what we accomplished. Not only am I to meet Kalandrel, but dinner is a small gathering of his family and courtiers who've been waiting for my entrance into their world. But on the other hand, I do look stunning thanks to the work of Ardialle and Thessel.

This is an entirely new experience that I'm determined to enjoy despite how terrified I feel. This may all end badly, but for a glowing moment, I'm soaking in everything I can.

Thessel escorts me to the room where my presence has been requested. It's a long walk and yet, it's over too quickly. Then, entering the room, it seems like a study of sorts with books along one wall, and desks and tables with comfortable chairs set at random. Suits of armor stand at attention between the four windows, and torches light the space despite the sun still setting the room aglow.

The young man had been leaning against a table reading, but he snaps the book closed and grins as he sees us.

"Prince Kalandrel, may I present Lady Heiress Orielle of Bassan-threl?" Thessel says in a teasing tone. Then she backs out of the room and closes the door behind her.

"So, you did receive my invitation," he says, moving in quick strides to greet me. "Wonderful to see you again, Orielle. How are you feeling?"

"Quite well, thank you. I have yours and your father's hospitality to thank for that, as well as the use of the court physician. He, Ardialle, and Thessel have been most helpful," I say as graciously as I can with a slight curtsey like Thessel taught me.

"No need for formalities, Orielle. I'm glad you're feeling better. That fall gave us all a scare. And the beast still lives. I'm not sure if you were informed: we couldn't save your guards and maids, unfortunately. They were dead before we arrived. We're thankful you were not hurt, though, and preparations have been made to return the bodies to Bassanthrel."

"Oh..." I say, unable to keep eye contact, and fiddling with my fingers. I know it's not ladylike, but I don't know what to say. My cheeks grow hot. "I'm sure their families must be devastated over the news. Thank you for seeing to that. This has been an ordeal...for you as well."

I annoy myself with my fidgeting, so I force my hands to my sides against the soft blue silk, and I meet the prince's gaze once more. It gives me a moment to study him. Blonde hair, but his beard is a dirty blonde. Blue eyes. The kind that are stark on one's face because the shade is so rare and deep. Dark eyebrows that look like they can cut a person with anger, much like his father's, from what I can recall of the king. He's tall with wide shoulders, and he's wearing a sword on his hip with a fancy hilt. I like how the silver leaves and vines curl around the handle.

"Great Kings! You really have changed," he says, grinning and looking me over just as I have him.

"I don't know how I've changed," I answer honestly. "To my I'm just as I've always been."

"Then I could tell you all sorts of things and you'd think they were true," he says, popping his eyebrows at me.

"Well, that's just not fair."

"You don't remember sneaking pies from the kitchens? Or knocking over the roasted pig? The dogs had eaten half of it before my father's birthday celebration, and we were both scolded in front of the entire party."

My mouth drops open, and my eyes widen.

"No."

"It's true."

"*We* did that?"

"*You* did. I just got dragged along as usual."

"I'm so sorry," I say, dropping my head. "I shouldn't have done that, let alone gotten you in trouble. I hope the punishment wasn't terrible. Please forgive me."

"I didn't mean to make you feel bad, Orielle," he laughs, taking my hand in what should have been a friendly gesture, but sends a jolt down my arm. "But no, the punishment wasn't terrible. In the strangest fit of fatherly compassion, our gracious king had us both scrubbing pots in the kitchen and sent us to bed without the wafer desserts we were trying to nab."

I glance up in surprise, allowing my hand to settle into his. Mostly because his sarcasm puts me at ease. I can do sarcasm. It keeps him at arm's length.

He seems alright so far. We'll have to see, though.

If he knew who I really am...

But I'm starting to like castle life and its coziness, so I hope he doesn't find out.

But I'm living a lie. And that's no way to have a real relationship.

But...telling the truth would be suicide.

But...

It's too much to think about and distracts me from the now, so I refocus on the here and now.

Here and now, there's a tingle in the prince's hand. A subtle sensation I can't quite put my finger on, an undercurrent that seems to ebb and flow like a pulse. But I pay it no mind because he's begun to speak.

"You used to love the library. You had such a fascination with magic. I know you don't remember, but I thought if you could see it again, it might jog something." He turns, now leading me farther into the room. I stare at all the books. The majority of them are leather-bound with different shades of brown or dyed covers. Dark blues, lavenders, green, and a couple are shades of red. It's a definite sign of wealth to have some of these richer colors. They take a lot of the right mix of herbs, which I find interesting. I run my finger along the dark blue spine of a particular hefty book.

"Beautiful," I say. "Where's this one from?"

"My great-grandfather had that commissioned. He was obsessed with The Great War. See these other books here about wars, strategies, and weaponry? He studied them often."

"The Great War? The one with the wizards?"

"Magic-users. There are more than just wizards."

"The concept is so strange," I say, gesturing to the blue book. "May I?"

"Of course. You used to make fun of that one."

"Did I? Remind me."

"You used to say it was silly of us normal people to think there was any hope of defeating an army of magic-users. We debated a lot on the subject. Even created mock armies to test your theories."

I laugh. "Well...who won?"

"Of course, *we* won in the end. You were being contradictory on purpose. You loved aggravating me."

"Must have been a sight to see or I might not have liked it so much."

"Oh, it was enjoyable for you, listening to me rant about armies and the tactical advantages used in the Great War."

"Well, you must have enjoyed it too, or you'd have found someone else to play with." I stick out my tongue and then remember I really shouldn't. He merely scoffs, but I look down in embarrassment.

"So, these magic-users...we won the Great War, or we'd not be standing here today...what happened to those who have gifts?"

"'*Gifts*' is a strong word," he says. "They have limited abilities, from my understanding. It's outlined here..." he takes the book and flips a few pages to show sketches of the magic-user's abilities in use. The pictures are beautifully done, with bold strokes. Peasant-attired people with a haphazard array of battle equipment. But some didn't need weapons. Their hands are outstretched, and rocks hover. Whirlwinds blow. Storms and lightning crash on the battlefield. The magic-users look angry and determined, and powerful.

I shiver.

"They still walk among us. Though we have safeguards, we've not been successful in eradicating those people from among our own. Ours is not the only kingdom that wishes to be rid of their kind."

"But magic could be used for good?"

"Your innocence is endearing," he says sarcastically but smiles tolerantly. "Who's to say for sure? Power corrupts people. It's like fire. The closer you get to it, the hotter it burns, the hotter *you* burn. Men fear losing what they have won. They fear people more powerful than them, for they will surely take it away, and why not? These magicians can conjure terrible, bloodthirsty creatures. They themselves can prey on the mind. They can turn a whole nation. Imagine if someone made you into a simpleton or killed someone you love...What would you do if you could crush their spine with the flick of your wrist? Would you do it? How many people could stop themselves? It's no simple matter."

I don't point out the irony in his wanting to regulate 'power.'

"To think people can command such things..."

"You used to love the idea. You mentioned once to my father that they might make good entertainers at court."

I pop an incredulous eyebrow, "Is this one of those things you mentioned telling me that may or may not be true?"

"Not at all. My father laughed. He knew your penchant for troublemaking."

"Isn't magic one of the things we shouldn't discuss?"

"Just kids being kids," he shrugs as he flips the book to another page. It looks like a list. "These are the known powers of the magic-users."

"Whoa..." My eyes slide down the list.

"Manipulation of the wind, storms. All the things you saw on the other page. But you'll notice here...they can travel through the wind and sunlight. Some read thoughts, others read emotions. It's said that the Dark Magician Thagyn cast spells to make himself live longer."

"Did the spells work?" "He was trying for immortality...but the general thought is that they did indeed make him live longer. Seems it sapped his abilities though."

"Strange..."

"You don't remember any of this, do you?" he asks, bending his neck to catch my eyes. I shake my head.

"I'm afraid not. But I can see why I was interested as a child. It's like a whole different world."

"I'll show you around tomorrow. Maybe some memories will return." He closes the book and returns it to the shelf.

"Why are you so eager to help me remember?" I cock my head at him.

"If you remembered everything we've been through, you wouldn't have to ask," he winks.

"That good, huh?" I say and then pause. "It's very kind of you to recount all this. Very patient and understanding."

"Of course, My Lady," he takes my hand again, and this time I feel the tingling ebb and flow of that deeper thing, but it seems like a warmth, but it's a color...and image...like the warm orange glow of a fire in the hearth welcoming a friend home.

It's a glow that settles in my chest but doesn't feel like it belongs to me. Like it's only settled here for a moment. And I can't control it.

"Come, we should meet the others for dinner. Mother won't like it if we're late. But on the other hand, she wouldn't be surprised." He places my hand in the crook of his arm and leads me out of the library. "Of course, father would send someone to look for us, fearing you might be up to your old pranks."

"Were we really so mischievous? You'll have to tell me the trouble we got into."

"Plenty of time for that," he says as we move through the large hall, stopping in front of two tall doors. Servants sweep a bow as they push the doors open.

"The Prince Kalandrel and Lady Heiress Orielle," a voice booms across the large room. It's lit with many torches and candelabras hanging from the ceiling. Servants line the pillars on each side of the room, some with platters of food (despite the laden table), some with pitchers. Lavishly dressed people weave in and out of the servants, hanging out in groups or moving amongst them. A tune rises from the players tucked near the doors on the far end.

These people move to create a tunnel as they bow to their prince. Some greet him, a few greet me as well. It all feels so strange. I'm not supposed to be here. I feel like a gilded peasant, but a peasant, nonetheless. Can they see it? Can they tell I don't belong?

And the food...there's a large duck...or goose in the center, surrounded by leafy greens and vegetables cut into different shapes. Steaming plates of rolls, sauce, and vegetables round out the entourage with a fruit bowl.

The smell makes my stomach twist with hunger. I could dine on the thick scent alone.

"The King and Queen," the voice announces, and the throng turns to greet their monarchs.

I'm curious as well.

The Queen is lovely. Blonde with flowing hair that curls lazily down her back like a waterfall. She's wearing a lavender silk gown and a golden chain around her neck with pearls, dripping off. Her fine chin is as high as Thessel teaches me to hold mine. And her eyes are gracious. She nods to the people who bow at her and the king.

I've seen the king in the physician's quarters, but I get a better look at him now. He has a sharp face accentuated by his sharp, peppered beard. His features are a little worn, with fierce crow's feet, but his eyes are cutting and sweep over his subjects in the same attitude I use to pick out bad sprigs out of my herbs.

Something akin to respect touches my skin. Purple-orange like a sunset. The feeling settles under my skin, moving through me like a living thing, and I notice it with trepidation. This is the third time tonight this strange sensation has hit. And I start to wonder, but before I go too far, the King and Queen have seated themselves at the head of the table, and the guests move to do the same.

Kalandrel pulls me along to a couple of seats near his parents. He presents me to them. A servant pulls out our seats. I give them both a deep curtsey.

"Your Majesties," I say.

"Good to see you again, Lady Heiress Orielle. And looking well. I trust Olid has taken care of you?" the king says.

"Indeed. Thank you for your hospitality. And for lending Thessel to me. She's been a great help." I direct that last part at the queen.

"Of course, we simply mustn't have a simpleton as the next queen. You'll do well to follow her instructions," she answers with a smile, and then turns to her servant.

I sit, feeling embarrassment in my chest and across my face, but I get the message. I'm under observation by way of the maids. I get the feeling we're not going to be close. A hand touches mine lightly, and I feel a sense of comfort wash like cold water across my fingers. Light blue like the ocean.

These colors and feelings start to worry me. They carry an essence of a being other than myself, and as I meet Kalandrel's gaze for a moment, I realize they belong to him.

Magic. I *do* have magic. And I'm sitting at the table of the king who'd have my head if he knew.

The other guests settle as the servants begin to move around the table. A new tune starts, a happier one that reminds me of dancing.

A servant carves a piece of the fowl for the Prince and then for me, while another fills our goblets. I thank them even though I can tell that the people around me are amused.

The servants wait for me to tell them how much they should give me, which I find awkward because I don't want to get that wrong. I ask for only a little, but Kalandrel scoffs and dishes more out for me himself. I think this is more food than I've ever had on a plate in front of me. And for that matter, the plate itself is very fine. As is the silverware.

The mix of herbs on the meat, the fresh crust smell of bread, and roasted potatoes reach my nose, enveloping my face like the heat of a fire. I bask in the warm, savory steam, suddenly feeling guilty for enjoying it. I wonder if my family is eating tonight.

"How have you found the city, Lady Heiress?" the woman on my other side asks. The couple across the table perks up.

"I haven't seen much since my arrival," I answer.

"The palace gardens are simply *stunning*. You *must* take a stroll with me sometime," she says, leaning heavily on the words 'stunning' and 'must.'

I know her. By sight, at least with her pale face, smile lines, and red-tinted mouth. She's nearly ten years older than me and wears a hat and veil over her hair. She's loud when she goes to the market. Loud and snide, comparing the wares of the vendors she meets, discussing the quality and artistry of the jewelry, and insisting that she has an eye for such things.

But she has money, so the merchants smile at her and compliment her 'eye' for details. Today, she wears a gown of purple and gold and casts a lot of glances at the single men. And *not* single men. Especially the king and his son.

"Perhaps," I answer without committing.

"Tomorrow? Before the execution?"

"I have other obligations on my time," I say apologetically, though I'm not at all sorry. But it's the first I'm hearing of the execution...

"Name the time, Lady Heiress. I eagerly await you. We will be great friends." She turns and starts talking with the gentleman on her left, then laughs loudly at something he says.

"They say you can't remember what the beast looks like. Is that true?" the woman from the couple across from us asks.

"It's true."

"What a shame. Might make it easier to find if the knights knew what they were looking for."

"The beast will be dealt with," the king interjects, as if closing the subject. The two take his hint, hurriedly averting their gaze.

"And what of the execution tomorrow? Have you decided what to wear?" the first woman asks, her hands wrapped delicately around her goblet. "I'm thinking of my blood red."

"You simply can't wear that, you wore that to the ball last Summer Moon."

"Oh no, it's been altered. The seamstress has styled it for *this* year. In fact," she pauses and leans across the table. "She says she's working on some designs that will be the fashion for next year." Her eyes slide toward the queen as if hinting.

I stop listening. Not because talk of dresses doesn't interest me, I'd like to learn more. But because I'm too anxious to keep listening to their tittering. I have bigger problems.

The prince has merely been watching, but his mother pulls his attention for a moment. She leans close, whispering something. He shakes his head and whispers back. But I sense he's a bit put off by her. Dark blue like the threat of rain. A color I'd always liked, but in this context, is perturbing.

I'm curious about her dislike of me. I wonder if she'll cause problems. If she's stirring up trouble right now.

My face heats as a thought comes unbidden to my mind...Would the 'gift' tell me? I *shouldn't* use it, and I'm not even sure how to control it. But if I did know how and I were in danger, I'd definitely use it to protect myself. I know that much.

I might be in danger now and not know it, and where would that put me? Is there a way to learn how to use it without putting myself in danger? Without anyone finding out I have it?

And it dawns on me that Orielle might have had a fascination with magic because *she* had magic. It only makes sense. I didn't have magic before I landed in her body. Now I do. It must be hers. And if she fooled everyone for so long, in the middle of court no less, can I?

Chapter 12

Maehdiorah

W e can find the girl faster if we look together, but I don't point that out to Elonrod. Melding our gifts would require a level of trust I simply don't have for others. So, we continue to look separately. He doesn't remember her voice. Only her face and a bit of her essence.

Neither of us has seen her. We're not certain she's *not* dead. And all we're going on is his 'feeling,' and that might be wrong. He insists on finding her, though. I'd have thought he may have had feelings for the girl, but he doesn't speak of her in that way. Something's gotten under his skin, though, or we'd have stopped looking long ago.

Part of me hopes she's dead. Especially, if I *am* the Dark Magician she had contact with. But, if it isn't me, she'll be more use to me alive. She may hold clues she's not cognizant of. And I need to know if there's another Dark Magician out there. They could destroy everything I've worked so hard for. And I'll need to know *exactly* how they came across the ancient ways...

As the sun's last rays die over the mountains, we don't have a choice...Or at least *he* doesn't. We'll have to wait until morning.

"Tomorrow?" he asks.

"Sure."

"Thanks." He arches his back and stretches after having sat for hours.

The camp is alive and bustling despite the growing darkness. Cook fires outline some of the homes in orange with families and friends crowded around telling stories or jokes. I'm not sure which. I don't care.

I'd love nothing more than to slip away to my tent and be left alone, but people tend to distrust those who don't socialize to some degree, so I sit amongst 'friends' for a moment, listening to their stories until Reathl, Elonrod's mentor, tells me I look a bit pale from the day's work.

"I *am* tired," I answer, hoping for an offered escape route.

"You'll find her," he says encouragingly, as one of the camp women hands him a bowl of stew and a thick slab of bread. "Elonrod's never wrong. It's uncanny."

"You think she's still alive then?" I ask.

"If he says she is, she is. Nobody knows that boy's talent more than I do." The old man has a weathered face with a few strands of wispy gray clinging to a mostly bald scalp. His earlobes have elongated with age. He's round with white hair on his arms and hands. Wiry white brows and a thick nose. Two strands of thick, white hair sprout from a mole on his chin. And he always seems to be fighting phlegm.

Reathl used to be the most powerful magic-user in the community. Until Elonrod. But the old man's not jealous as most men would be when they get replaced. He's relieved. I can see it in the way he talks about Elonrod. Like a proud parent who looks for any opportunity to tout their child's accomplishments.

Most of the community look up to Elonrod. Some act as if he's their leader already.

I suppose that could be another reason he's trying too hard to find the girl. To show his people that he can protect them. Which is also why the people have begun to speak of war as of late. Elonrod is their best hope for change. For a better life.

What they don't realize is that war will only be seen as a 'Rising' by the kings, and every effort will be made to put them down. Once the jar is opened. It cannot be unopened. They will be hunted and scattered and beaten down much more than they are now. At least now they enjoy a meal with relative peace. After a war breaks out, though, this will be a luxury and perhaps only a memory of times gone by. And of the people sitting here now, many won't be later.

But war *is* necessary. Kings don't change their minds. Prejudices get handed down from father to son.

We do indeed need a war to change all that, but not between magic-users and the non-talented. They need to be on the same side, working together. Fighting side by side for a change.

It's the only way to build trust. Literally putting their lives in each other's hands. They'll see.

"Tell us the tale of Auriella," one of the children says. My eyes flick over the child and then over to Reathl.

"When we've cleaned up," he answers to a chorus of disappointed sounds.

"We could clean while we listen," one bargains.

"Sometimes when I tell tales, you lot stop your chores," he returns, waggling his brows.

"We won't, I promise," says the first child.

"Then I'll start. But if I see any lollygagging, I'm not going on."

The children race about their various duties, cleaning plates, and bringing water. One of the older ladies hands me a bowl of stew while they listen to Reathl's booming voice.

"In the ancient times, there was a beautiful young woman named Auriella with hair the color of gold," he begins. I listen, but I hate it when storytellers start with 'in the ancient times.' They were right about Auriella being beautiful, though.

"She was a poor healer and lived a simple life, but she had a secret she kept. She had magic."

"Ohhh..."

"What could she do?"

"She was a healer, stupid."

"No tongue-wagging while I'm telling the story. And get back to cleaning those dishes." The children do as bid. Reathl continues, "One day the king's son fell gravely ill, so he sent out a proclamation amongst all the lands that whoever could heal the child would receive a great treasure."

"That's convenient."

"Hush!"

"Children, I'll not tell you again," Reathl chides. "So, healers and physicians came from far and wide, but none could heal the child. For there was a dark curse on the boy, and only magic could save him.

"Auriella heard of the boy's plight and wanted to help, but she knew after one look at the boy, she'd have to use her magic, which was forbidden. The king grew desperate as his only heir was slipping away. He promised Auriella gold, a position in his house, and anything her heart could wish for if only she would save his son."

"How did he know she had magic?"

"He didn't know. He just thought anyone could do it."

"What if she couldn't do it?"

"He'd do what kings do when they don't get their way. Throw her in the dungeon."

I no longer wish to listen to the tales of Auriella, the Golden Healer. She is a paragon, I know. A goddess and a beam of light to these people, but I am tired of hearing stories. And I tire of people for the day. There's only so much I can take. Perhaps I'll visit Lelioth tonight. That always cheers me up.

Stories are all well and good for the people. They inspire and uplift. But reality needs tending to. I take my stew away from the firelight, moving down the line of tents until I get to my own.

In past years, I shared with other girls my age. Some have married now. Some have died. Our good fortune expanded, and we've picked up more supplies. Those included tents, and now I have my own, for which I'm grateful. I love having my own space. Everything is mine. Nothing is foreign. Everything is untouched by curious hands, unseen by spying eyes. Nothing disturbs it.

I sit and eat in peace, thinking about the missing/dead girl Elonrod is so determined to find, and her predicament should she still be alive. It's possible we haven't seen her because she's hiding. If she is foolish enough to tell anyone about magic or her encounter with Elonrod, she'll be in a dungeon, no doubt. And if she's in a dungeon, it's likely we won't see her until her execution. The king won't miss an opportunity to make a spectacle of the situation as a warning. There's a chance we could slip in and rescue her before the killing stroke or the fire catches. We can travel through the sun, or if it's cloudy, we can try the wind.

But that would have to be good timing.

And what if the Dark Magician she's been touched by is me, after all? She may have to die to keep my secrets hidden. The life of one girl isn't worth everything I've built and all my future plans.

It's not callous. It's just weighing the number of lives I'm saving. Not only for this generation, but for many generations to come.

Chapter 13

Ellory

I wake with a purpose: Find a way to get to the lower town. As I lay in bed last night, plotting my way home, I realized I have the perfect excuse to swing by. I'll ask the prince for a tour of the city to familiarize myself with it. Inevitably, we'll see the lower village. We won't go down *every* street, obviously, but maybe I can convince him to take a detour.

That's just *one* solution for *one* day, though. How do I make it a regular practice?

I can't ask Ardialle or Thessel to procure me a disguise without causing suspicion, but I could procure one for myself...potentially. At the very least, I'll need a cloak that doesn't look too expensive. I've already gone through Orielle's things, and I've found one that's plain enough that in the cover of night, it'll blend enough...probably.

Speaking of going through her things...I've found a coin purse and a few small bangles, which I'm hoping Ardialle and Thessel won't notice are gone. I mean...technically they're mine, but I don't know how much the maids will take note.

And once I find a way in and out of the castle, I'll be able to come and go.

Thessel knocks at the door to my bedchamber. I know it's her because she has a special pattern to her knock. She doesn't wait for me to answer, though, walking right in, which I'm uncomfortable with.

"The prince stopped me to ask when you'll be ready," she says in greeting, "You'll need to hurry, so you don't keep him waiting."

I shoot out of bed, because disappointing the prince may have repercussions that steal me away from my plans. I move to the armoire and filter through the dresses.

"What's appropriate for riding? Also...how does one ride a horse?" My family was not rich enough to keep one, so I've no idea.

"With great care," she answers, "That's not one I can teach you without going with you to the stables. Just keep your dress covering you and sit side-saddle. Remember to keep your chin up, shoulders down, and back straight to lengthen your neck."

"We may need to carve out some time for proper lessons."

"No time now. Grab that green one. Let me have a look at it." I do as I'm told. She holds it out, eyeing it up and down. "It'll do. And it'll be easy to wash if you get dumped in a puddle."

"Not funny."

"Don't fall in a puddle then." She's bustling around quickly, trying to put an outfit together.

"Where's Ardialle?"

"Her father is ill. She's looking after him today."

"Oh...What should I do as a Lady Heiress in this situation?"

"Forgive her for being absent, of course."

"But do I send her something? Food? Medicine? What kind of sickness ails him?"

"I'm not sure. I didn't ask. And I suppose you could."

"I'd like to. How would I go about that? Do I ask someone? Do I go to the shops myself to pick out a few things?"

"It's a very kind gesture, and I know you mean well, so I'll say this...it's not normally done, but if you'd like, I'll put something together for her, and we'll give it to her tomorrow."

"Thank you. I trust your judgement," I answer, not mentioning that it does little good for Ardialle today. I realize I have no idea where Ardialle lives in the vast city. I'd never find it on my own, and considering the sickness involved, Thessel would never permit me to go. Or she'd tattle on me if I insisted.

Sometimes I forget who the noblewoman is here. Thessel runs everything with a tight hand, and while I know she means well, she *really* likes having her way.

We get me stuffed into the dress and my hair taken care of before she shoos me out the door.

"You're to meet him in the stables," she says. "Go down this hall till you come to the stairs, go down, take a left, and keep going. If you get lost, ask one of the servants to take you."

"Thanks, Thessel." I rehearse the directions in my head as I walk down the corridor. I do as she said...Down the stairs. Left. Keep walking, but the corridor looks like it's ending, and I'm not sure which direction to go. Several corridors lead off, and I choose one that goes left. I'm all turned around, but I notice that there are more servants here, so maybe I'm going in the right direction?

Several servants carrying laundry, buckets of water, and platters of food weave in and out as they pass and move around each other. I keep going, hoping to find some indication that the stables are near.

I find the kitchens instead. Not wishing to go through and disturb the cooks (because I'm pretty sure I'm not supposed to be here), I touch one of the servants' arms. He jumps in surprise and gives a swift, deep bow. Like down on one knee with his hands on the ground...I feel awkward about it.

He's young, probably around eight or nine, with a cap covering his unruly hair, smudges on his hands, and across his nose.

"I'm sorry. I didn't mean to startle you. I only wish to know which way leads to the stables," I ask.

"I will escort you, Lady Heiress." He blushes as he rises, but he doesn't meet my gaze.

"I don't wish to take you from your work," I protest.

"It will be my pleasure," he bows again stiffly. "If you will please follow me, Lady Heiress." He turns stiffly and takes me back the way I came. We go down a different corridor this time, down another staircase, and then another, and then I see daylight through an open door.

"There they are," he points to a large barn, nearly as tall as the gates, long and wide as if there are several rows of stalls.

"Thank you..." I say. He blushes violently. "Sorry, I don't know your name."

"Truv."

"Thank you, Truv."

"My pleasure, Lady Heiress," he gives me another stiff bow and rushes off to finish his duties. I lift the hem of my long skirt and step lightly in the boots Thessel picked out for me.

The stables smell like hay and horses. The scent is soothing, as well as the muffled movements they make and the munching of oats. I see several of the large animals' heads poking over their gates and then retract as stable boys walk by with tack and leads. I've seen horses in the lower town, scruffy and short, but these are different animals. Larger, sleeker, well-kept, and well-fed. A tall sorrel is led from the stall, prancing and antsy.

The prince stands near the sorrel's gate, speaking with a stableboy.

"We'll take Pris as well," I hear him say.

"Yes, your highness." The stableboy leaves.

"Good morning," I call out. Kalandrel smiles.

"Good morning, Orielle. Thessel wasted no time, I see."

"She's determined."

"That's what she's paid for. Keeping an eye on you. Come, you'll enjoy this." He takes me to a stall with a gray horse inside. "This is Pris. She'll be your mount today. Best you two get reacquainted," he says, swiping some oats from a bucket on the ground and dumping them in my gloved hand. His hand brushes my wrist, and even over the leather cuff, I feel the color of golden honey. Warmth, excitement. Care.

It's scary and nice at the same time.

"Hold out your hand to her." He takes my wrist and gently holds it out to the horse. She shuffles over lazily, stretching out her long neck and sniffing at the oats. Then she dips her fuzzy muzzle into the palm of my glove and scoops the pile with her lips. I remove the glove to stroke her soft cheek.

"She remembers you," he says. "Shame you don't remember her. She was your favorite."

"Still is," I answer, because she's the only one I know. She dips her head under my hand.

"She's asking for forehead rubs. Like this." He gives her head a good scritch right between her eyes. She seems to like it, eyes half closed as she leans into his hand.

"She's beautiful," I offer. Kalandrel smiles.

"There's so much I wish you remembered. But I guess we'll have to just make new memories."

The horses are saddled quickly and brought out of the stables for us to ride. The Prince places a hand on my lower back, guiding me closer to the large, gray mare and holding the stirrup for me to step into. Stepping into the stirrup, I grab a handful of dress to keep it from getting bunched or pulling in an unladylike way. The prince hoists me onto the horse, showing me where to put my feet and helping me fix my dress.

He slings up on his own horse easily. He rides the sorrel with the antsy feet. But the animal calms when the prince reins him around.

"Are you settled?" the prince asks. I nod, trying not to overthink this. I've seen it done. People do it all the time. It's perfectly fine. But the animal follows the prince's horse, rocking underneath me and feeling very unstable.

So far, I'm not enjoying it.

My horse trots to catch up with the Prince's. I don't like the jarring, up-and-down motion, and I clap my hand around the horse's mane, holding on for dear life. Prince Kalandrel laughs at my struggle. I look up to see him turned around in the saddle as my horse settles back into a walk behind the sorrel.

The gate to the city passes over our heads, and I see the yawning mouth of the iron spikes overhead. I can't help but imagine them falling on top of us. What if they do? I know the chain is solid, but accidents happen.

"Not so stiff. It'll be more comfortable if you relax," he says. "And less likely that you'll fall off."

"If I do fall off, this is the dress to do it in, according to Thessel," I say.

"*Planning* to fall off? Isn't that like predetermining that you will?"

"Not at all. It's acknowledging that I control nothing. And I'm less likely to be surprised."

"You don't like surprises?"

"Not particularly. Too many of them lately for my taste. *Everything* is a surprise lately. I'd like for something to be familiar. What about you?"

"Depends on the surprise. Get a new horse for my birthday celebration? Love that surprise. Find my betrothed has been attacked by a beast in the forest? Not a good surprise."

"That doesn't sound like a particularly good surprise," I admit. "What about the beast, then? Any word?"

"None yet. We hear reports of it attacking villages, but the attacks are random, and the beast seems to disappear. It hasn't been seen during the day, so it must be nocturnal."

"What do you think it is?"

"Not sure, but it has wicked claws and teeth." He shoots a glance at me. "You were lucky to forget that encounter at least."

"I don't feel lucky to have forgotten anything. I feel like I've lost a lot. Especially with the people I love." I'm thinking of my family, of course, but he seems to find a double meaning in the way his lips curl slowly. I wish I had his hand in mine right about now. Not because I like him, but because it might tell me something about what he's thinking.

"Yes, that must be frustrating. I'd certainly hate to lose that. But I'd like to think that if I did, you'd be showing *me* around, and telling me of all the mischief we got into." He winks. He has this grin when he teases that makes me want to tease back, but I can't make light of that kind of thing. It's not really fair to him that I'm not her.

"Of course," I answer.

"Well then, this is the upper city," he says, gesturing around to the buildings and the square where carnivals, festivals, and the like are sometimes held. The houses are much better put together than in the lower villages. Sturdy, with thicker beams, stonework, and doors that hang straight. Some houses even have iron gates and gardens. In fact, it's a sign of wealth to have a garden within the city walls because of the space they take up. Servants who work in those gardens are dressed especially well to show off the wealth. Fruit trees are coveted as well, some displayed in front of the houses, but the nobles who live here send servants with brooms and pitchforks to shoo those who try to collect the fallen fruit. Even the bird-pecked ones.

Though some nobles have larger estates in the countryside, this is where they stay when in the capital. And some homes here are owned by the wealthier merchants or citizens without nobility who have a lot of money. Patroned artisans...knights who've built up wealth...etc. Which annoys the nobles, who feel that they have more claim to the nicer homes. There are juicy feuds from time to time that I used to hear about in the streets. News travels.

I used to dream of living in one of these houses. That dream died a long time ago after the disappearance of my father.

"Merchants set up shop down this street sometimes," the prince says suddenly.

"Can we see them?"

"Are we shopping today? Not exactly what I had planned..." he teases, but he moves his horse. Immediately, he's swamped by vendors, bowing and calling him. They hold up their wares and rush alongside his horse. And mine. Some call to me, holding up silks, jewels, and pretty things. One even has several animals to keep as pets: pretty birds, dogs, cats, even a squirrel.

I just smile politely and keep following the prince down the row. Some vendors fall back, new ones take their place, but the prince says nothing to them, doesn't acknowledge them, and casts many glances at me and my horse to see that no one bothers me.

I've never seen him look so princely, back stiff, face stoic and unyielding. I admire him for it.

Down the line we go, merchants getting less and less rich, and when we turn the corner, I look to where my stand was.

There's a new stand. Fresh wood, sturdy look to it. And I can smell the treatment from here as well as recognize the workmanship. Gerdor made it.

My heart sinks, and I expect to see my mother running the shop, but there's Cassian instead. I have to keep my face from showing how relieved and sad I am to see him. He looks so strong and grown up there on his own.

I need to speak with him.

"Can we stop there?" I ask the prince, pointing at the new shop. He steers his horse towards Cassian and stops short. He helps me down and holds the horses as we approach.

I smile at Cassian, whose confusion etches his forehead. But he gathers his wits enough to bow quickly. He keeps his head down and his eyes averted.

"It's okay, boy," the prince says. "The Lady Heiress just wanted to see your wares."

"You have quite a spread," I say, touching the table lightly with my fingertips. It's much more solid and nicer than the old one, and

Cassian has a new stool. I'm relieved and happy to see him, but I also realize I have to stay aloof.

And it looks like he's done well despite the fact that I'd never really taught him about what I do...*did*. Some of it looks *better,* even. I'm impressed. How did he pick that up so quickly?

"Thank you, Lady Heiress," Cassian says, but he won't meet my gaze.

"Can you tell me about these?" I say, pointing to the flowery ones. Applegrif, a soft pink flower that grows near apple trees.

"Um...It's used for soothing headaches and stomachaches," he answers, shifting and picking at his nails.

"They're very pretty," I say encouragingly. He nods. This may have been a bad idea. Especially with the prince looking over my shoulder. "You seem uncomfortable. Are you alright?"

Even as I ask, I feel a tingle of depression and fear emanating from him. I don't even have to touch him to see the dark, raging blue of thunderclouds, the darkened depths of a boiling sea, and feel the emptiness of a broken heart. The heavy weight of responsibility and fear of not being enough. It's such a heavy and pervasive emotion.

It makes my cheeks burn because I know the feeling myself.

He swallows and nods. Keeping his gaze averted.

I feel so helpless, and all I want to do is reach out and tell him I'm alright. Tell him it'll be okay. I didn't go anywhere. And take that burden of trying to make ends meet back.

It *was* my job. I failed. I'm failing now. Especially because he has to deal with all of this.

He shouldn't have to.

I take my coin purse out of the folds of my dress. "I'd like some of the applegrif. Sometimes I get headaches. I may come again to buy more." And I feel giddy, having found at least one way to come back here from time to time.

He nods and pulls a couple of sprigs from the bundle.

"I'll get that for the Lady," the prince says, stepping forward. He hands a few coins to Cassian. Coins that are worth more than the sprigs. Cassian hesitates but lets the prince drop the money into his hand.

"Thank you, your highness," Cassian says.

"Good lad," the prince says distractedly as I tuck my purse and the applegrif away and smile at Cassian before leaving.

"You didn't have to do that," I say to the prince as he helps me back on the horse.

"I didn't know you get headaches still. From the fall?"

I nod, taking the reins. He leaps onto the sorrel once more and heads off.

"I'll have Olid informed. He'll make a tonic for you."

"I've spoken to him about it. He knows already. I believe he's working on something."

"Why did you stop there rather than the one farther uptown?"

"I heard Olid say to Edwin that there are different kinds of *unique* plants at the one lower down. He had the boy get some things there for me when I was ill. I wanted to see for myself." I hope that story holds. It *is* true.

"The new wood is certainly promising. They must do well for themselves. And Olid knows his herbs, so the merchant boy must be good."

I say nothing, but I smile in reply as the prince turns to look. I'm pleasantly surprised by Cassian's knowledge. I didn't know he'd paid such close attention to how I'd run the shop. Hopefully, he'll be able to make ends meet even without his apprenticeship. Now that he's gotten the attention of the prince, things might pick up as well. He can use that in getting his name around and known.

And I can frequent the shop on occasion...just to check in and provide money. Perhaps we can become 'friends' over time, and he can confide in me. Time will tell.

For now, I'm just relieved to have seen my brother. Sad that he's hurting and wondering how Mother and Mellen feel.

It'll be alright though...maybe.

No, it *will* be alright...right?

The prince doesn't take me through the lower village. He points out the way, though. I'm perfectly fine with the detour as we head toward the outer gate.

And with one weight lifted off me, I feel another settle in. I'm indebted to the prince. So far, I enjoy his company, but I must admit, I'm feeling hedged in by a promise I never made.

He seems perfectly fine, but...people can pretend. Show the sides of them that they prefer you see rather than what they are. And I can't forget that I'm an enemy to him, the king, and the kingdom. How would he react if he found out about the magic? Even with his feelings for Orielle, I'm guessing that wouldn't go over well.

It's not harmful magic. I can't actually hurt anyone...that I know of. So, it's not like I'm dangerous. But that wouldn't matter...And that's kind of unfair.

I used to not think so much about it. Now I have reason to.

The guards bow to the prince as he passes through the gate and onto the road leading north. I'm not familiar with the terrain here. Usually, I head south.

The trees are tall here, and the shade is cool. The city sounds fall away, and soon it's just us and the horses and the scent of pine.

"Sometimes it's good to get out," Kalandrel says.

"I agree. It's peaceful out here, but I'm surprised you don't travel with a guard. Especially with that beast."

"I don't normally bring a guard, but I should have thought of how it might be for you after what happened. We can go back if you'd like," He pulls up his horse, waiting for an answer.

"No, not for me. For your own protection."

"You think I can't protect myself?" his eyebrow cocks as he nudges his horse forward. A teasing smile curls his lips. "Ouch."

"That's not what I meant."

"Certainly, sounds like you don't think I can handle myself, so I have to wonder..."

"Believe me. I'd love nothing more than to say you can defend yourself against hordes, but I can't in good conscious lie to a prince. I know nothing of weaponry or fighting. So even if I offered an opinion, it would not be a judicious one."

"You're no fun to tease."

"Ah, but it makes it more fun for me. Isn't the challenge something you rise to?"

"There you are."

"What?"

"Sometimes the old you breaks through."

"You like the old me?"

"I love the old you."

I nod, falling silent because I don't know what to say. I do feel terrible about her death. He doesn't know he's lost her forever. His love.

If I knew what she was like, I could try to be her. But...that's not possible. Being someone I'm not would feel like a dungeon. Even with the pretty dresses, food, maids, and someone as kind as the prince seems. A pretty dungeon. I can't...

We fall silent, moving around the thick pine trunks. He seems pensive. I wish I knew what he was thinking.

"Have I offended you?" I ask finally. He shakes his head.

"It's not you. It's not fair to ask you to feel the same way. Or to even say it back."

My heart wrenches for him when I realize...

"Kalandrel, I didn't-"

"No, please. Don't feel pressured. It's not your fault."

"The last thing I want to do is hurt you. I just don't know who or what I am, let alone who anyone else is. I'm sorry. I don't know how to make it better. But I wish with all my heart I could. I really like the man I see in you. I think you're strong and brave and good. The old me loved you...right? Just give me some time?"

He pauses a moment, then gives me a side-eye.

"I noticed you left out 'handsome,' 'charming,' 'good dancer,' 'master swordsman,' 'great hunter.'"

"Ah! Well, it's a good thing you're here to fill those in for me. And I'm sure we could come up with more if we really thought about it." He smiles, and I smile too in relief. "Tell me everything. Tell me all the stories of us. Who I was. Who you were. What made us fall in love?"

"You want a love story?"

"Our love story...yes."

"We met when we were young, but I wasn't interested in girls and romance. You pretended not to be interested in romance, and you felt like you had to hide that girlish side of you under a layer of mischief..."

The horses plod on as he tells me of a little girl whose father visited the king often. And a little boy who was assigned to keep her company in a strange place. They became friends through different adventures chasing pirates across the seas, in the ponds and lakes, succumbing to the siren's songs, and eventually getting shipwrecked on an island with strange creatures. Many such adventures occurred, fighting giants in the far northern lands. Playing war against the kingdoms that attempted to conquer Drene.

He tells me how they rode horses together, took their educational lessons together, got into trouble together, and got *out* of trouble together.

He tells me how the two grew close. How they were sad when the girl had to leave, happy when she returned, and sent letters in between.

And how she teased him, and he teased her. And how he knew he loved her early on. And she loved him. And how she was perfect to him.

And we stop the horses near a spring that runs from a pond, and he helps me off my horse as I pretend to be that wonderful and brave-sounding creature he fell in love with.

And though my feet are on the ground, he doesn't let me go. And I feel a beating pulse from his hands, which are still around my waist. Deep red, the color of giving one's heart to another.

It hurts.

He looks into my eyes as if searching for that girl. He'll never find her. I wish he could. I never meant to take her place.

"Why are you sad?" he asks softly.

"I just wish you could have her back," I whisper.

"But I *do* have her," he insists. "You're here. And what you are is who you were. No matter if you can remember or not."

And my heart breaks for him, because if there was ever a time to tell him who I am, it's now. But there's no going back if I do. And if I don't, I'll have to forever hold my tongue, come what may.

So, I bite my tongue metaphorically and my lip literally and look down, because I don't want to disappoint him. He deserves so much better than me. Than a peasant girl.

But I can try to deserve him. I can try to make him happy, can't I? Could I be enough?

But he's not the only one in this scenario. What about me?

"Look at me," he says, gently lifting my chin. I do, and his whole face has softened with an intoxicating glow.

"I just don't want to hurt you or disappoint you."

"Then just be you. And that'll be enough."

I nod, feeling overwhelmed by all of this. This acting of a part mixed with my real emotions, and how am I supposed to feel right now? And how am I supposed to keep all my secrets?

And I'm about to look away in shame, but he leans in, closing his eyes. His lips touch mine, and I don't know what to do, but he does.

His emotions explode across my mind. Splatters of all sorts of colors clinging to his memories of us...of *her*. Blue for missing her. Red and orange for her friendship and love. Golden of comfort. Pink, when he thought she was cute. Purple when she teased him too much. Green when someone else was interested in her.

She was every color to him.

His love for her becomes a dream for me. Something I hope someone can feel for me someday. The real me. Love that I feel as myself instead of on someone else's behalf. I hadn't thought about it for myself. Too busy. Too stressed. But now I *do* want that. Except now, I can't. I'm stuck.

He pulls away and lays his forehead on mine. His mouth curls in a smile.

"You don't have to remember. I'll remember the old times for both of us. And we'll both remember the new ones to come."

Chapter 14

Maehdiorah

I should just find her on my own. It's only logical to see if the girl is a threat before Elonrod finds her, but an age-old sensibility cautions me. I've learned to listen to my instincts, but right now they're at war. One urges me to find and dispense with the girl. The other says wait...be patient. I have no idea why. What could come of waiting? Or perhaps it's not about what could come but what might remain if I choose not to act hastily.

I abhor moving without reason. I detest hasty decisions. Even though sometimes hasty decisions must be made to keep my plans in play. Having to pivot takes energy and focus. Extremely delicate measures.

And with people, it's always best to err on the side of caution. But in this case, there may be danger no matter what. It's a matter of controlling the danger, meeting the level, and bringing it all around to where *I* need it to go.

I'm only one person. It's very difficult to plan and execute an entire revolution over decades that will result in a new world order all on my own. Even if I've had time to strategize and practice. One wrong move can topple the whole thing and land me back at square one, waiting for another Elonrod or Thagyn. Preferably Elonrod...Thagyn sounded like a handful. But beggars can't be choosers, and it's not like I can control which personality the next great, talented magician will have.

And no...it can't be me. I have the abilities, willpower, and discipline, but this is not my story, and that is not my role. I have a different part to play. I *can*not be the hero.

My decision about the girl right now is to wait. Let Elonrod find her and trust in Fate. My fallback is that I can always dispense with her later. There are multiple ways to remove her from my path if she's an impediment.

So, instead of looking on my own, I wait for Elonrod to join me.

He's lost some of his cockiness as he strides into the clearing. He's unkempt, with hair that he keeps running his hands through, and a slant to his usually mischievous eyes. I can't understand why *he's* so invested in *this* girl (and I refuse to look into his head at this time.) Sometimes magic-users slip through our fingers. We can't save them all. We have to acknowledge that we're not all powerful.

The ancient ones understood this.

The Dark Magicians tried to thwart this.

He simply has to choose whether or not to let it bother him. I understand it's hard. Challenges his abilities. Makes him more fallible than he'd like to feel. But if there's nothing to be done, then there's nothing to be done. And he needs to understand and be okay with that.

"I've been thinking we should go back to Thorondar. We can take turns. Amplify each other's powers. We'll have a better chance of finding her," he says, plopping down on his log.

"If she's still there," I point out. "Why is she so important to you? Why this one? There are probably hundreds like her, and we might be able to save them if we can find out who they are."

"It's complicated."

"It's really not."

"We just need to find her."

"I'd rather not put my life on the line without knowing what for."

His face darkens. "I can't give you a reason that makes sense."

"Do you have feelings for her?"

"No," he says, shooting me a disgusted look. Truth. I can feel and see it, but I can't dig any further into his thoughts or emotions without violating his privacy, and there's always the chance he'd feel someone else in his mind. Trust is still important.

"Look, I can't explain it, and I won't ask you to follow me to the city." He stands abruptly, tilting his head to the sun. I leap at him just in time, catching hold of his arm before he blinks out of sight.

I'm dragged along with him through the beams of sunlight. It's one thing to look at. Another to dive in. It's like swimming against a golden river's current, trying to wash you downstream. Every fiber of your being has to be ready and willing to withstand and push. And one should definitely keep their eyes closed until they land. Using the sight of the mind and gifts to steer.

We topple through rays of sunlight onto the ground just outside the forest near Thorondar.

"You weren't supposed to hitch a ride. I wasn't expecting to have to travel for two," he growls, rubbing the shoulder he landed on and shooting me an angry look. I stare back as I rub my twisted ankle.

"You weren't supposed to just disappear. What if you'd been captured and killed?"

"Still might be."

"Let's find cover at least or try to blend in."

I wasn't planning on traveling into the heart of the enemy's territory, and being here without preparing worries me. We're technically already in sight of the castle walls and gates, so there's a good chance we may have been seen suddenly falling from the sky. So, we walk towards the road slowly, casting glances at the walls, listening for the alarm, and waiting for crossbows to be trained on us.

Nothing happens as we approach the road. We enter the city as if we belong there. No one stops us, and most people ignore us. Now that we're inside, we should find shelter or somewhere we can be left alone and undisturbed. Prying eyes could be detrimental.

"There's a water duct down by the well on the north side. No one visits it much. Most people on that side of town have their own wells or go to the community well in the square," he says. I don't ask how he knows, but it tells me he's more reckless than I'd imagined. How often does he come here? Or spy?

And I wonder what else he knows...it could be useful to our cause.

"Following you," I say, gesturing for him to lead the way. We can't use magic to travel here, so we walk through the city. Using the lower town as cover, we loop around the west side of town, then follow the city wall to the north side. There's little traffic where we are, so we don't draw attention. When we do, we act like beggars to make the richer folks ignore us. It makes them uncomfortable, and they move on quickly without making eye contact.

Finally, we find the duct.

The river comes through the town here. Or at least part of it flows through the moat created long ago, while the castle wall was built up to allow the water in through a grate. There's a small canal that carries the water through the city.

And where the water comes in, there's no one. Not even guards posted on the city wall, which seems strange. Shouldn't they be guarding a potential point of entry? I guess they don't in times of peace...but still? One never knows when enemies will strike.

Not my responsibility...Not my city to protect, so I let it go, but not without making a mental note for myself...just in case *I* want to use it.

Bathed in sunlight, we sit against the wall, listening to the water trickle lazily by.

"You still want to take turns, or do you think we can just search?" I ask before he sinks to the ground.

"Search, first. We shouldn't have a problem in the city. We can amplify if we can't find her." He situates himself so he's comfortable and wastes no time shutting himself off from the outside world and seeking the sun's gaze. I do the same.

Swept away by the images in the eddies of glowing yellow, I search for the girl.

The thing is, as we've seen over the last few days, there are a lot of peasant girls with dark hair. This could take a while.

We sit for some time. I've found several girls with dark hair, but I've not cross-referenced them with the essence I found of the family. I don't want to be too efficient, so I just keep track of the girls occasionally, branching out to see if there are others. I get bored, waiting for Elonrod to either catch up or find the girl on his own. But it gives me time to think. I do love being inside my own head. It's peaceful there.

Elonrod stiffens suddenly, leaning toward the sunlight as it's shift-
ed, and he's mostly in the shade of a wall now. Agitated, he opens his
eyes and walks toward the light, sitting in full sunlight again, shifting
his cloak around him like he's itchy.

"I think I've found something," he says, waving me over. "Come
here."

I do, though I don't really want to. I sit cross-legged in front of him.
And he pats my knee.

"Find me," he says. And I begrudgingly open myself to the gifts and
sunlight, reaching out tentatively to find his essence. I hate this part.

It's intimate emotionally and mentally. Not on an incredibly deep
level with the melding of gifts, but enough that it makes me uncomfortable. I don't like being that close to others.

It also makes it easier for someone to slip past the mental and
emotional blocks I have that prevent those who read thoughts or
understand feelings from reading or feeling mine. Not that anyone
should be able to slip past them even if we're connected on this level.
But it doesn't mean it *can't* be done.

There are things there that no mortal should know. Feelings no
mortal would understand. Those things must remain in darkness and
protected.

It doesn't take long to find him. His essence is strong and heavily spiced with magic. Our essences work together, interlocking like
hooking elbows, and we traverse up the river of golden light and
images together. He takes me to what he thinks he's found.

Skipping images of a girl. A pretty girl with really light blonde hair.

"You said her hair was dark," I say, pulling away from his gift.

"Shh...that's her."

She sits on a horse as the images skip. She's in the forest. Trees only let in blinks of sunlight at a time. And he's right. Her essence has a trace of Dark Magic, like a binding.

I recognize the imprint immediately. It *is* mine. Which is both a relief and a cause for concern. Relief because it means there are no other Dark Magicians to deal with. Concern because if word gets out about a Dark Magician...This could spoil my plans and put things into motion I'm not ready for. Her very existence threatens everything I've worked for. But what to do about her?

The girl is certainly not a peasant now. Not with those clothes and that fine skin. She looks nothing like the girl Elonrod described, and though I can feel traces of her family's essence on her, they've weakened with time and distance. The ties are *not* familial. They're mental and emotional certainly, but they're not connected the way families are. No wonder she was difficult to find.

It's painfully obvious now why Elonrod was so desperate to find her.

My face grows hot because if Elonrod can tell...if he can match the imprint embedded in the Dark Magic...He might start to unravel other carefully kept secrets.

I wish I'd known about her sooner...

She was a mistake. The thing is, there was no way to know what went wrong. It was all too fast. Too hasty (hence why I hate moving hastily). I didn't know she'd survived.

There's no way he'll let her go now. He's been searching for her and for the other since they were separated.

Curses.

It was never supposed to come to this. There will be too many questions. I have to pivot, but I'm not sure which way.

"We have to find her," Elonrod says. I open my eyes. He's staring wildly into my eyes with a fervor. "She needs us. She's gotta come back to camp with us. She's not safe here. If they find out, they'll kill her."

"We'll figure out how to get her out of here but think this through. She's clearly something else now. You saw her clothes? And who is she with?"

"It doesn't matter. We'll find a way."

He's losing his head. He's too emotional to listen to reason, and I'm sure he'd travel to her right now if the sun were strong enough in the forest. But he might mess things up. And we might get caught. And I need more time to figure things out.

"Listen," I say, grabbing his face and making him pay attention to me. "We have no idea what the situation is. If we want to keep her and ourselves from getting found out, we need to do it carefully."

"I can drop in, and we can get away no problem."

"Trust me. She's going to want to know she can trust you before she gets winged away to a camp full of magic-users. That's kidnapping. And if she's changed social status, which she appears to have done, someone is going to be looking for her. A high-profile person disappearing, especially through rays of light, is going to put some heat in our stew."

"No one says 'put heat in our stew' anymore. You sound like a grandmother." His brows pull together.

"I'm not wrong, though. We need to be careful."

"Fine. We'll do it your way. What do you suggest?"

"Just...wait. We know she's alive. We know what she looks like. Now we find out who she is, who she's with, how we can extricate her while causing the least upheaval in her life *and* ours."

He's not happy with it. He's been waiting for years to put his family back together. If he just waits...if he's patient, he can have his sister back.

He blows out a breath and straightens his back. Then he relaxes and searches for her again. I follow the path she was just on.

"She's with a nobleman. They seem...fond of each other. He has the king's crest on his saddle." His voice sounds worried.

I see her in patches still, and expanding my focus, I see him too. The man she's with. He's speaking with her, but we can only see, we can't hear.

She seems fine if I just look at her, but if I look...I can see she's afraid. Guilty. Sad. I also see desire.

The man, though...He has deep feelings for the girl that dance off him like heat waves bending the air. How sad for him. To be in love with a magic-user. His heart will break.

Elonrod and I sit in silence, watching his sister as she and the man ride to the castle and toward the northern gate.

"They're here." Elonrod leaps to his feet, and before I can stop him. He's racing down the canal. I curse and run after him.

He bounds over a bridge and through the square towards the northern gate. I don't want to cause a scene, so I don't call after him. I just follow, wishing I could use magic to travel right now. These cobblestones are killer under my poorly soled, leather shoes. They might as well be slapping my feet.

The reckless fool takes us to the busier section of the northern part of town, where droves of people are gathering and heading into the gate to the castle as if for a special occasion. The city gate is wide open with daylight spilling through. People there have stopped and moved off the road for a couple on horseback. She's one of the two. She sits on a gray horse while the man rides a tall sorrel. The people disperse and bow as he enters. Some call out to him, calling him 'prince.'

Curses. How did she get herself involved with the prince?

Elonrod has stopped in his tracks, staring at his sister with an intensity that lets me know he's reaching out to her with his thoughts.

She starts, and her head swivels, finding us in the crowd. Her face pales, but she quickly looks toward the prince. He merely points his horse towards the castle, still oblivious to us, a mercy of Fate.

She darts a glance at Elonrod one more time, and her eyebrows rise as if she's trying to speak to him before she tears her eyes away and follows the prince.

Elonrod's face lifts, and he turns to me, eyes lit up with joy.

"She saw me. She knows. I told her."

"What did you tell her?"

"That we're coming to rescue her."

"And what of the execution?" I ask, pointing to the bundles of sticks piled against the platform. Shamefully familiar sight.

His face drops as he looks around at the crowds as if seeing them for the first time.

"We missed one," he trails off, gazing around at the people eager to see what's about to happen. I reach out to listen and see into his mind, watching it work over how he could possibly save whoever it is accused of magic.

He can't think of anything. There are too many guards, dogs guarding the way in, and we look suspicious waiting here. Swooping in on the wind doesn't give him enough time to fight off the guards that will no doubt be present. Sun travel either. He'd have to cut the magic-user free, fight, and get away.

We're not prepared for this. Better safe than sorry in this case. Better not to be known.

"We have to let this one go," I whisper to him.

"No," he shakes his head. "There's still time. We'll think of something."

"Elonrod...you know it's not going to work. Not this time. If we had enough people to distract..."

"We can't just let it happen," he whispers. And I see the guards eyeing us because we've been standing in the flow of eager attendees for too long.

I take hold of his sleeve in a comforting way. A gesture of readiness for me in case I have to travel him out of here. "Leave now. Stay alive. Save your sister later."

He notices the guards, too, and nods.

"This isn't fair," he says as we turn away.

"That's why we're trying to fix it."

CHAPTER 15

ELLORY

We're passing under the gate to the castle, and I'm trying to wrap my head around everything when the dog starts snarling and barking. His large white teeth bare as he unleashes a guttural growl and lunges. The mare rears up and bats at the dog in warning. And I grab onto her neck to keep from falling off.

"Hold him," someone says.

"Sorren, down boy," says a guard who's got hold of the dog's leash.

"The Lady Heiress's horse. Someone calm her."

A servant races to grab the mare's head as she comes down and threatens to rare again. The guard with the dog reprimands the animal, hauling him backwards, line taut.

"I'm sorry, Majesty. We brought him down for security with all the people coming for the execution. He's normally much better about picking out the magic-users. Please accept my apologies. I'll have him back in retraining immediately," the dog's handler says as he pulls the beast back towards the gate.

"Yes, do that. Have another brought to the courtyard in the meantime. Security is still our priority," Kalandrel says as he touches my elbow. Fear and concern, light green tinged orange. The mare settles under the control of the servant, still breathing heavily and licking her lips, but I'm shaking.

Kalandrel hops off his horse and moves to my side to help me get off the mare. "One of those we train to sniff out magic. Unfortunately, he's not very good. Are you alright?"

Not very good? Ha! I disagree. That dog definitely knew.

But I say nothing and nod instead as I let him help me to the ground. He tells the servants to take the horses back to the stables.

"Come. Settle your nerves, Orielle. It's over now. No harm done." Kalandrel walks me back to the castle. "And we're just in time for the execution."

It's lovely...not the execution. The other part. His fussing about me and being completely enamored. It's nice. It really is, but I feel more trapped now than ever. I'd forgotten about the dogs. What if this keeps happening? With *all* of the dogs? They can't *all* be wrong. So, what conclusions must be drawn eventually?

He takes me through a part of the castle I've never been to before. It's open, airy, and lit with many large, pretty windows with swirling ironwork in the shapes of leaves and roses. There are stone statues here, some of past kings, some of animals. Many prettily dressed nobles have gathered as well in these open spaces, some sitting on couches and divans while others stand in clusters talking. Servants move among them occasionally with drinks and platters of small snacks.

They bow graciously at their prince, all smiles and kind words, and the enormity of their thoughts seems to collect like a cloud of gray mist, swirling like insincerity. I don't hear what they say as we pass through the middle of them to the other side, where a doorway stands open but guarded.

As we enter, the smells of the outside greet us: sun-warmed stone and dust. We've emerged onto a balcony, fat columned stones hold up a stone railing where the king stands with his hands planted. We look down on the courtyard. From here I can see the whole of the south side, the stables near the gate to the city, and the barracks and training grounds on the other side. And in the middle, a stand with piles and piles of sticks surrounding a tall post.

"Father," the prince says with a short bow. I curtsey as well.

"Cutting it close," the king says.

"I'd never miss it."

"I hear there was a mix-up with one of the hounds."

"He's had that problem once or twice. I was assured the hound would be put back into training. And I ordered another to be brought to assess the crowds."

"Good. We're almost ready here. Make sure things run smoothly."

Kalandrel bows again and releases me before leaving the balcony. I hear him talking with the guards outside, asking how the preparations are going and when we can expect to begin.

I'm at a loss, so I stand where I was abandoned (strong word, I know, but in the presence of the king...especially one who hates magic, it feels like safety has been stripped away). The queen enters from the opposite side of the balcony, eyes flicking over me and the king before she stands at his side. Her presence doesn't ease the tension at all as we watch the crowd gather and are ushered to the base of the platform. So many voices, some entertainment in the form of juggling, and a firebreather have arrived and delight the people while they wait.

It seems like forever until the prince returns, smiling heartily at me and assuring his father that all is ready.

"Greetings, loyal subjects," the king booms, waving his hands for attention. A hush falls over the crowds. "We are here to witness the execution of a magic-user. A crime which is one of the most treasonous in all the lands. Magic is forbidden. You all know this. It is unfair, unyielding, and must be eradicated. Those who use it do so for selfish reasons.

"We are lucky that none of us has lived through a Rising, and with acts such as these to ensure we remove the magic-users from our midst, we never will."

As he pauses, the crowd cheers, some clapping, some whistling. The king gestures to the guards below to take over. The executioner brings his torch as some of the guards start dousing the platform with oil.

"No, please," a familiar voice cries. "The children were dying. Please, listen to me. I did nothing wrong." The old woman, Ferdy of Ilfrain, looking much more worn and tired, moves towards the platform. Sobbing takes the place of her cries as the crowd heckles her. Someone even tosses old vegetables.

She collapses unconscious near the end of her walk, and the guards have to lift her limp body onto the platform. They tie her to the post at her midsection, feet, and neck, with her hands bound behind her. She wakes suddenly and screams.

Her cries pierce my heart, and I feel the cold stone of the railing against my palms. Terror sharp as a blade, crying out with every instinct to live. But inside that terror, I can feel the truth. No one was hurt by her use of magic. She only helped. And that *should* matter.

But it *doesn't* matter to the men who wait for the King's order. He gives them the signal. The executioner steps forward and starts lighting the wood bundles. The woman screams, trying to break free. The guards move back.

Fire takes hold...It moves greedily along the oil-soaked wood.

And I sit here, useless as a woman who only meant to help with the gift she was given, meets her end.

I can't watch, so I turn away. How can the nobles do this? How can they sit here, perfectly content to let this happen? It's maddening. I don't know if I should dignify this woman by letting this memory become imprinted on me, or if it's decent not to watch what shouldn't be happening. How do I honor a fellow magic-user?

The smell of smoke encompasses the balcony now, and I notice that some of the guards move back, covering their noses. I do too. Screams still tear through the air, but now they're heart-wrenching pain, and an extra, vile scent floats in the air.

"I'm not feeling well," I say suddenly, moving towards the door. Kalandrel follows. He motions for a servant.

"See that she's alright," then he turns to me. "I must continue here, but I'll check on you when it's finished."

I nod, feeling my stomach sour. The servant takes my elbow to keep me upright as we pass through the corridors and into quieter places in the castle. He deposits me in a thick chair just outside my quarters, and I thank him as he moves away to fetch Thessel.

It's not that I haven't seen executions before. Once or twice when I was younger. It's...that could have been me down there. That was someone who was good at heart, meant well, and acted with love. If this kingdom has no place for that, they don't deserve good people.

I rise, heat in my cheeks, determination in my step as I make my way to the library. I don't know if it's the best place to be but being surrounded by quiet that I desperately need seems like a good idea.

I make my way through what seems like familiar corridors until I find it. Then I breathe for a moment, touching the handle lightly and going in.

A cursory check of the room shows no one else present, so I close the door behind me and sit in one of the large chairs. A warm, guilty feeling spreads in my cheeks as I glance at the blue, leatherbound book. I don't want to get caught checking it out. But I don't know another way to find out about all of this.

It's not just the old woman. The boy from the market said I was his sister. He said I have magic. He's coming to rescue me.

But I have no idea how or when.

I'm not even sure I believe the part about him being related to me. I already have a family, so that seems nuts. But I'll worry about that later. After I escape.

For now, I just have to focus on not getting caught. I can't run into any more dogs. One instance is excusable. Two is only borderline coincidental. Three might as well be a death sentence.

And what about the prince? I'm torn about him. On one hand, I'm appalled at what he just helped bring about. On the other I feel bad for him. He's in love with a ghost. I don't want to break his heart, but he definitely deserves better than this. Than me. Than a betrothed and future spouse who lies to him. And to be honest, I've been avoiding the thought of being Queen because it just doesn't work with my brain...I can't fathom it.

I definitely *can't* be Queen with magic.

But...could I? Would I have enough influence to change the laws? To make it legal for people to possess magic? Can we avoid executions like the one today (even just the memory brings back the scent of burning flesh. It stings my nose and lingers)?

There's no way I won't get caught, though...

Either way, I need to learn more.

Thessel is a good source...for the 'queenly' part of things.

But for the magic, I'll have to check out the books. At least until Mischief Boy comes up with a plan or can tell me what's going on.

He looked scared. And the way he inserted his thoughts into my mind was incredibly disturbing...I don't like to think that someone can read my thoughts. But I can read emotions, and that's similar...I guess?

It's really embarrassing how little I know. But I didn't need to know before. It wasn't relevant till now.

I take the book from the shelf and start flipping through the pages. If someone comes in, I'll just say it was a book the prince showed me of the kingdom's glorious triumph over magic and those who wield it. They won't question me then. Especially with the aftermath of the execution being cleared away in the courtyard.

CHAPTER 16

MAEHDIORAH

E lonrod tells everyone in the camp that we've found his sister as soon as we're back. He runs from one end of the camp to the other, pumping his fists in the air, whooping, and shouting that he's found her. The children chase after him, sharing in his excitement because sometimes, things to celebrate are few and far between.

The elders stop their chores, shading their eyes against the sun as they watch Elonrod circle the camp and come back through. Winded and grinning like he used to, he plops down next to Reathl, who mends a shirt. Gomthen shuffles closer to hear as well. Most of the camp gathers to hear the news.

"I felt it. It's her. It's undeniable. You have to see her," Elonrod says.

"How did you find her?" Reathl asks as he sets aside the shirt he was mending. Elonrod quickly explains our trip to the capital city, but everyone has questions.

"Won't she be hard to rescue out from under the prince's nose?"

"What can she do?"

"What is she like?"

Elonrod answers the questions as best he can.

"Well then, how are we going to rescue her?" Reathl asks.

"With caution," I jump in. "The prince is in love with her. He'll not let her go quietly."

"No matter. We can hide her away. He'll never find her," Elonrod says.

"If he comes looking for her here, I don't see that we have much of a chance against his knights," I caution.

"She has immense talent. We'll teach her to use it. With both of us, we could be unstoppable."

I say nothing...that's what the Dark Magicians of old thought, too. Look where they are now.

"You're not going to ruin this for me, Telisan. You're smart and talented, too, but you know as well as I that she belongs with us. She'll put our cause leaps and bounds forward. And if you ever actually *tried* to use your talents, you might be of more help, also."

I cock a brow at him, but he makes a face at me like he knows my secret. Like he's challenging me. Foolish boy.

"If the prince is in love with her, he might change some laws for her," Reathl says with his bushy eyebrows rising into his forehead.

"Don't bring him into this. He's not good enough for my sister," Elonrod replies. "She's not staying there with *him*. A man who's had our kind hunted and killed."

"Those laws have been in place for centuries. It's not likely he'll overturn them. Even for love," I offer.

"Such a shame. Does she look like you, Elonrod?"

"Not really...no. She's actually...in a different body now."

"What does that mean?" Reathl looks from Elonrod to me and back.

"Her old body died. She's somehow inside the body of someone else. Something to do with the Dark Magic that's bound to her."

"She *has* Dark Magic?! That doesn't bode well," Reathl says, shaking his head and rubbing his grizzled face.

I wish Elonrod hadn't brought it up, but I couldn't have thwarted it. It's too important a detail to leave out.

"No, *she* hasn't used it. It's been used *on* her."

"For what purpose?"

"I haven't figured that out yet. She doesn't seem to have recollection of it being used on her."

The old man breathes slowly and shakes his head. "We'd better focus on getting her out of there first before we can unravel anything else."

"We could stage her death," I offer.

"Great Kings. That's morbid," Elonrod says with a scrunch in his nose.

"Think about it," I answer. "The prince won't look for her if he thinks she's dead. He'll mourn and move on. She'll be free."

He turns away, but I can tell he's mulling it over.

"I've heard tell of a beast near the capital. It's been attacking people. The guards are really afraid of it, but they can't seem to get rid of it. Perhaps we make it look like the beast got her," he says.

"That will work," I say, "A little blood and a cloak for them to find..."

"Yeah," he says, rubbing his hands on his knees. "Yeah, then they won't suspect us. We can slip back to camp without a fuss."

Reathl nods. "Sounds like a plan."

"We just have to get some things together," Elonrod says, his eyes light up the more he thinks of the plan and having his sister safe with us.

I'm happy for him to have found his sister. For the moment. She'll still bring up more questions with her tie to Dark Magic.

But...if they think it's a one-time thing that happened long ago, perhaps they won't worry about a Dark Magician. Then I'll still have time to execute my plans. I'll just need to steer in the right direction. Little by little. Step by step. That's how change is made.

Great things take time and patience.

CHAPTER 17

ELLORY

The door creaks open, and I jump. The prince grins and pushes the door open wider.

"I thought you'd be in here. Thessel said you never returned to your chambers. Are you feeling better?" He leans over my shoulder to see what I've been reading. My cheeks color, but I don't hide the book.

"Yes, I think it was the smell. I wanted to catch up on some things. I wanted to remember."

"That's cute," he says with a smile, kissing my hair and taking the book. "There's certainly an advantage to knowing this stuff. Occasionally, a magic-user will pop up within our borders like the woman, but we haven't had all-out war for some time."

"It seems...scary to face down people with those types of abilities. To be able to crush a person with a rock or sweep them away in a windstorm..."

"Well, you need not worry about such things. Clearly, we have this under control." He nudges my shoulder with his. I see warm pinks and glowing reds, beating hearts, and I remember his kiss.

I look away quickly. He laughs.

"You don't have to be shy. You didn't use to be."

"Tell me more about the wars."

"Because I distract you?"

"Not at all," I meet his eyes with my nose in the air. He moves so he's facing me now. It's hard not to notice how tall he is.

"Yes, I do."

"Are you going to tell me or not?"

"Once you admit I distract you."

I sigh, meeting his gaze because I don't want to back down. He smiles, and his blue eyes bounce from my eyes to my mouth and back.

He starts to lean in, and I panic. But then there's a knock on the door and a voice calls, "Prince Kalandrel?"

"Come," the prince says, pulling back only slightly, as the door opens, and a guard pokes his head through.

"The king requests your presence."

"I'll be right there," he says dismissively, and the guard leaves. He turns back to me and gives me a quick peck. Vibrant pink and luscious reds. "I'll be back."

He disappears through the door, and I return the book to its place before heading back to my quarters. Partly because I don't want to be here when he returns, partly because I'd like to rest. No one bothers me there except the Lady's Maids.

I wish I could talk to my mother about all of this. I miss her so much it aches in my chest. It never occurred to me that I might not get to watch Cassian and Mellen grow up. We weren't as close as I wanted, but I hoped that wouldn't always be the case. I just thought if I could get ahead with finances, we'd have more time. Mellen and I could eventually go shopping together for pretty things. We'd tell each other secrets. Be sisters. Tease Cassian about the crushes he had on girls.

But I left for work early in the mornings, came home after dark sometimes, and just fell asleep. There are only a few moments I really remember getting to spend time together as a family. Sometimes, over morning meals, if they were awake by the time I left. Some whispered conversations in the dark where Mellen would tell me about boys she liked. One time, we mended her doll together.

I thought there'd be more time to make more memories. To live.

To think Mischief Boy is right and that *he's* my brother is insane. My family is definitely my family. They have to be. I was my mother's miracle baby. I've always been her little miracle.

...

Stillborn...Her first baby was stillborn. The cord had wrapped around its neck. Its face was bluish purple, she said. Dead. She'd never been so scared, and the healers definitely couldn't find a pulse. She tried to revive the baby and said it was difficult.

That doesn't *mean* anything. Could be nothing at all.

But the girl whose body I'm in now...she fell. The physician said there was so much blood. He thought it was Orielle's at first, but when they found no wounds, he thought the beast hadn't touched her at all. That doesn't make sense, though. Why wouldn't it have killed her, too? Why would it have left her unscathed but not anyone else? What if it *had* killed her, too?

And if there were no wounds, could that be explained by magic? There's healer magic. I'm not sure how that works, but some *would* know. There was pain...such terrible pain in her stomach. Perhaps it was still healing? On the inside? Maybe that's why it took so long to transition?

And if *Orielle* died...and mother's first baby died...It could mean I'm not who I thought I was. Who I grew up being. That I'm not Ellory at all, just some spirit who stole a baby's body and was brought up in her place. I have no idea what I really am.

No. This is crazy. I'm going crazy. I just need to rest. There's a lot going on, that's all, and I'm just overwhelmed with the execution, Mischief Boy, and the prince. It's just all too much right now. That's all it is. I just need to rest.

I finally find the corridor with my room and slip inside, shutting the door and leaning against it. Luckily, Ardialle and Thessel aren't here. It's safe. For the moment.

CHAPTER 18

MAEHDIORAH

There's a game that the kids used to play called "older than the earth." Usually, it was an older child teasing the young children, but what they'd do was grab two sandstones and rub them together until the sandstones were mere pebbles. There'd be a pile of dirt where the sand had piled up, or sometimes the wind would catch the grains and carry them away. Then the older child would say, "You're older than the earth," and tease the younger children about being old. Of course, the younger children would be upset. (Which is dumb because if they sat and thought about it, they might realize that the older child also was older than the earth, and who cares anyway? But they didn't sit and think about it. They reacted because the older children had told them it was a bad thing. And they believed them. That sort of thing happens all to often in general, but I digress.) Sometimes the younger child would swipe at the older child, which turned into a game of chase, but that only inflamed the teasing.

Humans are sensitive to growing older, some going to great lengths to stay young or at least to not die. It's completely natural given their short lifespans. And their sensitivity has been passed down for generations.

They were the youngest race of those beings created by the Immortals. The last to be born, and the first to begin dying. And they've been trying to thwart Death ever since.

But a singular eye can poison a human.

And that's how Dark Magic works. With the humans it encounters. To escalate their desires. But over time, it twists.

That's why humans fear it. And it's with just cause. Our people, having heard that Elonrod's sister has been touched by Dark Magic, fear what she might bring. The council is called.

Amtira clears her throat as Gomthen raises his hands to silence the camp. We've met around the fires today so all can attend this council. Their fates are intertwined with this new information about a Dark Magician.

"We've all heard of the Dark Magic used on Elonrod's sister. And though we don't know from whence it came, Elonrod has seen that it's not her that wields it," Gomthen says.

"We believe it's safe to bring her here," Amtira adds.

"But can we know for sure?" one of the mothers says, her hand reaching around her child.

"I saw and felt the bond. It's not her," Elonrod says. "She has no markers of it. No knowledge of it. And I'd have felt a Dark Magician's power. There's nothing else like it. But no Dark Magician was there. Whoever it was isn't interested in her in the least. They're long gone."

"What exactly did the Dark Magician do?" a man asks.

"At first, I thought they'd bound her magic. She wasn't aware that she had magic at all. But now she seems able to use it. The Dark Magic is like a chain, but it doesn't seem to do anything. It's just there."

"Dark magic must do *something*," Gomthen puts in. Elonrod's brows draw together as he steps up onto a log to address the camp.

"Listen, I wouldn't put any of you in danger, no matter how much I've wanted this. She's not dangerous. She's simply bound. To what? I don't know. But *she's* not the problem. Whoever did this to her is."

"And we don't know who that is," Amtira says, turning to Elonrod for confirmation.

"No. I've felt no trace of Dark Magic anywhere else."

"How far have you looked?" someone else chimes.

"In Thorondar."

"They could be anywhere?"

"Yes."

"Then we could all be in danger."

"If the Dark Magician Rises, yes."

Murmurs and questions rise from the crowd now, pinning Elonrod, whose hands raise as if he's trying to calm them.

"Listen," he says. "We should be looking, but carefully. If they don't know about us already, we don't want to alert them in any way."

"We can't fight a Dark Magician."

"The kings won't rest until the Dark Magician is found. They'll be more vigilant than ever. Every corner of their kingdoms will be crawling with knights, and we'll all be found."

"Well, they don't know about it," Elonrod says. "And they may not ever find out if the Dark Magician never Rises."

"Dark Magicians always Rise," Gomthen says.

"This one hasn't," Elonrod says.

"Give it time. Dark Magic always twists the minds of those who use it."

Elonrod drops his arms for a moment, and his shoulders round a bit. His resolve tightens as he watches fear take over his people. He needs to lead, especially at this moment. So much depends on him getting this right. Everything weighs him down. And I sit back, watching with interest to see what he'll do next.

What kind of leader is he? It will come down to moments like this.

"Friends," he calls. "Calm yourselves. Think about what we know to be true. Right now, we're safe. Right now, the Dark Magician *hasn't* Risen and doesn't know about us. Right now, we have food to eat, tents over our heads, and we can practice our gifts knowing that we're alright. Let's stop thinking about what *might* be and focus on what is.

"We will deal with any problem that comes our way like we always have. Whether that's a Rising or a war with the kings. We have among us the greatest and most gifted of our time, and the more we gather, the better off we'll be. That's why we need to focus here and now on what we can do to better our situation."

The people have settled, listening to his words. Amtira's hands are clasped in front of her, and her face has smoothed. Gomthen's brows are still pulled together, but his good ear is cocked toward Elonrod. Reathl beams.

"So, what's your plan?" a man asks.

"I will rescue my sister from the castle. We'll stay vigilant, looking for other gifted people and the Dark Magician. Everyone will take precautions before leaving camp and double our scouts if we have to. We'll continue to hone our gifts and..." Elonrod's eyes dart around. "We'll prepare for war."

Noise and movement assault my senses. Fear and determination in their uproarious shouts and waving hands, while some become quiet and still. War is no small thing.

What's interesting is that the pursuit of life can sometimes lead to its end. And sometimes in order to thwart Death, one must court it.

But in scrapes and near-Death experiences, what a privilege it suddenly becomes to be older than the earth.

Elonrod meets me at 'our' spot outside the camp to plan his sister's rescue. He thought it best that we go alone. She'll recognize us, and we can be in and out faster.

"I can get her. That's not the problem. The problem is the beast. We need it to look like the thing actually killed her," he says.

Light breaks in patterns through clouds, casting shifting shadows on the earth. It's caught my gaze more than once today, because if the weather turns, we'll have a problem fetching the girl. Even wind travel can be tenuous during a storm. Lightning is unpredictable.

"If people see the beast elsewhere that night, it discredits our ruse. But perhaps she could have met her end another way? I guess it doesn't have to be the beast," he's reasoning with himself, not really waiting for answers, so I give none. "We just don't want them to come looking for her. A disappearance will cause suspicion...I can tell her to meet us. But she can't really respond. What if she can't get out by herself?"

I let him ramble and talk himself into a plan. I hate the way he plans things so haphazardly. It's confusing, disjointed. It's not in chronological order. But I listen and arrange things in my own head in a way that makes sense, putting the pieces together.

"We settled on night. Then she won't be missed until morning. We'll have time to set up the scene. You asked Elaress for a pig, right? The blood has to look fresh."

"She'll give us one. But she's not happy with the waste of meat."

"We can bring it back," he says. "Unless the beast eats it." He wrinkles his nose. "I want to know more about the beast." He pauses. "...you don't think that was Dark Magic, do you?"

"What was?"

"The beast."

"What kind of beast is it?"

"I don't know."

"I guess we'll find out. If it's a wolf or big cat, then we'll know it's not."

"We don't *need* it, do we?"

"Shred a cloak that's definitely hers, slaughter a pig for a celebration dinner, and leave its blood all over the cloak and the surroundings. Travel back to camp. Seems pretty straightforward. We don't need the beast to actually be there. We just need it not to be seen anywhere else. And then we don't have to worry about it eating our feast. Or holding it off while we work."

"See, this is why I bring you into these things. Sometimes you're like this wise, old crone. It's uncanny, but helpful."

I cock my head at him, brows crinkled and mouth shrugging. I don't think he means anything by it. Not that I'd be offended, just wary...I *am* old. But I don't want anyone to know that, and not for the usual superficial reasons humans have.

"You're welcome," he teases.

We'll have to settle for wind travel, which will take more time.

And it's best if we don't come in contact with Lelioth...I have a vision for how that ends, and this isn't it. He was not conjured for nothing, and it takes a lot of effort to conjure such things.

Lelioth was not cheap.

"So, since you like things very obviously laid out...I drop you off in the woods with the pig. I find Ellory and bring her to the spot where I left you. We make it look like she's dead and travel back here," he says.

"Yes."

"Okay," he beams. "Easy. We can do this."

"Don't say 'easy.' Saying that almost guarantees something will go wrong."

"You're so weird. Nothing will go wrong. It's too simple."

I blink slowly. Fool.

"Thanks..." he says after a moment, "For all of this. I know you prefer *not* to do things like this. The rescue missions, but I appreciate your help."

"You're welcome," I say.

"You're odd. But in a good way."

"Thanks...you're odd too. In a socially acceptable way, so I suppose that's fine."

He bursts out laughing and gets up. "I'll meet you here tonight?"

"Yeah, I'll meet you here, but the weather may not permit a rescue," I answer, pointing to the heap of clouds over the mountains. His mouth pulls down as he nods.

"I suppose we'll see." Then he shoots me one last look before heading back to camp.

He's like a huddled mass of energy held together by skin. It saps my own energy at times. I'm not fond of it. And I'm not fond of having to deal with humans in general. They're a lot of work. Especially rescue missions where emotions are heightened, and things can go wrong.

I'm not worried about tonight. I just need some time and space for myself. Sometimes I wish I could cut a hole in the fabric of this realm and step easily into another where humans don't exist, and neither does Time. Being in the dark, quiet sounds incredibly relaxing.

Unfortunately, I cannot just do as I wish.

It's fine. I work with what I'm given.

CHAPTER 19

ELLORY

Fretting doesn't look good, so I try to act normal when Thessel comes in to make sure my hair and clothes are perfect for dinner. In a way, I'm sad that I'll have to leave her behind when and *if* I get 'rescued.' Despite her being a spy for the queen, I've grown fond of her. But I'm also relieved that I won't have to hide anymore.

And maybe then I can relax a little.

I hate how little is in my control. But there's no use struggling against the circumstances. It's more than I can handle on my own.

Dinner is a smaller affair this time. I'm escorted by Thessel to a smaller dining area that's cozier, less well-lit than the hall, and has a cozy fire at one end. The prince is there already, and he smiles, moving to take my arm as I enter.

"This way," he says, leading me mock-gallantly to placement second down from the head of the table. There are four settings. One at the head, two on either side, and one for me. The prince takes the one next to me, and the silence stretches as we wait. I assume it's for the King and Queen.

"This is more intimate," I say, reminding myself not to lean on my elbows as I turn to the prince.

"They wanted to discuss the wedding with us."

My nerves tingle, and I can't help the nervous smile that spreads across my face as I look away. "Ah."

"Discuss is a misleading word...more like tell us how things are going to be and what will be expected of us both."

I nod and wrinkle my nose before realizing Thessel would tell me to stop because it's not ladylike.

The doors swing open, and the King walks in briskly. His eyes sweep the table, and his posture dips. He signals to a servant.

"Where is she?"

"Getting ready, Sire."

"She needn't look perfect for a simple dinner. I have affairs to attend to. Tell her to come directly." The servant bows and leaves quickly. The door shuts behind him as another hurries to help the King into his chair at the head of the table. He leans on his hand and rubs his head, not acknowledging either his son or me. We wait in thick silence.

It drifts like a tense living thing, ringing in my ears, only interrupted by the low roar and crackle of the fire.

Then the door flies open, and the fiery-eyed queen in all her glory sweeps through, commanding with the flourish of her dress as it sways and the cadence of her imperious step.

She passes a cold glance over me and her eyes flick to her husband, who eyes her as if waiting for her to respond angrily to his summons. She lets the servant seat her, her face porcelain-esque. Her dress is satin purple with golden fringe and designs embroidered on the sleeves. Her back is stick-straight, even as servants reach around her to set food and fill her goblet.

The king offers no rebuttal to the side-eye she throws at him. Instead, he ignores her and proceeds to ask his eldest son about the beast.

"They weren't able to capture it. But reports of its appearance have come to us. Some don't agree, but those who do claim it's a large, black beast that melts into the shadows. They say it's formless, except for its large claws."

"Then we know what caused it. Magic-users. I want the castle and our borders under tight security until we find who conjured it. We may have another Rising on our hands, and we can't have that."

My insides grow cold.

"The Guard will be notified along with the knights," Kalandrel answers. "We'll call in the reserves if need be."

"Yes, call in the reserves. I think it is necessary if the reports are to be believed. The people need protection. This can't go on." The king's tone is edged with finality, and color rises in his neck. His face is stone, but his eyes are fire. Then he catches my terrified stare. "My apologies, Heiress Orielle. It must be harrowing to hear of the beast after your ordeal." His tone is not at all apologetic. Simply formal.

"I wish I could offer something to aid your search," I say with a dry throat. I sip the water I've been given.

"We'll take care of it," he answers, shooting a look at his son. "We always do. But I suppose we should discuss the other matter. Clearly, your union is supposed to bring stability to the realm, strengthen the borders, and provide heirs. So, we'll be expecting that very soon after the wedding."

My cheeks flush, and I look at my plate.

"Does that embarrass you?" the king asks. I can feel his eyes boring into me, and I get the sensation of warmth, red-orange, determination, and daring. Obstinance.

"A little."

"Get used to it. Your business is now my business. I had mostly sons. Your duty is to provide sons, too, and you will do so."

I nod, not trusting myself to speak. I didn't know what to expect, but I wasn't expecting this.

When is that rescue going to happen? I could use it now.

What? You don't like being told you're just an object? a laughing voice impresses on my mind, and I steel myself against the strange and uncomfortably invasive thoughts of Mischief Boy.

I don't like that you can read my thoughts. I think back while still trying to focus on the king as he speaks about the various duties I'll perform as a mother and queen.

How else am I supposed to tell you the plan? Mischief Boy strikes back. An image of him flashes across my mind like a spark in the dark. He's grinning, and his energy is high. He's with a somber-looking girl. The one from earlier.

Okay...what is the plan?

We're faking your death, and we'll need to move quickly. Move to a window. Stand in the sunlight.

I don't think I can just leave. The king won't appreciate that.

Make an excuse.

My mind tumbles quickly through excuses I could use to leave. A sinking sensation floods my mind like I'm trapped, and heat fills my cheeks. The prince's hand grazes mine unconsciously, and a tug of energy releases like a conduit opening. And it's too late to stop it. He turns in slow motion as his face melts into concern. Slight orange touches the edge of my senses. His emotions, but something extra clouds his face, and sends colors and emotions through our hands. Surprise, questioning, fear. Lavender, muddled brown- green, light blue, and light green. I feel it in the pit of my stomach that somehow he just felt what I'm feeling in a very real way. He knows.

"I'm sorry. I'm not feeling well. I have to go," I say, and I lock eyes on his even as I rise and move to the door quickly. My hand over my mouth and the other around my stomach.

I hear the king mutter something, but I'm already through the door and in the corridor looking for the nearest window.

Find me, please, I think. *I'm almost there.*

Hurry, the voice doesn't laugh now. *The sun is about to set. We don't have much time.*

A shaft of warm sunlight strikes the floor just down the hall, and now I can hear the prince calling after me. I panic and run to the window. I feel his hand grasp mine just as I reach out and touch the mote of light.

"I'm sorry," I say again, my vision blurring as the dust in the sunlight merges and a figure melts out of the light like wax dripping from a candle. I've never been happier to see Mischief Boy. His eyes dart from me to the prince, and then he grabs my other hand. And I feel like I'm being yanked through a cascade of water, drowning me and filling my lungs and burning my eyes. I can't breathe. Everything is blinding yellow and weight and heat like stones after the sun beats down on them. It gets more and more intense, until it's almost unbearable. And for a brief moment, we're weightless, and then it feels like falling fast with the current of yellow-gold light. Plummeting and having no control whatsoever, like a doll in a petulant child's hands.

Suddenly it stops. The air cools enough not to feel like I'm getting a sunburn. I blink away sunspots, getting small images of the forest and hearing birds as my head rolls with vertigo. Mischief Boy tugs on my hand, trying to pull me into the dusky forest.

The prince tugs on the other.

"What is going on?" he says, whipping out his sword, though he sways on his feet. "Are you a magic-user?"

Breathing shallowly, shaking, and trying to pull away.

"I didn't know...I didn't mean to lie to you. I..."

"Yes, she's a magic-user, and she's leaving to a place your kind can't hurt her," Mischief boy says, striding closer, not fearing the prince or his sword. His hand leaves mine, fingers flexing as he prepares to fight. The prince's sword rises, and he pulls me back.

"You're both under arrest. Do not attack, or I'll be forced to kill you," he says.

Mischief Boy's eyes flick to me quickly and back to the prince.

"Don't threaten me. I can kill you without a thought. Now let her go."

"No. There will be justice in this land. There's no place for your kind."

An inhuman shriek fills the air, and my scalp tingles. Both men steel themselves against the sound, and Mischief Boy's jaw tightens.

The beast.

Wind shrieks in my ears, and a blur of dull color strikes the prince squarely in the chest. His grip loosens, thankfully, and he flies back. Then, Somber Girl appears suddenly, a little windswept, and locks eyes with Mischief Boy.

"Thought you had it covered," she says, glancing at me quickly. "We have to move now. Before he regroups."

"And the *actual* beast?" he says. She shakes her head, and her mouth tightens.

"We deal with it."

Mischief Boy grabs my hand again and drags me into the forest...toward the sound...Fear sears through me, but I don't have time to question either of them as we duck under branches and leap over stones and logs.

"Where is it?" he asks.

"Not sure. But it's close." She leads him through a tangle of bushes and down an embankment. The growing dusk makes it harder to see, but she knows where she's going.

At the bottom of the depression, there's a pig tied to a tree, snuffling and grunting as we approach.

Somber Girl shucks her cloak from her shoulders and throws it at me. "Remove your dress quickly and get into this." I don't argue, and I'm thankful for layers as I turn away, though, and pull the skirt up so I can shimmy out of it. I toss it over to her and wrap the cloak around myself. She shreds the dress with a knife, and then her eyes land on Mischief Boy, who is breathing hard and keeps looking around for the beast.

"What are you waiting for? Go," she says, gesturing with her knife. Mischief boy grabs my hand again.

"What about you?" he asks.

"I'll be right behind you," she answers, still shredding as a piercing howl cuts the air.

"This wasn't part of the plan, was it?" I ask.

"No," he admits. And he darts a glance back at Somber Girl. "I can't just leave you here."

"Please, go. I can wind travel too. Just take her and get out of here. I just need to finish this..."

"I'm not going back to camp, not knowing if you're safe. That beast could tear you to shreds, and I can't have that."

"Hold! In the name of the King," the prince's voice booms over our heads as he slides down the hill. His face lined with determination, he reaches the bottom, brandishing his sword as he rushes.

His eyes dart from the shredded dress, the pig, and me in the cloak. I fear it's too late to salvage their plan.

"Please, don't do this," I ask, but a bloodcurdling shriek pierces the air, deafeningly close, and a figure of pure black shadow flits through the treetops. Inhumanly fast and very large.

"Too late," Somber Girl says, planting her feet. Mischief Boy raises his hands as Kalandrel stops dead, sword raised.

"What Dark Magic is this?" Kalandrel asks. "Make the beast stand down or the whole of the kingdom will hunt you."

"It's not ours," Mischief Boy says.

"Get her out of here," Somber Girl says to Mischief Boy, gesturing to me.

"It'll kill you," he replies.

"I'll be okay," she replies, still watching the shadowy figure circling in the trees with inhuman speed. The beast pauses and snarls at the prince. Cat-like eyes glow dark, red as the creature marks its prey.

"We can't leave Kalandrel," I put in. "It'll kill him."

"Agreed," Somber Girl says, glancing at Mischief Boy with meaning in her gaze.

"Fine," Mischief Boy says, rolling his eyes as sets into his stance and raises his hands as the prince raises his sword. A glint of sharp claws wings out like a shadowy wraith, reaching for Kalandrel, and Mischief Boy pushes the creature back with bursts of wind. He slows it enough that Kalandrel can dodge and slash, but it angers the beast, who growls and then skitters back into the trees, waiting for another opening.

"You're welcome, Prince," Mischief Boy says.

"It's not over yet," Kalandrel fires back, preparing for a second attack.

Mischief Boy takes off across the valley past the squealing pig. He yanks against the rope tying the animal down, and the pig takes off into the woods, but the beast doesn't take the bait. Instead, it focuses on us.

Mischief Boy looks a little miffed but bounces back.

"Here, Beasty, Beasty!" he calls, and the creature slows enough that I see its eyes flick. Its teeth form from the shadows as he growls, and he moves quickly.

Somber Girl stiffens, holding her arm out in front of me as the beast leaps from the trees, claws glinting wickedly. Then she grabs my shoulders and pushes me farther back away from the action as Mischief Boy sends a violent burst of wind at the creature, pausing its flight. It drops to the ground, using its claws to dig into the dirt, flipping its head, and pinning its pointed ears against the barrage of wind beating at it. But it gains on him.

Kalandrel, understanding Mischief Boy's plan, scrambles up the embankment enough to get higher than the beast and then leaps at the creature, blade first. The creature hears him and whips around, swiping with his claws, but Mischief Boy knocks the beast aside with another sudden burst of wind. Kalandrel misses his mark, but he's safe at least, landing hard and rolling to his feet.

"You have to use both," Somber Girl calls out. "It can't be killed by steel alone. It's a creature of Dark Magic. You must use both."

Mischief Boy calls out, "You hear that, Prince? We have to strike together."

"Then follow my lead," Kalandrel says.

"You follow mine," Mischief Boy says. And his eyes close, and his hands upturn like claws. A cold draft sweeps through the trees suddenly, and they quake violently with the strength of the wind. It howls.

The creature regroups in the trees, snarling at the wind, shaking his perches, watching us, looking for an opening to pounce.

Thunder cracks loud and hard under a blinding flash of lightning, and I flinch, covering my eyes at the sudden burst of light. I hadn't noticed the storm rolling in, but it must have been Mischief Boy's doing because his hands are raised towards it as if holding up something heavy.

The beast slashes at the sky, thrashing as it leaps from its perch onto the ground again. It seeps back into the shadows, almost like it's dissipating.

"We can't let it get away," Kalandrel says, launching himself toward the creature.

"No, wait," Mischief Boy says as a bolt of lightning strikes the base of the trees where the creature tries to escape. The creature howls as the tree explodes. I cover my head.

"We have him. Strike him now," Mischief Boy calls to Kalandrel above the noise of the storm and the wind. And I look up in time to see Kalandrel rush the creature, which is back on its feet and about to dart into the shadowy trees.

Somber Girl moves now, reaching out with both hands clawed like she's holding a ball of something, and the air grays and swarms around the prince. Mischief Boy reaches out his hand, and a streak of lightning pops the creature from above, as Kalandrel's blade sinks into the creature's side.

The lightning should have killed Kalandrel, too, but he's protected as the swirling air suddenly pulls him away from the beast.

A terrible screech claws at the air as the shadowy claws flail at the prince and the sky. The creature begins to shrink and dissipate like smoke, its cries growing hollow and echoey as it melts into the shadows and then into nothingness.

Kalandrel's sword is still raised, and he's on his feet, staring at the shadows as if the creature will return. Mischief Boy finally lowers his hands, allowing the storm and wind to dissipate as well. He breathes heavily, also watching the shadows with suspicion. Somber Girl's hands drop to her sides as she stares into the dark shadows with a stone-like expression.

Mischief Boy moves to my side as the prince turns.

"Thank you, but I can't just let you go," Kalandrel says, sword raised.

"You don't have a choice," Mischief Boy answers, raising his hands in preparation for battle again.

"No, please, don't," I say, moving between them. "Isn't it enough that we're all alive and the beast is gone?"

"Magic cannot exist in peace in this kingdom. Those who use it are corrupted," Kalandrel says.

"*I'm* not," I say. "And I didn't choose this. It just happened. And I was terrified because I knew what that meant, living in the castle. And if I could have buried it or given it away, I would have. It's not my fault...I shouldn't have to live in fear that each new day will be my last."

"You've lied to me. That is corruption," he says, his eyes hard and angry.

"I *couldn't* tell you. Or you'd have had me killed like that poor old woman," I say. "And I prefer living and not having to hide in fear. I'm sorry I couldn't be what you wanted me to be. I know how that hurts you. I want you to know that I felt how deeply you loved. That's my gift. I feel. And I can't tell you how sorry I am that you've lost that. But I can show you."

I raise my hand and step carefully toward him while he raises his sword in response, and Mischief Boy grabs my arm like an anchor, as if I'll try to do something stupid.

"Please?"

"I can't trust you. I have no idea what kind of magic you wield. Apologies aren't enough for this kind of betrayal. From this moment forward, you will be a fugitive. We will come searching for you and anyone else like you."

I feel hope seep from my body. If he doesn't want to listen, he won't. And I can't make him, so I stop trying. Pain settles in my chest like a rock. Deep brown red like the earth when there's a fire so bad the smoke chokes the sun.

"You owe us your life," Mischief Boy says, his voice hard and low. He steps forward with his finger raised. "And the lives of the villagers who are saved by us destroying the beast. We didn't have to stay. We could have left at any moment, and you'd have perished, and your lands would never be rid of the beast. Without us, you'd be lying here while the beast fed on your entrails. And no one would find your body. Remember that, Prince."

He takes my hand and Somber Girl's, and the prince lunges forward.

"Stop," he demands, but it's too late. The shrieking of the wind grows in my ears like a storm. I clench my eyes against the drying sensation, feeling the wind tug at my cheeks and hair like it intends to rip me to pieces. Warm, cold, strong drafts, lesser drafts, but always the feeling of air moving against my skin.

And I just succumb, because there's nothing I can do but be tugged along. But eventually the sensation dies. I get my bearings, breathing deeply because I couldn't draw a full breath with the wind in my face.

There's a small makeshift village of tents set up in a clearing. Rocky outcroppings dot the rolling hills behind, and a stretch of aspens lines the tents to the left. People move around campfires that glow warm orange in the darkening world.

"He's back," someone says, and some begin to cheer and move toward us. Smiles and welcomes greet Mischief Boy, Somber Girl, and me.

I repeat various greetings back to them, looking from one face to another of the magic-users. People like me.

There are so many. It's surprising and relieving in a way. And I feel a weight lift off my chest. Mischief Boy stays near, taking it all in with a wide grin splitting his face as he endures backslaps and a hair mussing from an older man.

We're ushered to a fire to eat. And though I tell them repeatedly I'm not hungry after what happened, they fix up a bowl of stew for me anyway.

"It's just our way of welcoming you," a woman with a long, thick braid winks as she dunks a chunk of bread into my bowl.

And I notice that among the chaos, Somber Girl has disappeared.

"She's much prettier than you. You can't possibly be related," the old man winks at Mischief Boy.

"Well, whatever happened, she's safe with us now," Mischief Boy responds, beaming. And even though we're not touching now, I sense how much this means to him. A reunion. Joy, relief, Hope. And all of this is overwhelming and confusing all at once because these people are so welcoming despite not knowing who I am.

Mischief Boy is so kind. And risking his life like that...

And I'd been so scared for so long...

This feels unreal...

And what does this mean for me? What does this mean for my family?

Chapter 20

Maehdiorah

I broke away as soon as I possibly could and went to my tent to grieve.

The unexpected hiccups in our plan proved useful. When I saw that the prince had traveled with Elonrod, I knew our plan was near failing. The prince was a witness. It was too late to pretend the beast got her. So, I called my pet.

Leli came to meet his doom. His life was always meant to end. He was always going to perish at the hands of magic-users and the ungifted. It was his purpose. What I'd summoned him for long before letting him loose into the world. But knowing doesn't take the sting away from his death.

I broke my own rules. I grew fond of him. Attached.

The pain he was in...when they stabbed at him...the fear as lightning popping in his face. My poor, sweet boy. Watching him desperately try to escape and not being able to. Looking to me for help. And I betrayed him. I let them destroy him piece by piece, even telling them how it must be done.

And in his dying moments, I felt him fading away, waiting for me to save him.

To hear a thing you raised call for you while you watch it die...

I shiver, rubbing the stone fondly, hoping he understands why it had to be done. Why he had to feel the pain of dying. He's not entirely gone. He's with me still in the stone where I stole back his essence before the end.

It would have been easy to save my beast, but I *had* to hold back. It was his time. It was his destiny. Lelioth's death will bring about good things.

I had wished for a more public display, but at least the prince has seen now. He knows what magic can do. His life was saved by magic-users. His kingdom also. He can't deny our viability and utility. And we have worked together to thwart Dark Magic. Proof of what we can accomplish together.

And he can't ignore our existence, which brings us to the next step of my plan, because he'll surely tell the tale to his father, who will mobilize his army. It's too late now. We must enter step two.

Step two is a little more complicated, but it seems that there may be more dramatic ties than I had anticipated. These 'complications' will either fuel the fire and cause the prince to come at us that much harder, or the winds will shift, and he'll be more understanding.

I'm betting on the former. At least for now. He seemed very betrayed by his 'love's' turning.

I don't fault her for it. Living a lie, pretending and working with what she had to further his feelings for her. Self-preservation...and in fact, her existence proved useful. I'm glad I listened to my intuition to keep her alive. Things are falling into place in a way I couldn't have anticipated.

Love and loss are powerful motivators.

And the prince will be more vigilant in his cities. He will hunt us. It's inevitable. And the wishes of these people to fight for our lives will be fulfilled. Fight, they will. And die too.

We will make use of it for sure.

As for the girl, she is safe and well-cared for here, though I suppose it's nothing like having a castle and servants at one's disposal. I must admit part of me condemns her for her speech to the prince in the woods about renouncing her magic if she could, but the other part of me understands she has no idea what any of this *really* means either. She's only had magic for a short while, after all, after having been indoctrinated since her birth to avoid it at all costs. She doesn't know better.

And of course, Elonrod is thrilled his sister is reunited with him at last, and I no longer have to spend my time working with him. Which means I have time to myself again.

It's relaxing. I missed solitude.

I'll enjoy it while I can.

I rub the stone in my pocket again as if rubbing Leli's ears. One day, I'll conjure him again, but not yet. There's no need to. Not at this juncture, when things are tense.

And I suspect that Elonrod will soon have the council notified that the Dark Magician still lives and conjured the beast. This will spread fear, and they'll want to find the Dark Magician as quickly as possible.

And if word spreads to the kingdoms that a Dark Magician lives. There will be chaos in the lands. No one else in known history has caused as much damage, killed as many people, sowed so much destruction as Dark Magicians.

Their fear is warranted.

CHAPTER 21

ELLORY

The people here are kind and giving. I feel more at home here than in the castle. I do miss my family, though, and that's something I'll bring up with Mischief Boy, or Elonrod, as he's called here. We didn't have much time to talk last night. The people fed us, asked all about what we'd faced, and the beast. I met a lot of them. More faces and names than I can remember. Then Elonrod showed me his tent where he'd made up a bed for me.

He didn't stay, though, and for that I'm grateful at least. It'll take me a while to get used to the idea of him being my brother. I've never had an older sibling. I'm not sure how to feel about it. I don't feel about him the way I feel about Cassian and Mellen. They've been there for most of my life. Elonrod hasn't. It's just...a lot. And different.

And I know this is strange because I hardly knew him, but I kinda miss Kalandrel. I know it wasn't me he was in love with, but it was...nice. I hope he's okay and got back to the castle safe. But I'm no longer stuck, and that is a relief. Free perhaps to have that dream now...You never know.

"Ellory, you up yet?" Elonrod calls through the door, knocking on one of the poles. It's nice to be called by my own name again.

"Yeah, give me a minute," I say, slipping my arms into the sturdier, more peasant-like dress I've been given. I'm grateful for their help, the food, the clothes, and the place to sleep, and I'm excited to get started and help them out. To be useful again.

"I'll be by the fire," he says.

"Okay," I call back just so he knows I heard him. Then I brush my hair back and braid it. It feels nice to have that kind of control back over my body and not have to submit to Ardialle and Thessel. I hope they're doing alright. By now, they've heard of my treason. That can't be good. I hope they don't feel too betrayed.

And I wonder if the prince ever found the pig...I know Elonrod and Somber Girl, Telisan, didn't go after it.

They were trying to stage my death...with pig's blood. I find that disturbing, but on the other hand...Nope. I got nothing. It's just something I'll have to accept and move on.

Morning sun shines on the camp, and birds sing in the aspens on the east side of the camp. The tents have been set up in two rows with a pathway between them. Cookfires dot both sides, some with large pots, some with roasting spits, and there are lines for hanging washing as well.

These people have a system. They've been living like this for a long time. Elonrod is indeed by the fire in front of his tent. The ring looks fairly new, and he hasn't much wood nearby, so I assume he eats at someone else's fire. He seems important here. So that makes sense. Popular. Social.

"Good morning," I say, sitting next to him on the log he's pulled up for us. A small pot of something waits on an iron grate nearby.

"Sleep well?" he asks, grinning from ear to ear.

"Well enough after what happened last night."

"The prince was so scared," he crows, stirring up the fire. "Remember the look on his face? Thinking he could take me on."

"So, you're pretty powerful then?"

"Did you not see what I did last night? That was epic."

"He's the most powerful magic-user for some time," says the old man, Reathl, who hobbles to our fire. He seems like the type who likes to talk a lot and share stories. He sits on a stone across from us. "He'll help us in the battles to come, that's for sure."

"We're going to war?" I ask Elonrod. He nods.

"There'll be no peace for our kind until we establish ourselves in the public's eyes as people not to be trifled with. When they see our might, they'll stop fighting us."

"I thought you were a peaceful people?" I say, looking at the families across the way and down the road. They seem happy and content.

"We are, but patrols are always looking for us, pushing us from kingdom to kingdom. We have no place to call home because the kings take and take. They fear our power," Reathl says as he shifts on his stone.

"We can't keep running and hiding," Elonrod says. "You heard the prince last night. They've given us no options. They want us dead. We have no choice but to defend ourselves."

"War talk?" a woman across the way chimes in, as she stirs a large pot with a heavy-looking stick. She's the same woman from last night with the thick braid who gave me food.

"Of course," Reathl says. "Always war talk. Always survival talk."

"We're all getting tired of running," she directs at me. "The children don't know a normal life. They're growing up thinking this is all there is."

I don't answer. I don't have to. It doesn't matter what I have to say.

"So, Elonrod says your gift is Empathy," Reathl redirects. I nod. "How much do you know?"

"Not much. I can touch someone and see what they're feeling. Like in colors, sometimes images."

"And when did you start noticing this gift?"

"When I landed in this body." I dart a glance at Elonrod and the old man, wondering if he's explained my weirdness to the old man. There's no tick of surprise in either of them, so he must have.

"Must be a good vessel for magic then," he says.

"Vessel?"

"Bodies are merely vessels for magic. Conduits. Magic lives in the spirit of a person. If you try, you can feel the extent of Elonrod's power to get an idea of how that works. Or he can project it to you."

So...these powers that I have now were never Orielle's. They're mine. Always have been. I just...couldn't use them with the wrong conduit.

Hmm...

"What else can you do?" I ask Elonrod.

"See if you can feel it," he replies, moving the grate onto the fire and the pot with it.

"How do I do that?"

"You said you've felt things before? When you were in physical contact?"

"Or when a person feels something strongly."

"Right, so you can actually reach out with your gift to sense another's emotions. You just have to open yourself up to it."

"But a little at a time," Reathl warns. "Too much can be too over-whelming. It's your first attempt. You don't want to burn out."

"Burn out?"

"It sounds worse than it is," Elonrod dismisses, and I sense his eagerness to try my gift. Warm pink like the glow of a sunset. "Just focus on me. Breathe. Here. Take my hand."

He plops his hand onto mine so the palms touch. And I immediately feel a rush of emotions like the ones he felt last night. Joy, hope, energy, in addition to eagerness, and also pride.

"Feel that? Now follow those emotions. Let them in. They flow over your skin now, but they can sink in. Explore them." I shift on the log to get comfortable and close my eyes to 'see' them better.

Hope is dawn. The line of red against the horizon. The slight yellow above the treetops when the rest of the forest is dark blue. A pinprick of light when the rest of the world is dark. And it doesn't sit still. It grows bigger or smaller with each wave of emotion, influenced by those around it.

As hope is dawn, joy is the sunrise. When the first yellow splash of sunlight strikes, and you can almost see it crawling across the land. Shadows fleeing before it.

Pride is a little different, harder to pin down, but the way it feels is a lungful of breath. I want to say it's bluish-purple, but it keeps shifting. It doesn't stay the same.

And I realize that the colors I'm seeing for different emotions can be different based on how deep they run and what else a person feels at the time. It's strange, but amazing. There's more to it than I imagined.

"See? Fun, right? That's only the beginning. You haven't opened yourself to them yet. Like you feel them on the surface, right? But you gotta let them sink in. It's like 'seeing' them with another sight."

"I'm not sure how to do that," I say, keeping my eyes closed.

"Imagine it's like water or air. These emotions flow. You can feel that, right? How they move?"

"Mmhmm."

"Right now, they flow around you, and you're in them like a pond or a pool. When you feel the ebb and flow, you can start to see the pattern it creates. Then you can pull it toward you and push it away. But first, you need to know what it feels like to …put your head under, so to speak. Almost like…let it drown you."

"That doesn't sound like a good idea," I say.

"Yeah, that might be a bit much right now," Reathl chimes in.

"She can do it," Elonrod replies. "Focus on me, Ellory. You can. And I'm right here."

"How far is too far? And what does that even mean?"

"You'll be fine. I've got this."

"How do you know?" I ask, opening my eyes. He removes his hands and drops them into his lap, heaving a big sigh. The food sizzles in the pot and smells delicious. He takes a minute to stir before answering.

"You feel and see emotions. I hear and see thoughts. You asked what else I can do. It gets complicated because there are many gifts, and they don't all act the same. Sun travel, wind travel. They require different skills and sensitivities as well as different levels of ability. Some people can see the extent of someone's power as well. It's hard to explain unless you've seen or felt it, which is why I wanted you to see and feel mine.

"I know you because of your essence. The piece of you that makes up who you are. It's similar to mine, so it's possible you have the capabilities I have, if you train. Your last vessel wasn't a good conduit. You'd have known you have magic. You'd have been able to use it because you would have been using it. It would have come naturally."

"Explain that to me. How can I have magic but not be able to wield it?"

"Like Reathl said, spirits carry the magic. The ability to wield it is something the body either has or doesn't have."

"This happens to people sometimes? You can tell?"

"The essence carries that spark of magic, yes. We can see it in their essence."

"How?"

"The easiest way to describe it is like a piece of life itself. It's an energy that some people don't have."

"So, I might never have conducted magic in my other body."

"Not likely, if you hadn't already."

"But this body can?"

"Not to your potential, but yes."

"My potential is being hindered. But I have it. So the real Orielle must have had magic?"

"It's possible...If her essence had the spark. The fact that you can feel empathy so naturally speaks to the viability of the vessel. It takes a lot of work to reach out to magic, but your body just 'feels' it. That's pretty incredible."

I nod, thinking a moment, and then say, "So, your vessel is great for conducting magic?"

"Yes."

"But if we're related..." I say, thinking back to those horrible thoughts that I hadn't really been the baby my mother had.

Most likely, he projects into my mind.

"Don't do that. It's creepy," I say out loud. "How much of that did you see and hear?"

"All of it."

"What do *you* think about it all?"

"Based on what I remember, it's possible. You should have had an immensely capable conduit like me. Plus, your vessel before this one looked a lot more like that other family you grew up with, so...probably not the original."

"Not all siblings have the same capabilities," Reathl cuts in. He stirs the food this time. I get the sense he's trying to manage Elonrod's expectations for me.

Elonrod rolls his eyes. "I know, but...You get it. With a powerful conduit, she could have been like me."

I'm not sure if I should be offended by that or not. I know he didn't mean it in a rude way, because I can feel emotion behind it. And I explore the emotion, studying it more like a living thing than the impression it's been. If I let it wash over me, what will happen? If I stick my head under?

The color itself is a bright blue, but with tinges of darkness underneath. In studying the color, I find it's hollow. There are hues, but they overlap. They're layered. Like dipping one's hand into a lake. The water one brings up is not blue or green, but the immensity of the lake itself makes it seem colorful. Especially in the reflections.

Emotions are much larger than I thought to have that kind of depth, that richness of color. But how deep? How immense?

The color shifts slowly, like a living thing. It draws away like a timid animal, comes closer with curiosity, booms with sudden flashes, and fades into the background, being replaced by other strains of color overlapping like waves. It's a constant flow.

Exactly, Elonrod's voice echoes in my mind. *See the ebb and flow. Feel the pattern.*

I don't know how to dip my head, though, I think back.

Can I try something?

I guess.

An image presents itself to my mind, like when he speaks, but it's like he's there with his hand outstretched.

Reach for me, he says. *Just imagine yourself reaching out.*

I don't know how...and I don't know why, but I can't do it. I don't know what I'm supposed to do or how that's supposed to feel.

Am I going to have to do the big brother thing and throw you in the pond?

I don't know what I'm supposed to do.

Push your feelings towards me. See me? Imagine an emotion, imagine the action, feel it deeply, let it take over you, and then push it towards me.

Fear is an emotion I'm familiar with. Stress and anxiety, too. I think back to not having enough money, worrying about being caught in the castle. The terror of the prince's hand grasping mine just as Elonrod emerged from the beam of light, and the feelings do come. My heart picks up.

You're struggling to connect with them because you push your feelings away and stuff them down. Stop that. Sit with them. Acknowledge them. Be with them.

I root myself there in the emotions, like I belong there. Like I always have. Like they're the only things to exist, and there's nothing outside of them.

Great kings, this is uncomfortable. And it feels like heat, I see brown and muddy orange, and a bright purple that threatens to blind me. They dance and swirl in a threatening way, like they intend to drown me, and I grit my teeth against it because my inclination is to hide from them, but I *do* sit with them. Letting them buffet me from every angle, like being slammed into by a ferocious wind.

They don't let up. But I do see a pattern emerge, and as I follow it, tracing its movements, I feel lulled. Suddenly, my head feels cottony and swoony. Like I'm floating above it and not in it. Like I'm being dragged by an invisible force into some strange and unknown area of my mind I've never been to.

It *does* feel like I'm underwater, though I can still breathe. There's darkness all around me. Cool darkness, with penetrating streams of color. And here I notice how the currents of color flow, shaped like people, and after a moment, I realize it's the shape of Elonrod, and the other is Reathl.

It's like I'm seeing them as they were a moment ago near the fire. But now they're made of color against a vast backdrop of black. Beyond them, I see faint wisps of color too, but they're fleeting and too far away to see clearly.

And for a moment, I bask in the strange glow of energies. It's calm here, quiet. And I feel as if I'm in a dream. Floaty, but I still have autonomy. I try to focus on my own body for a moment, seeing a strange mix of colors that I don't quite understand. Instead of unraveling all of it, I "look" to Elonrod instead, reaching out with my ethereal hand. There is a similarity here I can see between us. Like the essence has a life of its own that's etched in bright light. And his feelings are more vibrant to me because of how similar his essence seems to mine. Recognizable. Familiar. It's like he's marked. Eddies of color and images. The feelings color his exterior, but something else pulsates beneath the surface. But there's a barrier. I only see faint traces of whatever lurks there.

And vertigo seizes my mind for a moment as the dreamlike world tilts. Something hard, like a weight, seems to clasp my brain, and I feel like I'm starting to melt. It gets harder and harder to feel the currents, and the colors grow dim and far away. Exhaustion shutters my 'sight,' and I sink under it as the once vibrant world starts to grow black.

A tug on my mind and a touch on my hand pull me back to the surface. But with the contact comes broken images that move fast. A small boy with scared, watery eyes. A happy boy, a little older now with scruffy dark hair with a younger version of Reathl. The older man looks at the boy like he's the whole world. But fear and doubt lay heavy over both.

I open my eyes finally. Bright sunlight glares at me from above, washing the world in warm light. Elonrod grins, holding my shoulder as I slump. Propping one arm against the log to keep from falling over, I fight the urge to sleep. The ground looks oddly comfortable right now, and there's a haze over my vision.

"See? I told you it would be fine."

"Just be careful not to go too deep without someone experienced around," Reathl warns, digging into his gruel.

"We'll practice. She'll get used to it," Elonrod says. "Soon you won't need to nap after every time you access your gift."

I offer to help at the camp where I can. I mention my affinity with herbs, but it seems that Telisan has that covered. I've noticed she's not as somber as I thought. It's not sadness. It's more...stone-like. In every interaction. For example, I thanked her for her help rescuing me, and she just nodded, saying nothing. Her eyes looked right through me.

I get the feeling she'd rather be alone, so I don't seek her out.

And when I say, 'get the feeling,' I don't mean literally. I just mean in the sense of social cues. She can't be read. Even Elonrod can't crack her. He said so.

I don't blame her after what she must have gone through. A lot of people here grieve in different ways for their losses. I feel for them. But I must admit, I'm wary of their zeal for war.

And when I mention my fears about my other family starving, Elonrod doesn't get offended. To my surprise and gratitude, he simply slips through a ray of light and disappears. An hour later, he returns and reports that they're all fine.

My mother is engaged to Gerdor. I'm surprised in a gut-punch kind of way, but happy for her. I wish I could be there for her to help her get ready for her wedding day. And I'm glad she'll be safe and taken care of.

Mellen still works with Aidela, learning different skills.

Cassian is a stable boy at the palace now. Seems the King's Stable Master stopped by the shop for carrots and apples for the horses and offered Cassian a position. My little brother makes more money now, and the income is dependable compared to the hit-or-miss days at the shop. It's better for him, I think. He's more suited to stable work than herbs anyway. And with my mother moving to the carpenter's shop soon, Cassian will have the little hut for his own family someday if they don't sell it (which they might do or rent it out for more income).

Their good fortune is everything I've ever wanted. It's a relief, but jealousy twinges in my soul. Gerdor takes better care of my family than I have or could have ever done. He's better for them anyway, it seems. And it makes me feel like I wasn't good enough. I'm *not* good enough technically.

But it's not where I belong. I'm not her real daughter, but what we were to each other was real. I can keep that to look back on. I can hold it close and let them live their lives without me.

I'll forever miss and love them. And I will see them again. Even if it's from afar, and they never notice me.

"It was a harsh time," Elonrod says. We're sitting at our small fire with a few of his friends and neighbors as the darkness of night closes in. Well...*Our* neighbors, I guess. "Winter was just starting, and I was just a boy at the time, probably three or four, but I remember there being a lot of mud and falling snow. The snow didn't stick, and the wagons had a hard time moving through the deep, sticky ruts."

"We'd been taken in by some village folk on the border of Sarenth and Gesh. Tiny villages near the border of Northern Merendhere. The border patrols found us and started harassing us, so we were on our way out to find somewhere else to live. But the knights came. Looking back, it must not have been that many men, but it seemed like it. They had orders from both kings to round up the magic-users and execute us. We were weaker in those days. Just a small group of us, but the knights were still so angry. I remember their faces full of hatred. They moved through our camp quickly, shackling us, whipping us, pushing us into the mud. Mother was pregnant at that time with you. She was scared. I remember the cold iron of her shackle bracelets against my chest as she held me close to keep me from being hurt by the men. I remember the way her hair tickled my shoulders, and how her heart beat frantically."

His feelings drift like the smoke on the fire. I can see them, and I remember the image I saw of him as a little boy, scared and crying.

"Our mother only possessed a simple understanding of magic. She was harmless, but they didn't think so. I remember her waddling, holding onto a supply wagon for support as we marched. Her face contorted with pain, and she said you were coming. She was taken away. I was left alone."

"Reathl planned our escape. We fought back the knights and ran away. Some were lost in that fight. I don't remember their names. I wish I did. And I looked for my mother the whole time we were escaping. I didn't want to leave without her." His eyes are clouded and shinier than usual, but he clears his throat to hide it.

"I haven't stopped looking for her. Reathl used to say that whether she lived or died, she was a loving mother, and we should honor that."

"Yeah," I answer weakly, still overwhelmed by the history of a family I hardly know. It's awful to hear about our mother and what Elonrod went through.

"Lots of us have stories like that," says the woman from across the way, Erian. "No warning, and the knights would be there, kicking in doors, dragging children away from their mothers. Still happens. That's why we're so careful about where we stay and for how long. We scout ahead, and we have guards who watch through the wind and sunlight."

Someone else chimes in, telling of their own struggles and survival. I listen, but their tales come with a lot of grief and sorrow. The more

I feel it, the more it rubs me raw. It's easier than I expected to tire of having this 'gift.'

But like when I got over-sensitized at the market, I drift off into daydreams and thoughts. I return to Elonrod's story. What happened to our mother after she was taken? What happened to the baby?

What happened to me?

CHAPTER 22

MAEHDIORAH

I sit alone inside my tent, thinking and stirring a spiced soup I made myself.

I'm not hungry, though. I thought I was when I cooked, but now...soup isn't appealing. Nothing is really, but I know I need to eat something. I only take a few sips because I went through the effort of making it.

I've always hated how much maintenance a human body requires. We have to breathe, or we'll die. We have to eat, or we'll die. We have to drink, or we'll die. And there are thousands of ways to die besides. Being a human is a lot of work. We spend so much time just making bread. From the planting of wheat to harvesting to milling to prepping and baking...Not to mention how much time we spend sleeping that could be better spent doing other things.

It's inefficient. I wish there were a better way. Especially after living as long as I have. It gets tedious to do the same thing day after day, as if there aren't more important things going on in life that need attention.

There are days when I don't want to spend that time to keep living, but the body is fragile if one doesn't do the work to keep it up. It's too easy to wear oneself out. It's too easy to get sick.

Yet another reason life is precious to these people.

There is a legend long since lost that talked of others who valued life so much that they tempted Fate and made deals with dark beings. Deals with dark repercussions that they weren't prepared for.

And what we have and know now of magic is far more limited than it used to be.

There are a lot of things these people will never know. And all the knowledge that will disappear as the years roll on saddens me. However, it is Time's way to always move forward. And what will be will be. I'm not here to right *all* wrongs or change the future in that way.

And so, I listen in when the council meets about Ellory to determine what and who did what they've done to her.

I need to know what they know.

So far, they have no evidence of who it was. Which is good. I wouldn't want to have to start fresh again. I've been down this path too many times before. It tires me just to think about having to wipe the slate clean and begin again.

And I'm lucky that the others can't read my essence. Well...not lucky. Smart for placing the block in the first place. Being private has its benefits. If not for that, I'd have been found out a lot sooner than intended, and everything would be destroyed.

I'm safe for now. My plans can continue.

In days past, I'd tried the very thing I'm trying now, but the pieces were out of place. Not everything was within my control then. I've learned. I'm more careful, but sometimes even the best-laid plans can be overturned by idiots. Sometimes, one makes the mistake of believing their opponent is smarter than they are.

That is a deadly mistake.

And I've learned my lesson. Some opponents will sacrifice countless lives to capture just *one* magician. It doesn't make sense. But they do it anyway. Some execute poor plans, find themselves in a bind, grow bored, and do something impulsive that hurts themselves more than us. It almost seems unfair to take advantage of those situations, but I'd be a fool not to.

And still...some are just chaotic for the sake of being "unpredictable." But chaos has a sort of predictability if one looks long enough. Certain patterns emerge, be they a specific attack pattern or a time of year.

The race of men is never as clever as they think they are. It solidifies the downfall of the arrogant. And the delusionally audacious.

I sound incredibly prideful inside my head when I talk about my plans as if I'm the only one who can execute them. But if history is an indication, I *am*. That's not prideful. It's merely a fact. No one knows what I know, or we'd be in real trouble. No one has seen what I've seen, experienced what I've experienced. And they're lucky they haven't.

Don't get me wrong, these people have seen incredibly terrible things. Pain and suffering bind them. But I've seen horrors compounded over centuries.

I've seen Dark Magicians Rise. I've seen the awful things they do. And I've seen them fall. (But those are stories for another time.)

I've seen rivers cut gorges and seas dry up. I've seen new mountains erupt from the earth and others fall away. I've seen glimpses of things no human has ever seen, and while I'm by no means what these people might consider a deity, I'm not entirely human anymore either. I haven't been for some time. Some might even call me a monster.

Humans have to die. It is one of the marks of being a human. I don't have to.

Sometimes I wonder about the backwards flow against nature I've caused. The ripples that spread outward haven't all been good. And though the battles of the good and bad powers that maintain this world were resolved years ago, I remain. One of the last to know the darker elements of magic and what it can really do.

I set my bowl of soup aside. It grows cold anyway. I don't feel too bad about it going to waste. It's mostly broth with a few roots and spices I gathered from the forest.

I've asked myself many times if I'm ready for what's to come. I was much more confident of my plans as I was making them, but I always get nervous when it begins. I second-guess myself, which is never a good thing because nerves can cause one to sabotage their own plans even without meaning to. The truth is, it's never easy. Once the parts have begun to move, it only gets faster and faster like a cart rolling downhill. At a certain point, it's too late to try to stop it. That's why it's crucial to make sure everything aligns perfectly before it gets out of control. And to be ready.

I have done my best. I've put years of planning and failures into this attempt. Pruned, nudged, and placed the pieces. I've sacrificed centuries for this, bled, watched many die, and drowned in the wails of the broken as well as the hope of these people.

Of course, I've had insurmountable obstacles that forced retreat. Of course, I started from nothing, built and rebuilt, watched everything crumble to dust over and over again. Wanted to just give up, run away, and never return.

But that's not who I am.

And what would I be doing in solitude? This problem would occupy my mind tirelessly as it always has.

Every problem can be solved. Every fight has an end. If I fail, it's only because I haven't been strategic enough, tried hard enough, or seen the right angle yet.

I've learned from past mistakes. I've been careful. One kingdom at a time. One step, one step, one escalation. All carefully planned and executed. This time, I've accounted for the idiocy of human nature and given the cart the push it needs to accelerate on its own down the hill.

I hope it works this time.

The incantation that displaced Ellory was messy and imperfect. I was rushed. The guards were on us, and they were taking magic-users away and killing others. And I could feel my body failing me.

The times that these people look back on with horror...a lot of them came from The Culling of Cordain. King Arathanzan had been lenient to our staying on his border, but his patience with us had run out. Fear, too many magic users testing limits, interacting with his people, and moving farther within his lands...He ordered his knights to seek us out and imprison or kill us. Many died. Many were never seen again. People I'd known.

Just because it wasn't new to me doesn't mean it wasn't hard to witness and experience. I still see the knights, the blood, the magic-users begging for their lives.

One of the things that's most harrowing is fighting the knights, getting free, and watching as they take away others who weren't so lucky.

It grates on the soul. Time and time again.

And though I narrowly managed to escape with another magic user, she couldn't handle it. She shook, whispering to me about everything that passed as she peeked from our hiding place, watching as others were taken, beaten.

She was going to get us caught with the peeking and hysterical whispers. And I contemplated knocking her unconscious. I told her to stop looking, but she couldn't. And finally, she broke. She rushed right back into the fray to save one of her close friends.

I saw her make it halfway across the dusty street before being tackled by knights. She tried to wind travel, but she couldn't carry the weight of the knights.

As they dragged her away, she shouted for help. But I didn't save her. I had been wounded, trying to save her in the first place, and was too weak to fight off the knights again. I might have escaped on my own, but the vessel was dying. And I was scared. I hadn't been in such a vulnerable position in some time, and I vowed I'd never get that desperate again.

There was no use in getting myself caught. So, while her screams for help died on the walls, I kept silent and hidden.

I remember a pregnant woman being drug and dumped in the alleyway. She screamed in pain. I don't know why they left here, but they did.

An old woman came and shoved her dirty cloak into the woman's mouth while she helped the pregnant woman up, despite being quite thin and wiry herself. Then, with the pregnant woman leaning on the old crone, they checked to make sure the knights were busy before the old woman took the hobbling mother to her small hut.

I planned my route to the old woman's hut. If she could hide the screaming woman, perhaps she could hide me as well. My capacity for wielding magic was running low, and the vessel grew tired as it leaked blood. I had energy for one more act, but it was fading fast.

I lifted myself and hid behind the walls and in the crooks of buildings as I stumbled to the little hut. Dangerously low on options, I just needed to see that one of the magic-users survived and had enough capacity for wielding that I could escape.

Knights ran by, and I had to duck behind an old wagon. Crawling underneath, I ran to the hut, but they saw me. I heard them clanking after me...And I started the incant as I ran, and I felt them getting closer and closer.

Collapsing at the old woman's window, I glimpsed the old woman bent over the pregnant woman, whose head was thrown back and her face squeezed in pain. There were pigs hunkered farther back in the hovel, squealing too, but that's all I saw before the flash and then darkness.

I'd made it, but I didn't become cognizant until the new vessel turned three years old. By then, the marks of the knights and The Culling were beginning to fade. And I was subjected to growing up all over again, which meant that my abilities came back, but slowly. Only as much as the vessel could take. It took time to build up its capacity.

The old woman's name was Cela, and she brought me up after 'my mother' was taken away by the knights. We fed pigs, tended the garden, and went about our daily affairs, and didn't talk of magic. But she did tell me the story of my coming to be there. Cela had told the knights that I'd died, and she'd removed my body so the mother wouldn't be upset. They hauled the weak mother from the hovel.

I asked where my mother might have been taken. Cela didn't know. And she warned me not to go looking lest the knights take me too.

I stayed with her until I could travel on the wind, then I left to hide myself at one of my safe places.

I go back to the old woman's house from time to time to sing her garden into a plentiful harvest and the pigs into health and breeding. Her vegetables are the envy of the town, and she tells the villagers all the same thing: It's patience and knowing your herbs.

Good woman. I owe her my life, but I repay my debts.

As for this body. It was more powerful than I'd expected, and when I first met Elonrod, I knew immediately who he was. But he didn't know me. Or at least he didn't know this body, which is for the best.

Ellory survived somehow. Her spirit was supposed to move on, taken by Death, but the incant and the binding Dark Magic might not have melded properly. It seems the binding magic, which was supposed to encase my spirit into her tiny body, bound her spirit as well. Likely she can't die until her body does.

So, her spirit jumps from body to body accidentally.

She'll return to her body if I give it up. If that day comes, she'll feel cheated and angry. But at least she and her brother and everyone in this community will be free. And that's worth their animosity. Not that I care either way.

"There might be another way," I've heard before. "You don't have to take lives to make this happen."

Trust me. There isn't another way. We send our own to die in war, and how is that any different? Because it was random? Because the killing blow wasn't ours? Because they might have made it?

Or...we could trade one life (or several) to get the job done far more efficiently.

And that is my aim. And in the end, my plan and deeds, as dark as they are, will conserve lives.

I'm willing to do what they aren't in order to achieve peace at a much lower cost.

I do get tired. So tired. But someday, all of this will be worth it.

Chapter 23

Ellory

The village is not without problems, but it's more peaceful than ducking and hiding. The children attend lessons and test their abilities under the watchful eyes of Reathl and sometimes Elonrod. Mostly, the people get along, and when they don't, a third party is called to settle it. Elonrod sits in those meetings.

In a way, I'm proud to have a brother who'll be a leader someday. But at the same time, I'm not really sure where I fit in.

Orielle's hands, once soft, have grown calluses. And though I wear a headscarf and try to keep the sun off my face, I'm still developing a tan. I can't help but wonder how she'd feel, knowing someone is inhabiting her body, ruining it.

How should I feel about it? Guilty? Should I try to honor her memory by mitigating what damage I can? Who's to say she'd even care? She is dead after all, and though I believe in ghosts and spirits, it's not like I've been haunted by her...

Though that might be a bit dark. I shouldn't think that way.

All I can really do is hope her spirit is happy and at peace.

As for where I fit in, I'm just trying to help where I can. And learn what I can. Elonrod is eager to see if I can do other things, like travel, connect with the earth, or storms. We've not stumbled upon anything yet, but he does say I'm talented at Empathy, and that's heartening. As a brother, he's great, but I'm still learning to accept him as kin. We've led two completely separate lives, and it takes a lot longer than a few days for me to get to know someone enough to trust them.

Living for survival doesn't teach a person to trust easily.

As a person, he's vibrant...loves being the center of attention, loves that his people adore him, loves that he'll be their leader someday, and loves practical jokes. Which I hate...(sounds like he'd have gotten along well with Orielle).

And despite his vibrancy, there seems to be a hollowness inside. Like he tries so hard because he's afraid he's not enough. But I'm sure that'll go away as he matures and practices what he's learning.

I'm bent over Erian's giant pot, helping her sift through the clothes she's been dyeing. After stirring with her giant stick, I no longer wonder why her shoulders and forearms are quite large. She's strong as an ox, obstinate (in a sweet way), and hard-working. Her hair is dark, and it strays in wisps from her head rag. She's also tall and has sparkly brown eyes. The kind that you can tell are laughing.

She laughed when I took a turn stirring the clothes, but it's not a skill Orielle ever had to learn, so the muscles just aren't built. I pull clothes from the pot of dye now, occasionally rubbing my shoulders and arms as Erian's eyes still crinkle in laughter.

My hands are green now, but that'll wash out in a few days. For now, we hang the clothes to dry and let the color set.

"Ready to wear in a few days," she says. "We'll do blue next."

"Ellory," Elonrod calls. "I need you."

"Thank the ancient kings," I mutter. Erian giggles.

"Not till you know what he needs you for. Might be worse."

I only smile in reply and dunk my hands into the wash bucket before scooting to the tent, Elonrod and I share. He holds a bow, and there's a knife on his hip.

I didn't know he knew how to use them. But I guess it makes sense he'd have learned.

"As your older brother, it's my duty to teach you the way of the world," he starts with a twinkle in his eye. "And the way of the world is we eat what we kill."

He hands me the bow. I take the thing, running my hands over the sleek wood. I've seen them used. I know the basic concept, but this feels weird, and I'm not looking forward to learning. He has a look on his face that I've come to understand means he's not taking no for an answer.

"So, you're teaching me to hunt?"

"Why not? You can't just dye clothes all day. We can't eat them."

"Alright," I say, because I really don't feel like arguing. I feel hot, sweaty, gross, and smelly from working. Things that used to not bother me so much, but...kinda do now that I've spent time in the castle and didn't have to do these sorts of things. Part of me feels like I've let the old me down. Like I've gone soft. Part of me yearns for comfort now that I've had a taste of a comfier life.

Elonrod bends down to grab a quiver that's leaning against the tent pole. He's grinning from ear to ear, eyes sparkling as he slings the quiver over his shoulder.

"Let's go."

We walk through the aspens on the lower side of the village, following the river for a bit. He explains that animals have patterns when they forage, seek shelter, meander, etc.

"We're after deer. We don't want to waste arrows on smaller game. That's what slings are for. Rocks are plentiful, so use up as many of those as you like on a rabbit or squirrel, but they don't work on deer." He grins like it's a joke. I smile because I don't want to seem rude, but I am distracted. Something in him feels desperate. It's a tingling in the nerves. The pricking of hairs.

"You met with the scouts, didn't you?" I say. He nods.

"Nothing important."

"You're lying."

"We agreed not to read each other's emotions and thoughts."

"Then tell me what's wrong."

He stops, looking through the forest for a moment, but his mind is elsewhere. Then he looks at me with sadness in his brow.

"The knights are on the move. Patrols have increased. Not just in Drene, but Cordain, Merendhere, and the smaller territories. We're looking for a safe place to move to."

"Already?"

"They don't know where we are, or they'd be on their way here. But we have to stay ahead of them. There are some options for where we go next, but don't tell anyone right now. Nothing's solid."

"Why didn't you want to tell me?"

"I don't want you to worry."

"I'd prefer to worry about what I know than worry about things I *don't* know."

"I'll be sure to tell you things from now on," he says. Then he tilts his head. "You know, you could be included in these planning sessions we have. You ought to be. You might have inside information that could help us."

"I know nothing of the castle. I lived there, but they were mostly concerned with turning me into the next queen and making sure I didn't embarrass the kingdom."

He holds back a laugh, twisting his lips, but his shoulders shake.

"I still have a hard time imagining, but it would serve them right. A magic-user as queen."

"It's not funny. I was found out. The prince knew what I was before you got there. If you'd been one second later…"

"I'd have rained havoc on his kingdom for harming my sister. That's for sure."

I fall silent because he's so loyal with so little to go on.

"I heard that," he passes me a side-smile.

"You promised."

"So did you," he sticks out his tongue. I stick mine out back. But it is nice having an older brother. What would that have been like in the lower village of Thorondar? I would have had help. Or considering that he was there at times…maybe he wouldn't have been much help after all.

"Alright, are we going to do this or what?" I ask, gesturing with the bow. "We've been out here a while, and I don't have the slightest idea what I'm supposed to do."

"Here, watch." He takes the bow and pulls an arrow from the quiver. "So, you'll put the arrow here, see? Along this mark." He points to the indent in the wood and the dark band that rings it. I watch as he places the arrow against the bow, using his finger to guide it along the band.

"Poke the prongs on the back over the string like this...Then you'll put your fingers here." His ring and middle fingers hook around the string. Then he stands straight and tall, testing the ground with his feet and breathing before he pulls the string back.

His stance now is strikingly focused and tight compared to how loose and goofy he usually is. It's off-putting. He still *looks* natural...it's just not what I'm used to.

"I'm only going to fire, so you get an idea of what that looks like," he says, staring down the shaft of the arrow, eyes intense. The string is so close to his cheek, it makes me uncomfortable. Like it might smack him if he lets go. But when he looses the arrow, nothing bad happens. Just a swoop, thud sound as the arrow embeds into a tree not far from us.

"It's simple once you get the hang of it," he says, handing the bow back to me. "Wanna try?"

I *don't* want to try. Not really. But he's trying to teach me something, and with the threat of patrols and knights, it's probably best to have some defense. So, I take the bow, let him hand me an arrow. I place it like I saw him do, shifting the arrow so it lies properly, and aligning the prongs with the mark on the string.

"Watch your arm. The string might be a bit long," he says, as I try to pull the string back. It's surprisingly hard. Harder than I expected.

He made it look so easy. I'm already sore from dyeing clothes, so this seems impossible, but he laughs.

"Okay, maybe you'd better practice pulling back without the arrow first. Just don't pretend to fire. Always let the string down slowly unless you're shooting an arrow at something. Make sense?"

I nod as he takes the bow. He starts moving through the trees again, pushing branches aside as he goes.

"If we see something, I'll shoot it this time. But next time is your turn."

"Elonrod," comes an unmistakable voice from the wind, and a person materializes from a gray streak as the air passes through my hair and tugs on my clothes. It's still strange seeing people do that, but it's not time to sit and ponder it. The man's face is etched with fear.

"They've found us," he says. "They march now."

"Is Reathl evacuating the camp?"

"He's given the order. He said to fetch you."

"Go. We'll be right behind you."

The man nods, and the wind picks up again as he turns into a streak of gray and disappears. Elonrod grabs my hand, and the world becomes a blur of golden-yellow. We tumble out of the sunlight into the road between the tents.

The villagers hurriedly pack, pulling tents down and bringing wagons and carts to carry their things.

"How far out?" Elonrod asks Reathl, who stagger-waddles between tents, helping and directing. His face is red and puffy.

"Only a few miles."

"How did they find us so quickly?"

"No time to guess. We have to move. We'll discuss that later."

"We won't have time to get all these things," Elonrod says, looking around. Then he starts moving among the people shouting, "Just take the essentials. Take the animals that can move quickly and the children and move out. I'll need anyone who can withstand the armies to help me hold them off while the others get to safety. We can always rebuild what is lost."

Panic rises as families stop packing their homes and look for each other. Mothers call out to their children, and already some move towards the grove of aspens.

"Theliod, you've scouted a new camp? Lead everyone there. Take the wind and sun travelers first so they know where they're going, and they can come back for the rest."

Some magic-users rally to Theliod as he starts calling for those gifted with travel. Others gather around Elonrod, waiting for instructions. He starts sifting them by their capabilities.

"Remember, we don't have to stay and fight. We just need to buy time. Be careful. Everyone ready?"

"Yes," some say, some nod. All look afraid.

"We move on my mark." Then he looks around. "Where's Telisan?"

"Here," she says, ushering a gaggle of children toward Erian.

"I need you," Elonrod says. "I know you have more in you, despite how you hide it. Now is the time to use it."

Her jaw tightens, but her eyes remain stone as she hands off her charges and steps into Elonrod's circle. I don't know where I should be because I have no helpful gift. I should probably be helping the old and the children move to the new camp.

"Be safe," I say to Elonrod, as he gives me a quick hug.

"We will. Help establish the camp when you get there. The people will need you and your gift."

I'm not sure what he means, but there's no time to ask. I watch him lock hands with one of his warriors. And they all disappear in streaks, a couple in gold, the rest in gray.

Theliod has disappeared with his travelers as well, but they start popping up one by one and taking the old and weak. Those who can move have started disappearing through the grove in a pack, so they can be found by the others.

Erian motions at me to move with them, and I hurry to prop up an old man who's stumbling even with his cane.

We arrive at the new place. I'm one of the last to be 'traveled.' We're in a sort of half-bowl, backed up against gray, stone cliffs, where a clear waterfall trickles down the mountainside. The ground is mostly flat, gravel-like in some places. On the other end of the 'bowl' is a forest of aspens and some pines. It would be beautiful under different circumstances.

Already, families scrounge for wood. Long sticks for tent poles, smaller ones for fires. They haven't brought much with them, and though the travelers are tired, they speak to Reathl of returning to the old camp to reclaim some of the smaller animals, tools, bedding, and food. He urges caution, pushing their powers too far has costs, but he can't deny that we could use some of those items.

It's crazy how everything they worked for can be taken away in an instant. It's no way to live. Neither is hiding and running. It's not fair.

I wish I could help. I wish I could travel like they do, connect with different elements like they do. Instead, I have the gift of feeling how they feel...What good is that?

I start scrounging too, piling wood in the central, designated fire pit (since we only have so many resources, we now have to share). They pool the things they've managed to bring. And as some of the travelers feel rested enough, they disappear one by one to bring more things.

I look for herbs and food in the forest. Since Telisan is gone, I figure we might need some, and it's one of the only tangible skills I have.

CHAPTER 24

MAEHDIORAH

I hadn't planned on helping Elonrod stall the knights, but when he asked, I couldn't refuse. He knows too much, and that's not ideal, but I have a character to play for now, so I go. Though going is an admission that he's right, he may not know the extent to which he's right, so I have to be careful. I just have to help enough, stay out of the way, don't draw attention, do a little here and there. This isn't the *big* battle we've been heading towards. That comes later. This is only a skirmish.

I detach myself from a wind traveler at the spot appointed by Elonrod. The ancient pass of Yahanmark goes through the valley here. The cobblestones, barely visible through the long grass and young trees that have grown, are what's left of a once-great civilization. And through this valley is the easiest way to get to our camp.

Hidden in the trees, we wait for the knights. They shouldn't be far if the scout's information is correct. But the silence is thick and heavy with fear.

We're not even sure how many there will be.

And over the rise, we hear the clink of metal, the strike of horses' hooves against stone, and the creaking of saddles. A few magic-users stiffen, but Elonrod focuses on the sound. He's reading their minds.

They're bored, he projects to us. *Hold until I give the signal*. I acknowledge his orders with a glance. Louder and louder the sounds get until I see the shapes of horses coming this way through the trees.

Someone near me starts to breathe quickly, and they shift in the trees. They're going to get us caught, so I reach out slowly with my hand to touch their shoulder. She turns, face white, hands shaking. She's young. Dirty blonde hair, wide blue eyes. Allisthe is her name. I try to calm her with a look. She settles, but only a little.

The horses are nearly upon us, their figures pass through the middle of us, and we stay still, keeping hidden and out of sight. Seconds beat against the blinding sunlight, waving in patches on the ground, and I can tell there are still more to come, but Elonrod's voice calls, "Now."

Chaos ensues. Wind knocks at the knights, hammering from both sides. Magic-users appear and disappear through the sun and wind, harassing them.

"Keep formation," a knight calls, and the king's men move together, swords drawn now, watching the streaks of gray and gold that zip to and fro.

One knight tracks a streak of gray, finding its pattern, and slashes at it. The wind traveler tumbles to the ground, holding his shoulder and groaning. The knight charges towards him, but his captain calls him back. Elonrod appears next to the fallen wind-traveler, and they disappear in a streak of light.

I move carefully through the trees, watching the magic-users, keeping back and occasionally fouling a knight's strike or grabbing at a horse's hoof with wind, to send the war mounts into a frenzy. Even the most disciplined and finest horses panic when the ground seems unstable. It's one of my favorite tricks because the knights can't fight it; they can only hang on and attempt to regain control of their prancing mounts.

With a few more horses shying and raring, the others begin to panic as well. Herd mentality. The knight's formation breaks, and while they attend to their animals, magic-users continue to flit among them. But I can tell the expense of magic tires them. They're slower to ride the wind, tumble out instead of landing gracefully, and as the knights regain control of their mounts, they begin to bear down harder on the magic-users.

Now they know our numbers are few.

Now they trace us as we move.

They're prepared for us, and that brings their fury down harder.

Elonrod senses our weakening, telling the worst off to fall back. He brings a storm to bear. And as more of our kind tire, some begin to fall under the weapons of the enemy. Elonrod looks for me and motions for me to join him. I rush to his side as he raises his arms to call the sky's fury on our enemies. I lay a hand on his shoulder, focusing his power, seeing what he sees, feeling what he feels, watching as he pulls clouds that weren't there moments before, listening to the crackle of thunder and the fizzles of lightning grow.

"Kill him," one of the knights says, lunging towards us, and I send a sharp gust into his horse's chest. The animal pauses only briefly, ears flat, mouth wide and frothing. The rider manages to hang on, bent into the wind, holding onto the saddle. He kicks the mount onward.

The storm is raging overhead, lightning strikes in random places, and as the rider bears down on us and the horse closes in, Elonrod hesitates. He won't lose the storm completely if he wind travels, but he'll have to concentrate to get it back, so with a brief lapse in his storm, he reaches deep within himself and claps his hands together. The sound of thunder explodes across the valley, and a powerful gust of wind launches forth, throwing the horses and knights from before him. Trees bend and dry limbs crack, grass flies, torn up by the root, revealing the old cobblestones, which too start to shift and move, some becoming dislodged and rolling.

Then he stops, and steps back, breathing heavily, a sheen of sweat on his forehead while his storm has subsided to a meager threat of rain overhead.

"Fall back," he calls to the magic-users who've stayed behind, and they start to disappear, some touching the bodies of the fallen to take them back. I see Allisthe with a scratch on her cheek and water in her eyes, as she touches the body of her betrothed, but as she attempts to travel, she and the body tumble from the wind. She tries again, but this time, she can't make it onto the wind at all.

Elonrod rushes to her side, grabbing her and the body, then he motions for me to join him.

I take one last look at the fallen knights and their mounts, who start to rise and rally. Then I join Elonrod. We whisk away to the new camp.

CHAPTER 25

ELLORY

My kin start trickling in, some wounded, some just exhausted as they stumble and fall from the wind and sunlight. Those who've been setting up camp rush to greet their friends and family, asking for news and hurrying the wounded to the central fire pit to be tended.

I twiddle my thumbs, waiting, and asking occasionally after Elonrod.

"He said fall back," is all I get in response. "He's holding them off for now."

No word on when he'll return.

Minutes seem like lifetimes, but I busy myself with passing out the healing herbs I've found. Erian and the other healers get to work. Healing magic is fascinating to watch. Healers, like travelers, connect with certain aspects of nature. But instead of wind or sun, they connect with herbs, plants. They use the properties to ease pain and help the mending process. But in the instance of one man with a vicious-looking cut on his arm, the pain and bleeding are bad enough that he has to be held down.

"Use your gift," Erian says to me as I move to help hold the man. She gestures with the past she's making.

"Use my gift how?"

"Calm him."

"I don't know how to do that."

"It's like how Elonrod projects thoughts into people's heads. Project calm. Ease his pain if you can."

"But I-"

"Please," the man begs through gritted teeth, and I nod.

"I'll do my best," I answer, opening myself to feelings and emotions. I have to relax for a moment, because I see a lot of fear and pain all at once. So much that it would be easy to be overloaded by it all, but I try not to succumb. I focus just on my own feelings. My own concern and anxiety for Elonrod, and the hope that he comes back safely.

Nice...I have to find something nice, though. So, I dig deeper. What feels nice? Eating food around the fire feels nice, laughing and talking with my kind. Learning these new skills, becoming part of their community. Their acceptance.

But it's not enough. The man still squirms in pain, and I know I'm not doing this right.

Something stronger then. My family? That memory is orange ringed in the dark blue halo of night. The fire in the hearth is small, the food meager, but it was one of the nights Cassian and Mellen were awake past their bedtime.

Mellen was playing with her doll, brushing her fingers through the doll's straw hair while she tried names on it. Mother bent over the fire, stirring the coals to last a bit longer, while Cassian fiddled with a piece of wood and a knife Gerdor had given him.

I remember thinking, even in the quiet of the moment, that this was what I worked so hard for. To see them happy, safe, and healthy. To let them know that they were loved and cared for. And that they could feel the security of knowing I'd always be there to take care of them.

And tears fill my eyes, but the memory is too pure to spoil, so I feel it fully. I sit in the middle of the emotions, the cozy warmth, the soft glowing orange wavers like a fire in a hearth, slow, steady, but snapping and crackling. And there's a calming blue haze overlaid. I seek out the pattern, harness it, and fall into that place in my mind.

I see the man's form. Pain is blinding red and flashes of angry white-yellow. Sickly green fear radiates from the edges of his being, pouring out into the dark world, and I reach out to his being with my orange glow. I touch his arm, pushing the warm orange emotion out into this dark world.

And then something interesting happens. The soft orange glow doesn't overtake the pain and fear. It binds itself to it, though, wrestling with the pain and fear, and I wonder if I need to bolster the emotions, so I go back to my image, soak it in, and then push the emotions back out.

The colors blend and lessen, and the effort starts to weigh on me. Recognizing the vertigo, I claw to the surface before I succumb to the darkness.

The man has stopped squirming. Still breathing shallowly, his tensed body sort of falls onto the cot, and his eyes half close.

"Thank you," he says, as Erian dresses his wound. It's not fully healed. But it will heal better and quicker now.

"Elonrod's back," someone says, and I rise. Erian motions for me to go to him, so I do. Running to the spot where he fell from the back of the wind with three others in tow. Telisan, a girl I've seen but don't know, and an unmoving body, covered in blood. As Elonrod relinquishes the body to the crying girl, he looks at me, eyes shiny.

"How many returned?" he asks. I don't have the answer. But Reathl answers, and he nods, swallowing hard, and surveying the camp and his people. He swipes a hand over his eyes and forehead and clears his throat.

"What were we able to bring from camp?" Reathl walks with him to show him the preparations they've made. He's hailed as a conquering hero, but he accepts their praise with a heavy pain weighing on his soul. He assists where he can and directs Reathl to find a place to dig graves.

Eight new graves are piled with rocks, the flowers already wilting. Spirits are low. Reathl, Elonrod, and I sit around the fire after most of the magic-users have gone to sleep.

"There's only one way to make this stop," Reathl says. "At one point, we'll have to stop running and fight."

"I know," Elonrod says, but his face is haggard and bleak. The weight of everything hangs on his shoulders. Now I see the extent to which they rely on him. He's their hope, because he's their *weapon*. Their best shot at a new life. And he constantly feels the responsibility.

Reathl's eyes haven't left Elonrod's face.

"I'll make a plan," Elonrod says, tossing his stick into the fire and rising. He goes off by himself into the forest. I follow, because maybe I can ease some of his fear and stress a little.

It's dark and I trip over bushes, my dress tangling in them.

"I'm fine," Elonrod calls over his shoulder.

"No, you're not," I reply. He stops and allows me to catch up.

"I just want our people to be safe and not have to do this time after time."

"That's what you're working for, isn't it?"

"And it's terrifying, but if I don't have that terror, will I make the right choices? This is all so much, but I *have* to do it because no one else can. The fate of these people is on me. Whether we live or die is on me. The people we lost...it's because I failed."

"It's not your fault."

"It is. Because they look to me to keep them safe, and I didn't."

"You did your best."

"My best isn't good enough. That's why this is so hard. If my best was good enough, we wouldn't have lost people. I'd be strong enough to save everyone."

I pause a minute, letting the fear just exist...There's nothing I can do to ease this burden for him. So finally, I say, "What are you going to do?"

"My best," he answers sarcastically. Then he drops his head. "What happened today...that's only the beginning. The knights will come again. More this time. They have the numbers. They have allies. If all the kings sent their armies...But they don't even need that to wipe us out. We're not warriors."

"What choice do we have?"

"None."

"Then...at least we know what we're fighting for. We'll fight know-ing we tried to make this world better for ourselves and for the ones who'll come after us. We're not the only ones with magic. Maybe our feat will inspire others to fight for their freedom as well."

"Maybe." He scrubs a hand through his hair and blows his cheeks out with a sigh. "Today was a mess. We were unprepared and had no plan. I should have had a plan. Should have covered their backs better. Should have had more scouts watching farther out. Had a better start on evacuating."

"You know for next time."

"Yeah...having to gain experience to learn kinda sucks though. Eight graves. I've known most of them my whole life. I know their stories. I was taught by them or taught them. Worked alongside them. Fought alongside them...They shouldn't have died."

"I'm sorry," I say, putting a hand on his shoulder because it's the only thing I can think to do.

His mouth is bunched in grief, and he heaves a sigh and pushes his shoulders back. "Better get planning. We'll have to dig more graves, but we don't want to dig more than necessary."

Chapter 26

Maehdiorah

Elonrod feels trodden down. The hero needs a hero. But he can't have one. He must do this on his own. He must rise to the occasion of his own accord, and he must survive, or he'll never be able to stand up against what comes after. There is far worse in his future.

A war meeting has been called, and Elonrod asks for me to be there specifically. I do as asked, because he's the undisputed leader of our community and a war hero now. We sit together in a tent, Reathl, of course, Elonrod, some of the strongest magic-users, some who've guided community decisions in the past, and many of the warriors from the skirmish yesterday, still bandaged and healing. Ellory ducks in as well and sits near her brother with her hands in her lap. Her face shows concern, and she looks around at everyone as if she's reading their emotions. I sense she's more at ease with her gift now.

Elonrod welcomes everyone and begins prattling about the battle yesterday and how our losses are heavy. Then he launches into a speech that highlights Ellory's main points from their argument last night about fighting for the people next to them. He goes on to show a map he's crudely drawn of the nearby territory and possible sites for battle that will give us an advantage while still keeping secret the whereabouts of those who can't fight.

Planting one hand on the table, he leans over the map, pointing to various posts he's outlined, and though he speaks confidently, he also speaks with an air of finality. He's asking his friends and family to go out and die. And I can sense his guilt and fear.

His people nod and agree. This is what they've been waiting for, wishing for. Freedom. A chance to live under a fair and just law and system. To not hide or be hunted. To not have to worry about their loved ones never coming home.

The plan is made. And the magic-users begin to filter from the tent, preparing themselves for the moment of battle. They will need strengthening in their gifts, stamina, and in fighting with conventional weapons. I rise to leave, too, but Elonrod motions for me to wait. He waits for the others to leave, including Ellory. Then he looks me dead in the eye.

"You know how I know you're more capable with magic than you let on? It's because no one amplifies like you. You know exactly how to touch the tendrils of magic, where to look inside a person, and how much to help each individual. It's not natural for others. But you never had to be told how to help anyone. You already knew. And that means you know exactly what it's like to wield it yourself.

"If we're going to survive this fight. I'm going to need you to put off whatever issues you have with wielding your magic. We need to survive this. So, we need you. Your kin need you. *I* need you," Elonrod says, eyes grave and demanding, leaving no room for argument.

If I still let pride override logic like in my earlier days, I'd have goaded him. But that won't serve my purpose here and now, so I don't. I just nod instead. He breathes a little easier. "Thank you."

I leave the tent, thinking that for all his past arrogance and pranks, he's growing into the leader he'll need to be.

CHAPTER 27

ELLORY

The camp is in chaos. Elonrod has set up an efficient system for scouting, though, sending several men and women at a time to varying distances to keep an eye out. And a few at a time search through the sunlight. They watch the main roads, of course, and passes since we're not *on* any roads. Elonrod has given orders for the scouts to keep their distance and never be seen or heard by the enemy. We can't afford to lose anyone. We've lost too many already.

Elonrod scouted our evacuated camp by himself, refusing to let anyone go with him. The knights burned everything they found. We suppose they did so in case we tried to come back and reclaim our things. Can't blame them for being smart about it, but it's a loss to us, and that brings down our spirits.

We work day and night, resting when we collapse or we're too tired to function. It seems the magic-users had a supply of weapons that they had built up, but they weren't able to take them all when we evacuated, so we make up for that now, honing what we can into sharp points, crafting handles, shaping arrows, and practicing our gifts. I practice pushing emotions because Elonrod thinks it would be a good idea if I could help our side with courage in the heat of battle and perhaps debilitate the other side with fear or sadness. Unfortunately, I've learned that building those kinds of skills takes a lot of time and energy. Neither of which I have an ample supply of. I can do a little for one person. I try to expand that range to two people or even a small group. I'm able to feel what it would be like to do so when Elonrod asks Telisan to amplify my gifts. I can't explain that feeling other than it felt like flying. The energy, the power, the directed perfection and stability of it...It's like it wasn't me at all. It was some being way more powerful building, sustaining, and forming that magic, making it flow, making it bigger, stronger...and somehow far more accurate. It was incredible.

It felt so amazing that I just sat for a moment in stunned silence while Elonrod grinned and said, "It's great, huh?"

I just nodded. I'd love to be able to do that on my own, but I'm limited. So, I keep practicing.

And there's also an hour or two a day when we practice using weapons.

I learn archery. Not merely for hunting but for killing people. Enemies. Setting up targets, a few other archers, and I learn how to aim at the knights and the chinks in their armor, how to aim at a distance, and how to take care of our bows, strings, and build more arrows. Building them is tedious, but necessary, and it's important to do it correctly or they won't fly straight.

I also learn basic fighting with a dagger as well. Very simple moves of blocking and jabbing. Swords are too heavy for me, but I keep lifting them and practicing with them on my own. Perhaps one day I can build up the strength and endurance...but for now, I keep a dagger tucked into my belt.

And I help Telisan gather healing herbs. She's strange. She works quickly and efficiently, but her eyes glaze over as if she's not really there. Her face is stone, and she hardly speaks. The others aren't put off by her, though. Oddly enough, if I look at Elonrod in the right light, he looks a little like her. Especially with the weight of battle settling on his shoulders lately. But fear and stress have a way of changing one's face.

And a lot of faces are filled with fear these days.

The scouts come and go at different intervals, and if any don't arrive on time, Elonrod goes after them himself to check that they're alright. We've not lost anyone so far.

He's careful to mark any movements of the knights on his map, so he knows where they are, where they've been, and their likely course. The majority of them head towards our former camp, thinking we must not have gotten far.

We didn't. Not far enough.

Collapsing into our beds after all we can do, we sleep soundly, but the sounds of preparation can still be heard as we drift off, weapons clinking, people teaching, scouts telling of what they saw...I hear them in my sleep.

I feel my kin's feelings. I feel the overwhelm and dread. The terror that haunts them worsens in the darkness of night. I do what I can to ease their fears, but against this...there's not much to be done except prepare as much as possible and wait for the inevitable.

It's the tone of voice that strikes fear into every being present as the man drops from the back of the wind. He calls out to Elonrod, and before he even speaks, we know.

The time has come.

The knights have come within the boundary Elonrod set to serve as our warning that they're close. We don't know for sure that they know where we are, but we don't want them to. So Elonrod decided that when they got this far, we'd go out to meet them.

Preparation halts, and a deadly silence grows over some, while others stare at their young leader. He nods, jaw tightening.

"We've done all we can do," Elonrod says. "Tonight, we rest. Tomorrow, we go to battle."

I didn't know what I was going to feel about all of this. It's certainly different talking about the possibility rather than meeting it head-on. I feel the nervous energy of everyone around me, and I don't even have to *try*.

It's night, and I shift on my blanket from one side to the other, staring into space as if it holds the answers to what the future will bring. It's too unpredictable and yet...perhaps not? We could be easily overwhelmed by the king's forces. But hope tells me it could end well, too.

Either way, I want to see my family one last time, because we simply don't know what will happen. I ask Elonrod as a favor to take me to the lower village.

"It's too dangerous," he whispers through the darkness. "They'll be on high alert, and if anyone sees you..."

"I know," I answer sullenly. I'll be a dead woman if I'm caught. We let the silence stretch for a long time. It's so strange to think of where I was just a few weeks ago and where I've ended up. It's surreal. Like I could still wake up in my old body, on my cot, and take the herbs to the market. Set up like it's a normal day, and be cranky about the sun, heat, smells, and the lack of buyers.

I'd die for that life now. To be back with my mother, Cassian, and Mellen. But would I give up the friends I've made here? The gifts and Elonrod?

I'm not so sure. None of this is simple. None of this is easy.

"We have bigger problems now," Elonrod says in response to my thoughts.

"You promised..." I remind him, rolling over on my stomach so my makeshift pillow (which is just a bunched-up cloak) squishes into my cheek. I can see his outline in the dark. And through the tent flap, I can see thousands of stars.

"These are war times," he whispers, "Privacy is a luxury. Besides that, you were thinking loudly."

"I'm not so sure I like having an older brother," I shoot back.

"Yeah, you do," he says, shifting and getting comfortable on the ground.

"What do you think is going to happen?" I ask. He's silent for a moment.

"I don't know."

And he lets it hang there in the dark. The sound of crickets rises in the grass outside, and the creaking of trees in the forest is haunting.

"Whatever happens, we'll be together," he says, holding out his hand. I put my hand out as well, and he clasps it. "There's so much I wanted to teach you before all of this happened. So much you can learn. I've put a lot of hope and pressure on you, and I know that can be daunting. But I'm glad I found you. I'm glad you're here now and that we got to know each other. Life is going to be hard for a while. But we'll both be there for each other, right?"

"Right," I answer, squeezing his hand.

"It's going to be okay," he says, and he takes his hand away, repositions himself on his blanket, pulls his covers up, and folds his hands over his stomach.

I breathe a moment, watching him settle and slightly jealous at how calm he looks.

"If I die-"

"No. Don't talk like that," he warns, and his sharp tone tells me he means it.

"Visit my family for me? At least see that they're safe?"

"You'll see them yourself when this is over. And if *I* die..."

"That's not allowed. G'night," I say, pulling the covers over my head to end the conversation. He scoffs.

"Hey, I listened to you," he says. And I can feel the energy shift in our small tent. "Take care of these people. Hide them somewhere. Keep them safe. Give them the life they deserve."

"I can't do that. Only you can."

"Yeah...right." He turns over now, his back to me, and I get the impression he doesn't want to talk anymore. So, I say nothing more.

I guess we'll just have to see.

CHAPTER 28

MAEHDIORAH

S o...the magic-users find themselves once again at odds with the mighty kings. And Beregon rides with his men to meet us. Lines drawn on opposite sides of a field lined with trees and short cliffs, where blood will be shed on both sides. No one will truly win here today. We have no hope even with our abilities. The others simply don't have the capacity to wield enough magic. And the king will try to wipe out the magicians he claims plague his lands. But he will lose knights in the process, sending barrage after barrage to their deaths.

Many will weep tonight.

And for what? So, the king can hold his head high, pretending to do the 'right' thing by suppressing magic and those who wield it.

Elonrod led their forces here to the spot he chose for battle based on its defensibility for us, and we watch as they assemble. There must be a few thousand knights brandishing their weapons and crying war under the snapping purple and gold banner of their king. A golden crown rests on the field of purple cloth with boxes surrounding it in flapping fringe. Berry purple, it is. The kind of berries that stain the hands deep red.

Catapults creak as they rumble into position behind the lines of knights. The big wooden masses shudder, and the magic-users around me shift and mutter. Tension grows, and the hairs on my arms raise with their fear. Surely, they can't have thought that the king *wouldn't* have sent everything he had against them.

Fools.

A call comes down the line, and several magic-users move together, clasping arms, some staring at the sky, some staring at the ground, others with their eyes closed to focus on the flow of energy and nature. Some as weapons, some as amplifiers. I'm relieved I've not asked to be one of them. I can move freely.

"We have to get rid of them, or they'll wipe us out," one of the magic-users near me says to his brother, pointing at the larger weapons.

"Let's do it," says the brother, and they both drop out of formation. They disappear on the back of the wind. A swirling gray dust devil springs up not far from the knights, swirling as it picks up speed and girth, spitting dirt and grass as it ravages the ground. It surges, nearly drowning out the thunder from the storm as it bears down on the knights and their catapults. Several knights run or throw themselves to the ground, cries ripped from their mouths and lost on the wind.

One foolish man stands against it, hair flailing wildly from under his helmet as he strains against the wind, holding himself up with a pike in one hand and swiping his sword at the wind with the other. Dust spits into his helmet, and he grabs at the cage of metal around his face, falling to the ground.

As the brothers distract the knights, a storm builds. Bubbling black clouds spread across the sky like a stain, blocking the sun's rays. Winds rise, tearing at the grass, and lightning cracks, followed by booming thunder.

We may not win today, but we will give the kingdoms a day to remember.

CHAPTER 29

ELLORY

The earth beneath our feet rumbles as it quakes, and the sky overhead cracks with thunder, sending shivers of lightning over the fields. The light bounces off the straight rows of armored men already in disarray as a dust devil pounds their ranks. The fading light leaves the encompassing clouded, night-like blue-gray with which to see by. And suddenly, tremors of undulating earth sweep the field.

"Our kin won't be able to hold it long when the knights advance, but hopefully it'll confuse and dishearten the enemy," Elonrod explains. We stand atop the hill overlooking the fields. Our chosen site from which the archers will fire at the enemy.

This place is far enough away from camp that the enemy won't get to the children and the elders. At least some will live on. Hopefully in peace and left alone, but who's to say? We've done our best. We *will* do our best.

But I wonder, will it be enough? Will any of this be enough?

I suppose it's too late now. The dreaded time has come. Heat rises in my face, and my head spins.

"Elonrod, I just want you to know…"

"Me too, Ellory. I'll see you when it's over," he says, and I sense his fear echoing my own. It eats at the heart and holds onto the lungs, barely allowing me to breathe. He clasps my arm quickly and retreats off the hill with what resolve he has, taking his position at the head of the army.

"Freedom!" someone down the line of archers yells, and our magicians let loose a torrent of ripping thunder, crashing lightning, and earth-shaking as our enemy rallies enough to charge our main army in the valley below. Lightning explodes across the enemy's front line. Tendrils of shocking, white light reach out to snap at the knights cased in metal. It's beautiful and terrifying at the same time. The sudden flash, the streams arching off the main bolt, the glow of the ground, how fast it hits and retreats. It's mesmerizing…but horrible to watch the destruction it wreaks. Sections of the enemy's front lines drop while others scream in agony. Those who were lucky enough to remain untouched back away, staring at the sky as if they can dodge the next strike.

A few of their fallen rise, which empowers the ones behind who rush forward to sustain their brethren, and they all keep coming, some limping, holding their arms or chests, stepping over the bodies of the dead.

"I think we made them angry," says Erian, and I nod as another crack of lightning, blinds and sears the enemy's lines. But it seems they're over the initial shock now, coming in an endless wave, dodging and darting through the strikes, and some make it through to where they're near enough for our arrows.

Fear wells up inside me like a hot burning sludge, worming into my throat as I lift my bow and aim down the shaft, then I lift it in the air like I was taught to give the arrow more reach, holding steady as I wait for the order.

"Fire," Erian calls, and I loose my arrow. Watching it blend with the other arrows peppering the dark sky as they rise and then fall. Thin streaks against the field. I try not to see what I've done, but I know some arrows have made their mark from the cries below.

I shudder and quickly nock another arrow, the tremble in my fingers knocking it from its perch, and I have to reset it to take aim. My arms quiver, and my body convulses with fear. I suck in a deep breath, trying to stop the panic welling inside of me. This is no time to break down.

The storm still rages, though the dust devil has died down. I see the knights scurrying to assess their machines and right the catapults. One hangs at a crazy angle, but it appears that one is still in working order. The knights swarm like ants, trying to lift it back up. Unfortunately, they're out of range of our arrows, and unless someone can take out the catapult from afar, we'll be bombarded.

There are still dozens of knights on the battlefield, nearly halfway up the rise that Elonrod picked to receive them. And even as lightning blasts them in spats, they cover their heads, duck down, and continue running.

Worse yet, our position has been compromised, and some of the knights peel off the main ranks to deal with us.

"Keep firing," someone says, and I loose another arrow into the ranks of knights. Pull, nock, release. Pull, nock, release. Repeated over and over. The hill is steeper, slick with wet grass, and littered with sharp rocks, but the knights keep coming, even some with arrows sprouting from the gaps in their armor.

There are about forty, then thirty-three, then thirty-one. And though we're trying to pick them off, they gain ground rapidly.

"Retreat," Erian calls, and we do, moving back to the shelters and perches we created. One of the wind travelers grabs my hand, and we move into the trees on the ridge, where we have quivers stashed, and can still have the high ground. Some of us climb trees or wind travel up.

From where I perch, clinging like a kitten to the trunk of a sappy pine, I can't see much of the battlefield, but I can hear the clash and ring of metal, and I shiver at the sound, hoping...

We target the threat, aiming at those coming towards us. My shots don't do much good here. I'm shaking with the exertion of having to pull the string back over and over, but I keep firing, swapping my emptied quiver for a new one.

Some knights overtake a few of my kin, slashing them down and stealing their bows and arrows. They sidestep behind trees as they fire back at us. A puff of gray wind streaks by me, narrowly dodging an arrow and slamming into one of the knights. They tussle on the ground while the rest of us keep firing.

One of my shots takes a knight through the knee chink while another grazes an armpit, glancing off the armor, before the knight disappears behind a tree. He rolls off the other side, rushing to the base of my tree while I struggle to reorient my bow and arrow around the trunk. Finally, I get lined up as he whips out a knife and winds up to throw it.

The dark fletchings of my arrow disappear through his neck, and he freezes as another magic-user drops from the back of the wind to end him.

As the knight falls, I see dark blood trickling from beneath his helmet and down the front of his breastplate. He sighs out a breath, and I swear I can see the glint of his eyes staring at me. I don't have time to contemplate what I've done. What I've *been* doing. The others have closed in quickly, and Erian's haggard voice calls retreat again.

He would have killed me. He would have killed me, I repeat over and over in my mind, trying to block the image as I drop from the tree, landing hard in the leaves and the dirt next to the fallen knight. The smell of rotting leaves fills my nose.

As one of the knights barrels towards us, screaming at the top of his lungs. Three arrows instantly sprout out of him, and he staggers against a tree for a moment, then raises his sword and keeps coming. Streaks of gray filter through the trees, and some of my kin start to disappear. A wind traveler appears next to me suddenly, her blonde hair wispy and frizzed by the wind. She reaches for me, but before our hands lock, an arrow slams into her. We turn in surprise as the knight advances on us.

More knights pour over the hill and into the trees behind him, outlined by the storm.

"Run," says the wind traveler who's fallen to the ground as she tries to suppress the bleeding. I grab her hand, but she pulls away, whispering, "Run."

I do, pumping my legs as fast as they'll go, intending to meet up with the main force.

Chapter 30

Maehdiorah

It's my job to keep as many of these people alive as possible. If I could use Dark Magic, it would be easy. But I can't...*shouldn't*.

As the main army soldiers on amidst the strikes of lightning, random gusts of wind snatch screaming knights into the air, dropping them from great heights, which in itself is an unnerving scene.

Even with as many as have been picked off, there are still a great many to go, and now they've attended to their remaining catapult and proceed to load their projectile. Just as the knights prepare to fire, a large bolt of lightning slams into the wooden frame. The shock and heat splinter the sides of the great machine, and it collapses under the force, as knights dive out of the way.

I can't imagine the kings will be pleased that we broke their toys, but we have more immediate problems as their ground force is nearly upon us.

We ready ourselves. I sense a surge of magical energy building in Elonrod as he stands next to me. Something builds in him akin to the fury and the unrelenting torrents of a raging sea.

"Help me," he says, suddenly over the crack of thunder as he holds out his hand. I take it, immediately feeling the rush of his magic and the pull of mine towards him. I feel him asking our abilities to meld together. I allow only a portion to be revealed to him, enough to give what he asks for. As his thoughts and emotions swirl, his plan takes form in my own mind.

And with a sudden burst of energy, a shockwave rattles the ground in front of us, the land rolling like a blanket that's been flipped. The knights who were almost upon us are tossed like dolls under the rumbling of the earth. Bits of earth crack under the strain, but another wave shudders through the ranks, rolling through the reserve ranks and knocking them to the ground. Horses panic and prance, knees buckling. Some of the terrified animals rise and run, kicking at the ground as they do so, while others buck and rear to gain freedom from their masters.

Shakily, the knights gain their feet once more, but another rolling wave knocks them to the ground. I see one of them smack the ground while another looks back at their captain, who rolls to his knees and lunges off the ground.

"Advance!" he shouts at them, frustration in his raspy voice. The knights do as they're told. Warily, they follow their captain who surges forward, but when the prince reins his horse in and charges onto the battlefield, his men take heart. And the reserve army follows him now, too.

Kalandrel races down the middle of the battlefield, dodging the bodies of his men, blade outstretched. His battle cry rises above the storm, as does the cry of his regrouping men, and they break into a run as his horse tears past. The full swarm bears down on us once again. And our magic is stayed for the moment while our own regroup and rebuild their strength.

"Keep to the plan," Elonrod calls, his hand still gripping mine. "Use what we can. Do what we can, and when things start to turn, you know what to do."

Sounds of ascent reach my ears, and I breathe deeply.

"Nervous?" Elonrod asks me.

"For this? Always."

"This is what we trained for," he answers and then thunders at the rest, "Bring out the infantry. The rest stay back."

The magic-users shuffle behind us, and I feel a surge of magic energy leave as he prepares for another barrage of earth. I call more of nature's magic, willing it to flow through me as if I'm merely a conduit, and I feel Elonrod shaping it even as it soaks into my being.

He waits...The knights close in, and Elonrod unleashes another torrent of earth, undulating the ground beneath their feet, and knocking the prince's horse out from under him. The gray animal flips, legs flailing as it goes down, and desperately tries to rise. One of its legs no longer looks right, and the animal screams, as it staggers on three legs, eyes wide. The animal panics, tries to flee, and goes down again.

The prince rises angrily, lifting his visor to spit dirt and then slamming it back into place.

"Charge," he commands, and we wait for the brunt of their attack.

CHAPTER 31

ELLORY

I'm one of the last magic-users out. I've watched them all blink away on streaks of gray. And I'm hoping someone comes back for me before the knights catch up. There's one last place where we stashed quivers, and I grab the rest so the knights can't use them against us, but I don't stop to fire. I keep running towards the sound of battle, but I hear the knights not far behind.

"Shoot her," one says.

"Throw me the bow."

Terror gives my legs new life as I turn and run. I should break through the tree line soon. I should be behind the line of magic-users, and I'll have a whole bunch more knights to deal with, but I won't be on my own. As I see the break in the trees, I can hear the knights closing fast. The clomp of their feet, the clunks of the metal, and I'm sure at any moment they'll run me through.

The quivers bang together on my back and fall off my shoulders down into my elbows, spilling arrows, but I keep running. There's no time to retrieve them. I glance behind me quickly and see one skid to a halt while he trains his bow, as another keeps running, sword raised, as he closes in. My heart sputters as I raise my bow to block his sword, but it's too little, too late.

Then a streak of gray descends, whipping through the trees and slamming into the man. The other knight shifts his aim from me to the other magic-user. I drop the quivers quickly, jam an arrow onto the bowstring, and pull back, yelling "watch out," to my kin who scuffles with the other knight.

The archer knight pulls his aim back to me as I loose the arrow at him, and dive behind the partial cover of a tree. His arrow skitters off the bark, shaving bits of wood that spatter the air. I ready another arrow and dip out from cover, finding him again and shooting. My arrow digs into the dirt by his feet as he moves aside. I duck behind another tree, my arms screaming with pain. Quaking, I pull back the string once more and dive out from cover, just as my kin finishes off the knight and whirls onto the back of the wind, knocking the archer knight off his feet as well. I release the string slowly, so I don't have to keep holding the arrow as Reathl contends with the man.

But other knights are on their way.

"Reathl," I call. "We gotta go."

He darts a glance at the knights closing in and disappears in a streak of gray, landing by my side, grabbing my arm, and whisking me away. Wind claws at my hair, the surroundings whoosh by, and suddenly we stop just behind the main line of defense. I stumble, catching my balance and gaining my bearings.

The storm lessens in the sky. Some of those who conjured it have fallen, but even as some lay bleeding, I see them reaching to the sky as if trying to drain the last bit of magic they can to help the rest of us.

My people's line of foot soldiers contend with the knights, bravely pushing, being pushed, cutting with howls, and falling with groans. It's a harrowing scene to see so many bodies, and for a moment, the heat of sickness washes over me. Then I see a familiar figure calling to his men to fight despite the barrages of magic swiping at them from all sides.

Kalandrel.

My heart drops into my stomach, and guilt washes over me.

He fights with the fury of a storm, swiping and slashing, but none from our side can stand up to his skill. And they fall. Too many fall. But maybe I can get through to him. Of course, he must be angry with me still, but enough to kill me? I know it's a fool's chance, but...It's a chance?

If I can get to him, will he let me speak? And *if* I can speak to him, can I get him to listen? And *if* he listens, will he stop all of this? Not to forgive us and let us into the kingdom, but to at least stop hunting us, at least? Let us live in peace?

Can he see us as people, too? Not as monsters?

I duck and dodge through our side, moving through the lines of magic-users still using their gifts to contend with others, smaller bits of lightning, concentrated bursts of wind, etc. Once through their line, I pick my way carefully through the mass of fighters contenting, some one-on-one, others ganging up on the enemy.

I'm no match for Kalandral. But there's no turning back now, and I'm crazy for doing such a reckless thing, because I'll surely die if he's let bitterness win, but if he hasn't? If there's still a shred of him left that has feelings for Orielle…and the thought of using his feelings for her feels manipulative and small, especially since I'm *not* her, but…

I don't want to lie to him. So, I won't. I'll be strategic in what I say. In that, there is hope.

Hope is the reason we've held out so long. My kin and me. My family back in Thorondar, Elonrod, looking for his family…and sometimes it pays off.

I pull the dagger from my belt as I dodge the last group of knights and magic-users between the prince and me. He slices through one of my friends, and with a sickened heart, I watch them fall to the ground. Kalandral looks up, his gaze meeting mine.

"You." His face contorts with pain, betrayal, and deep sadness.

"I never meant to lie to you," I call above clanging metal, grunts, and war cries.

"You manipulated my feelings with magic."

"I didn't know I *had* magic. I couldn't control it. Didn't know how to use it. I couldn't have manipulated you. I am what I am, and I can't change it, nor did I choose it. Please know that," I yell back as his blade strikes overhead. It slams into my dagger, pushing me backward, and I stumble. Tripping on someone as a sudden wave of betrayal, hurt, and disappointment burns against my skin. I want to drop to the ground and weep.

"You didn't say anything. Why did you not tell me?" he asks, stalking towards me, shoulders hunched and angry, blade up and ready.

"I couldn't tell you," I explain, "The way you spoke about magic in the library…and I was meant to be your queen. *Me*. A magic-user. I was terrified." He slashes again, but slower and less aggressively. I deflect the blow, holding his blade on mine, locked together but only by his good graces.

"I would have been executed if anyone found out. Even if *you* didn't want it, your father would have burned me as mercilessly as the old woman, and I never did anything wrong. I harmed no one. I don't even have the ability to defend myself now."

The sheer force of pent-up emotions washes over him like the crashing of his blade on mine as he regroups and strikes again. I block it, but with my arm still sore from shooting, I can't hold out much longer. This will have to end eventually, whatever that comes to. He strikes again, waiting for me to catch up.

I feel *him* now. He hesitates, though his core is white hot and puckering like a fire spitting ash. It forces its way out of him so hard, so recklessly that it manifests in his strikes, but from within comes an emotional struggle.

The red and pink swirl through the hot anger, brushing against me, but his eyes cut like his father's, and though he wars against his emotions, he's duty-bound. He can't reverse his orders. Orders his king gave him. I feel it roiling in him.

"Please...see *me*," I say, reaching beyond our locked blades to him. He jerks back and sidesteps as if he's squaring me up.

"How can I trust you?"

"I only lied out of self-preservation, but if you need proof, end this." I stand back, dropping my blade. He swings at me, and I close my eyes, steeling myself against the feel of his blade cutting my flesh, and though I flinch, I stay mostly still and wait. Sounds of battle break through our moment. I breathe in and out a few times, and the blow never comes, so I open my eyes again.

He's standing with his blade near my throat. His jaw is tight, his eyes full of pain and regret.

"We can't reconcile this. There will never be a place for magic in the kingdoms."

"Then do what you have to." His eyes crinkle with pain, and his mouth grimaces.

But before he can do anything, a well-meaning magic-user drops from the wind, rushing the prince with a spear.

"No," I scream as the world slows. I feel myself diving into his path and knocking the prince back. Pain explodes across my middle, and my hands shake as I stare at the long stick embedded in me. Shock blossoms across the magic-user's face as his weapon digs into my midsection. He's trying to stop, I feel it in the slowing down of the spearhead, the panic that bursts across his mind, and regret.

"I'm sorry," he breathes. "I'll fetch Elonrod." And he disappears on a puff of wind.

Pain eats me, gnawing at my stomach, and my clothes cling to my body in a heavy way they hadn't before. Light-headed, I sway on my feet.

"Pull it out. Pull it out," the prince says, grabbing me and helping me to the ground before I collapse. "Men! To me. I need a wall right now and send a physician."

"It's too late for that," I say, because I feel the painfully familiar shift of my soul detaching from this body. It's creepy that I know this feeling now. Slowly…carefully. Bit by bit, it prepares to leave, like gathering itself together. It's terrifying to know what this feeling is. And what it means. My hands quake, and my face feels feverish as knights file into a wall near the prince to keep the magic-users at bay. I feel cut off from my kin. From Elonrod.

Oh, Great Kings. This is going to kill him.

What do I do? How do I fix this? My mind feels like a blank white slate, and I hate myself for not being able to think of anything to say or do before I die. One doesn't often have to think of their final acts, and though I knew it was a possibility I might not survive, I didn't think about the actual dying part...

"It's going to be fine. You'll be fine," the prince says on his knees beside me suddenly, holding my hand over my chest and propping me up slightly with an arm under my shoulders. "We'll take you back to the palace, inform your father that you're safe and okay. We'll negotiate his release, and we'll revisit your...'gifts' when things cool down."

"He's in custody?" is all I can think to say.

"My father though the might have been hiding your gifts."

"That's not fair," I say. And it really isn't. Whether Orielle had gifts or not.

"There's still time to make it right."

"No...you have to listen to me," I say, tears welling in my eyes. "I'm so sorry. I never meant to lie to you. I didn't want to break your heart."

"No, don't say that," he says, "I'm going to take this out now. This is going to hurt. Bite down on my glove." He shoves a dirty, sweaty, leather glove into my mouth, and I'm struck by how soft the leather is before a ripping sensation sizzles at the ends of my nerves as a sharp jerk removes the spear. Pain radiates through my abdomen all over again, and I scream, tears slipping out of the corners of my cheeks. My stomach feels oddly cold as I hear a thunk of the wood being tossed aside. Then the prince's hand covers the wound as he tries to close it himself.

"Physician?" he calls to his men.

"We've sent for him, highness, but the battlefield still treacherous. He may not arrive in time."

"Get him now." He stares at the wound, eyes darting, then he says, "Is there a *healer* from your side?"

Words come floaty through my mind, and my vision is hazing.

"I felt how much...you loved me. It was the most beautiful swirl of red, pinks, but it had traces of you in every emotion," I say, my breath feeling whisp as the air thins. "I wish things had been different."

"They can be," he says, hovering over me once more to hear me. He grabs hold of my hand again, kissing it softly as tears well in his eyes. "What color do you see now?"

"Red and warm pinks for love and care, swirling grays like confusion and threat of storm on the horizon. Light green for fear and dread. Warm light of honey...that's part of you. And dark blue of loss," I answer slowly, feeling the pulse and ebb of my blood leaving me too quickly. My limbs tingle with cold.

"That sounds beautiful. Keep talking. Tell me what else you see."

"It's starting to fade," I answer sadly as the emotions are harder and harder to see. But I reach out with my hand, grazing him lightly to push a little bit of it back to him. I'm weak, though. I'm not entirely sure it gets through before gray over takes the colors slowly as magic leaks away from my body, and I'm suddenly afraid. What if I don't come back this time? What if this is the end for me?

I don't want to die. Again. For the third time.

I feel his forehead press against mine, his tears dripping onto my face and tracing paths down my cheeks and into my hair. He quivers with unshed tears and emotions that beg to be let loose.

I haven't the strength left to help him. To make his sadness go away. Succumbing to exhaustion, cold settles in fingers and toes like the first frost of winter.

At least Elonrod had a sister for a little while. At least Mother has someone to love her. At least my family will be taken care of, and Cassian and Mellen will have brighter futures. At least Kalandrel will have a new start.

I can accept that.

I'm sorry I wasn't stronger for all of them, but they deserve better.

I choke, trying to breathe and relinquish even the strength to keep my chest rising and falling, letting the darkness fold over my vision like a blanket.

The End

SNEAK PEEK!

ONYX MIST (BOOK 2 OF THE ONYX SERIES)

I breathe slowly, deeply through my mouth to keep silent, half hidden by the trunk of a tree. It's barely dawn, and the forest is blue gray with the odd quiet of a world still waking. Dew drenches the forest in a musty-earth, decaying-leaf smell that makes my nose itch, but I can't stifle the offending smell with my tattered cloak. I have to remain perfectly still. Any moment now, they'll appear. But...they'll only come as long as they don't know I'm here.

Over the hill, the flicker of a deer's ear barely seen in the bushes tells me that the herd is coming. For the moment, they're unaware, which gives me the advantage as they come for the water in the small valley.

There's an opening near the water's edge where I'll be able to get a shot. For now, I wait.

Brown-red fur appears in patches through the bushes and disappears in turns. Sometimes it's accompanied by the snap of a twig or the rustle of stiff branches which is a good sign for me because if they were afraid, they'd be quieter. Deer are excellent at sneaking through foliage, even thickly grown places like this. In fact, if spooked, they can disappear so silently, I wouldn't even know they were gone, but here they're not afraid, snuffling and lipping the bushes to get a bite, chewing. One lifts its head, staring into the distance as its jaw works. She turns to scout another direction before dropping her head again.

I breathe out silently, gratefully. They haven't smelled me. My scent should be carrying the opposite direction which is why I picked this hiding spot.

A couple of deer step out of the bushes to the water's edge, dropping their heads to drink.

I tighten my grip on the drawstring of my bow, moving slowly, so I don't spook the animals. This bow is hard to pull back, and I can't hold the string for terribly long, so I have to time everything perfectly and hope everything goes smoothly. I point the tip of the arrow at one of the deer, approximately where I'll be holding and aiming, just to get a feel for the space. Then the bow tilts up as I pull the string back smooth, slow, and firm. I nose the arrow where it needs to fly. The taut string slips through my fingers as soon as the arrow aligns with my target. A sharp thwap sounds as the string snaps back into place. I try to follow the arrow with my eyes, to see where it strikes as the deer scatter at the sound, rustling and then going silent as they dive into the brush. They disappear within seconds, and I'm left alone in the little bowl.

I can't see the fletchings of my arrow indicating where it landed, so I can't tell if the arrow hit or not. No need for stealth now, I jog to the edge of the pool searching for the arrow or any traces of blood. There is none.

I curse and kick the ground. I can't keep losing arrows. They aren't cheap and making them isn't easy. I walk the area, searching the ground and the leaves for any signs of blood. Since the arrow has disappeared, it stands to reason that it may be embedded in the animal still. Widening my search, I keep looking until I notice a brushing of blood on a bush and a spatter on the leaves below. The animal is hit.

My heart picks up as I follow the trail that I can piece together, always looking ahead and marking the trail behind in case I get lost or have to backtrack, which happens occasionally.

Surprisingly, it doesn't take long to spot the heap of fur tucked under a bush. I breathe easier, as I check the carcass over. The arrow is broken, unusable, but at least I have a deer now, and that's ample compensation. I take hold of the back legs and start pulling the animal down the hills to the village of Brun.

It's a long trip when I'm encumbered with a deer carcass, and it would be worse if the deer were heavier. I sweat as the morning sun sweeps over the hillside pouring yellow through the leafy trees. I puff out my cheeks with heavy breaths, grunting as I pull the carcass aside to avoid rocks and bushes. Yes. This is a pain. Yes. It's a repeated pain, but it's worth it to have food and something to trade with. I have very little choice if I want to eat and have *some* comforts out here in the wild.

I woke up in a new body not long ago (maybe three weeks? I should have been better at keeping track of time), and now I live in the woods, not an outlaw, but as an outsider for sure (partly self-inflicted) which suits me perfectly for the time, because I'm disoriented here. I don't know where Elonrod and the magic-users are and what happened after I died. I don't know who this body belonged to.

She is the more pressing issue. Meeting people always comes with the chance that they'll recognize...her...me.

When I got stabbed in the war, I wasn't sure I'd come back. But here I am, breathing and trying to figure things out. And there have been difficulties in this new body: an intense, all-over body type of sickness where I pass out for hours at a time.

I sincerely hope that whoever this girl was, she was done using this body before I entered it. I don't like saying it because it's awkward to think about having to get used to a new body but...she's taller. I'm kind of enjoying the height...and reach.

I've tried to make her look different, cutting and dying the hair, smudging mud on the face whenever I go into the village. The short, choppy haircut was a series of mistakes due to lack of experience and using a pond as a looking glass. I gave up making the sides equal and just cut chunks. Now it sticks out in places, but I added a small braid to one side. The girl's hair was red. I dyed it light blonde. I suppose to remind me of days past and because herbs for that are plentiful out here. Her hands are now calloused and have dirt embedded in the fingernails. Her clothes *were* nice...before she died. When I awoke in them, they were covered in blood and had frayed tears in the fine-looking fabric. (But like Orielle's body, no wounds to indicate how she died, so I don't know.) Now her clothes are buried in the mountains somewhere northeast of here. I'm sure questions have been raised about her disappearance. Search parties will be launched if they haven't been already. Mostly because she'd been somebody. An important somebody.

She'd probably be ashamed of what's become of her body. *I'm* ashamed of the callouses and terrible haircut, but I have very little control over this. I don't *choose* whose body I land in. I just try to justify what I'm doing and have done in these bodies, slipping into their lives, lying, hiding, stealing clothes (which I did as soon as I could find an unattended clothesline because quite frankly, I needed *something* to wear). If not for survival's sake (because apparently, I can't stay dead) then for the sake of something I don't understand and can't fight. Something with magic...

I know it's not my fault, but that doesn't help.

I still feel like a leech.

So, I cultivate the look of a woodland dweller, all dirt and coarse-ness, and hope no one looks twice at me. It's worked so far.

But as for the other pressing issue, I've no idea where the others are. I can't ask a whole lot about magic-users without raising suspicion, so I mostly just ask for news of the country, nod somberly at whatever I'm told, and then slip back into the hills.

Many Thanks!
Acknowledgments

This book was years in the making. YEARS... And it was an absolute struggle to get written.

So when I thank those involved, I mean it from the bottom of my heart.

Marissa for listening to me and letting me bounce ideas off of her. She gave me a ton of great ideas to write into this book as well which made the book so much better. Thank you! You're advice was invaluable.

My friend Jeramee for being a cheerleader for me through the whole process of writing. You'll never know what it means to me that you were always there. And also for being like "Oh! Cool book covers!" because even that little bit of validation was like, "Yeah! I can do this!"

My aunt Cindy for being willing to read the mush that is my writing and give honest feedback.

And on that note, I want to thank ALL of the beta readers willing to provide feedback. I got a TON of great edits from y'all, and I appreciate that. And just your willingness in general to give the book a chance. And then for letting me send books 2 and 3 for your perusal. That was a lot of faith to place in me, and it doesn't go unnoticed.

And a thank you to those who connected me to more beta readers. It could have been a complete dumpster fire, but you were willing to take that chance. (I'd put a laughing emoji here if I could, but I'm not cool enough to technologically inclined so...just imagine that I did.)

My mom for believing in me. Always. Like... every time I write a book, she's there to clap for me. Thanks, Mom!

ABOUT THE AUTHOR

D.B. Forest writes high fantasy and tiny psychological thrillers that are... Ish? Like they exist and contain words which counts.

Currently self-publishing the Onyx Series, a 5-book fantasy series that started as a quick throwaway story and ended up taking over my life for a year and a half. I used to be meh about it... Now I love it. Yay! Character development for ME.

Also author of "Scythes of Onyx" and "Tales of the Immortals," short stories set in the same universe as the Onyx Series. The universe keeps expanding because characters just keep doing things. In fact, I'm writing another 5-book series snuggled right smack dab in the middle of the short stories and the novels. It's HARD, but I love 'em so...

I have an ellipses problem I'm not ready to address, a tendency to use italics, and a habit of starting sentences with conjunctions (you'll see). I'm not even trying to be professional at this point. Just having fun with this whole bookish adventure of writing and self-publishing. I am indeed human (and not fantastic at grammar. Exhibit A), so there will be typos. We could make a game of it though. Highest count wins! Prize: Emotional damage borrowed from fictional people. Woohoo!

I am not responsible for what my characters do, but I do accept angry letters on their behalf considering I'm probably just as surprised as you by how the stories go. I tried to tell them. They just do whatever.

When not wondering why my fictional people won't listen to per-fectly reasonable advice, I can be found hanging out with my dog who believes I should do that full time. He might be right. We'll see how this goes.

Want free pics and stuff for the Onyx series? Grab them here.

ALSO BY D.B. FOREST

Books in the same universe

Onyx Shadows

Onyx Mist

Onyx Dust

Onyx Whispers

Onyx Essence

A Dance with Fire

Scythes of Onyx

Tales of the Immortals: A Ballad of Love

Tales of the Immortals: A Song of Death

Dystopian Action/Adventure

Let's Call it a Game

Smoke in Our Veins

More to come! Are you as excited as I am? I'm like, "Let's GO!"

Follow the progress here

SCAN ME

DIVE INTO THE ONYX SERIES!

Because this story is just one part of a universe.

You're more than welcome to follow along this journey or more accurately this explosion of randomness. I can't promise it will always be entertaining...but there will be terrible jokes and chaos.

Interested in keeping up with the releases? And also getting pics from the books? And see the character chaos and me weeping over the complications of corralling characters who act like a house-full of toddlers who definitely don't take direction while I follow them around begging them not to destroy the furniture and eat their veggies?

SCAN ME

And if you want to follow on Instagram where I post a lot of this randomness, check me out at @dbforestauthor

Also, just feel free to say 'hi.' I don't bite. That's unsanitary.

PLEASE LEAVE A REVIEW

Your voice matters.

Plain and simple. A casual browser may or may not buy this book because of what you tell them in your review. That's why reviews are so important to authors.

So...I'd be INCREDIBLY grateful if you left a review to let people know what YOU thought of this book.

But also...if you don't want to, no pressure.

Thanks a million!

-D.B. Forest